Brit Chism

Mnemosyne's Daughters

Contents

This book of short stories is dedicated to my older sister Linda Marie Chism-Touchstone across barriers of distance, time, illness and life-death. Thank you for teaching me to read.

Eurydice

"'Who was Eurydice?' you ask. Not a very interesting woman according to mythology. By all accounts she was a beautiful oak dryad who danced in the Grecian forest. Her father was Apollo, her husband was Orpheus, and she died of a snake bite while fleeing from Aristeus, a sexual predator. There you have it—an oak dryad defined by her relationships with men."

Eurydice LeBlanc threw the tabloid, *The Weekly Gumbo*, across the coffee table.

"I might as well be a pole dancer in a bar," she said to no one.

The banner headline from the coffee shop rag asked, "What's In Your Name?" from where it had landed on the polyurethaned cypress floor.

She changed clothes into lululemon gear and athletic shoes. On the porch of her Bywater house she stretched her muscles, then ran to Crescent Connection Park. She began at the east end by Bartholomew Street and by the time she reached the graceful Piety Street Arch she hit her stride. Mentally she checked off landmarks: Mandeville Street Wharf, Toulouse Street Wharf, the Moon Walk, the Riverboat Terminal, the Aquarium. She would pass the Riverwalk then head into the newly trendy Warehouse District and return home via Rampart Street to St. Claude Avenue. The Bridge Run was only weeks away and she felt good about it.

At home she rubbed an ache in her lower back, and stripped off her athletic wear, then relaxed into the shower.

The chubby mailman lifted the lid on the mailbox with one hand and picked up outgoing mail, dropped letters and flyers into the box, and slammed the lid shut with one smooth motion. "Two points," he said, like he had dunked something, although it was obvious he spent more time at the table than on the ball court. The metallic thud of the box's lid let Eurydice know that she had mail.

She wrapped herself in terrycloth and sorted ads from bills and personal stuff. One letter, posted from a clinic on Rampart Street, was marked "confidential" and addressed to her. She googled Delgado Clinic and discovered it was the V.D. clinic of the Orleans Parish Health Department. As she opened the letter and read, it became apparent that she was being notified of exposure.

"What the fuck?" she said aloud and dialed the telephone number from the letter.

"There must be a mistake," she said into the phone. "I don't want an appointment, I want to speak to your supervisor to make sure this doesn't happen to anyone else." She listened and took a deep breath. "OK, book me an appointment. This week, please."

At the clinic she was told to sign in. Yes, they had sent her a notice of exposure, and if she would please just fill out the form, she could see someone. She signed and sat down in the waiting room among piles of pamphlets and a huge and diverse cross section of New Orleans residents.

A tall, black drag queen sat down beside her.

"I love your dress," Eurydice said.

"I'm Miss Mnemosyne," the drag queen said.

"I'm Eurydice. How do you do?" She extended her hand.

Mnemosyne touched her hand with a thumb and two fingers. "Pleasure," she said.

She wore a wide brimmed hat beneath which sat sunshades trimmed in tiny fruit. She moved these down her nose and looked over them when she wanted to inspect something that had caught her attention, and then pushed them back up to hide her eyes and throw shade.

"You got the clap?" asked Mnemosyne.

"I got a notification letter by mistake."

"I've heard of that actually happening. It's possible. Somebody's idea of a sick joke. Quite juvenile I should think."

"That's what I thought, and so I decided I'd come up here and straighten this out."

"Good for you. I like to get to the bottom of a problem myself. You know they require the names of your sexual contacts to treat you?"

"Well, I've only slept with my husband."

"Then you will have no problem with finding out who your contact was, who had them send you a letter."

"No, you don't understand."

"Sister, I understand plenty. This is not my first tour of the financial district."

"Financial…?"

"Toulouse Street, Burgundy Street, Rue Dauphine, St. Louis Street? You know, the financial district, where the werkin' grrrrrrls werk it."

"Oh, my."

"No judgment here. Don't sweat it. They require you to watch a safer sex video and take a post test. Then they give you meds and tell you not to drink any alcohol. You'll do fine."

"But this is a mistaken notification."

"You think? Who's your boyfriend?"

"My husband. He plays guitar in a band called Orpheus."

"Oh, he's cute. I saw them up the street in Armstrong Park. They played for the NO/AIDS Task Force fundraiser."

"You know him?"

"Everybody knows him. Groupies all over the place."

"Groupies?"

"Yeah, honey. I heard he plays both sides of the fence."

"Both sides of the fence?"

"You know. Straight up. Down low. He don't care if it's silk panties or silk boxers hittin' the floor. He just knows he's about to get some satisfaction."

The ward clerk called a number and Mnemosyne stood up.

"That's me. Do I look fabulous?"

She pirouetted for Eurydice.

"Fabulous," said Eurydice.

The Bridge Run drew closer, and as good as Eurydice felt about the event, she would not be able to participate. She put on her sweats and running shoes and warmed up, stretching on the porch. The sunshine felt good as she walked to the very end of Connection Park, near the naval yard. The winding, landscaped paths beside the river soothed her. She crossed the train tracks near the Piety Street Arch and as the Mandeville Street Warehouse came into view she became aware that a man was following her. She ran toward the warehouse in hope there would be more people, perhaps longshoremen on their front end loaders, or hanging out smoking on the loading dock. No one. It appeared locked up tight. The landscaped grass had grown tall and needed mowing. The sprinkler had left water over the cinder path. As she splashed through a low, wet spot she felt a sudden pain in her ankle and saw a large water moccasin retreating into the grass.

Three months later, *Les Delices*, the support group for divorced wives and discarded girlfriends, met in the card room of a Bywater Gay bar. They used to meet up at the main library on Loyola Avenue, but they got too rowdy and left there by request. This bartender needed some daytime patrons in the bar, and the women wanted a place to meet without harassment, so he welcomed them.

"I feel like each time I die and come back there's less of me," said Eurydice. "Maybe it's the pills. I don't get all of me back. I can't put my finger on it, but I don't rember."

"Hi, Stump," the group said. These friends called her "Stump" on account of her peg leg. She'd had a rough few months.

"Hi, ya'll know my story already. I think I've told you? You know there's five rivers in the underworld? Lethe's the river of forgetfulness. The river of oblivion."

She stopped as if trying to remember where this conversation was going, then continued.

"How can I mourn what I've lost if I don't rember… remember what it was?"

"It's ok if you can't remember all of it. Just do your best," said one of the group.

Eurydice thought hard about that day, and her face grew stern.

"The prick at my ankle was noticeable. Painful. I knew something was bad wrong right away. Maybe it was the fear—running from the would be rapist—sweat, fast breaths, racing heart that juiced the venom. It was a big snake—he'd been under that wharf for a long time. As I fell, that other vermin straddled me. Then he saw the snake retreating into the grass."

"He stood up and stood over me for a minute, looking down. Like he couldn't decide if he wanted to fuck me or if I was so full of snake venom he didn't want to stick his dick in there. 'Help me, I'm snake bit,' I said, 'Call 911.' But he ran away."

She grabbed a Kleenex and wiped at angry tears.

"The leg swelled, turned cold and blue, then mottled purple, and finally, black. I couldn't stand up and my throat was closing. I thought, 'No one knows I'm here.'"

"I woke up in the ambulance. The EMTs were frantic as they worked. Floating above myself I heard, 'defibrillate,' 'epi,' 'asystole,' 'we're losing her.' Then the waters of Lethe covered me, and I forgot."

Eurydice rode the merry-go-round in City Park. A cloud of Formosan termites ascended from the old wooden structure. The light was unnaturally bright—Sunny Brilliant—a photographer would call it, with hard-edged, black detail-less shadows. It had a surreal quality, like a De Chirico painting of a wedding.

Mnemosyne, the Maid of Honor, pushed her fruit-edged shades up her nose and handed a bridal bouquet of tropical flowers and tropical fruit to the bride. A snake slithered from the bouquet. Between her thumb and two fingers she held out a packaged condom to Eurydice and said, "Pleasure." The carousel turned as the figures floated up and down.

The calliope sounded out-of-tune as Eurydice, in her white gown and accompanied by her belaureled father, Apollo, stood in a tiny church. She reached for the gold ring. A huge snake hissed at them and retreated beneath a pew on the carousel. Apollo pulled an arrow from his quiver and shot the snake.

Orpheus rode in on a ship bobbing up and down. Jason and the Argonauts were his best man and groomsmen. Orpheus played the lyre as groupies tore off his clothes. Mnemosyne played guitar and sang with them all in a reggae band. They syncopated and rocked, "By the Rivers of Babylon."

The would-be rapist straddled a bridesmaid and snapped a selfie. Then he jumped off the carousel and ran off in the direction of the old golf course. Eurydice chased him as wedding guests threw king cake babies at her. She closed the lead he had on her as they ran beside Bayou St. John, and pulled a large pineapple from her bridal bouquet and threw it at his head. It exploded.

The Sunny Brilliant light faded as a cloud passed, turning the dreamscape to winter gray. Her breath condensed into white clouds and the hem of her gown was filthy with mud. All around her the weeds had grown tall. She raised the hem and looked at her ankle. A water moccasin was stuck to her leg.

"Asystole," said a voice in the ambulance.

"Push a bolus of epi and continue CPR. What's your ETA?" asked a radio voice.

A cloud of flashing red and orange lights delivered them to the emergency department at University Medical Center.

Two years before at an uptown rave, the band was taking a pee break and Apollo LeBlanc had bellied up to the bar for a shot. He wiped some white crystals from the corner of his nose onto his finger, studied them and sniffed them back into his nostril.

Eurydice stood beside him shaking her assets and looking good. She stripped off her top, down to her athletic bra.

LeBlanc noticed and grinned.

"Cuervo shot," Eurydice said to the bartender.

They clicked glasses.

The guitarist downed his in one gulp. His eyes bulged and watered.

She sipped hers and watched him blow out a breath that should not be aimed at open flames.

"Whoa," he said.

"What color are your eyes?" she asked.

"Emerald Isle green. Just like my granddaddy's."

"Where'd you learn to play guitar?"

"In the garage. Nearly drove the neighbors crazy. I wanted to be just like Jimi Hendrix. I read he had seduced over a thousand girls and had invented more guitar sounds than anyone, ever."

Onstage, the drummer began a riff.

"Gotta pay the rent," he said and put three fingers to his eyebrow in a scout salute. Then he was back onstage, shining in the light.

"'A thousand girls,' I shoulda gotta clue," said Stump.

The *Les Delices* women all around the card room made comment: "Should have."

"I hope you know a good gynecologist."

"If orange is the new black, condyloma is the new V.D."

"Smooth."

"Silver tongued devil."

"Could he sing?"

"He played guitar in a band called Orpheus. Pretentious? You think?" said Eurydice.

Eurydice looked around the room at all their faces. Faces that wore that look that scorned women twist their faces into when worthless men are discussed. They too had experienced *the gaze* identified by the post-structuralists, the women's studies scholars, Jacques Lacan. Whether these women had ever read a word of philosophy, they knew from personal experience *the gaze* had yet again been cast upon one of their own with a bad outcome. *The gaze* that diminished autonomy, reduced worth, lessened agency, and objectified.

"Never fall in love with a musician," Eurydice said. "It was always about him. He sucked women dry starting with his mama. 'Apollo Scion LeBlanc, Jr.' is what she saddled him with at birth, so it wasn't entirely his fault."

Eurydice and Lizzie noshed at Cafe Degas near the racetrack.

"What did I ever see in him?" said Eurydice.

"Maybe he was the forbidden bad boy?" said Lizzie.

She is one of the few friends from Les Delices that "Stump" has gradually let into her inner circle. Her inner circle means women's lunches and power meetings over coffee. They do talk honestly, deeply without regard for consequences of a social or business nature. All have something that sets them apart from the norm.

Lizzie has always been of Sappho's tribe, so whatever success she has had repairing cars at Metrix Garage has been of her own making. Her garage. *Hers.*

"I guess it's the James Dean thing. Live fast. Love hard. Die young. Sad part is you pull other people down with you," said Stump.

"I didn't want to marry James Dean. I wanted to BE James Dean," said Lizzie.

She took out a Gitanes and lit it, then rolled the box into the sleeve of her tee shirt. A fleur de lys design stretched tight across her ample bosom. On the back, printed inside a larger fleur de lys, "The milk of human kindness has gone sour." She stretched her legs beneath the wrought iron table, tilted her head back, and blew a blue cloud of smoke toward the ceiling.

"Mama said she always knew I was a lesbian by the way I nursed as a baby. Happy. Content."

"In the myth, Orpheus had a high old time with the argonauts. Sailing around the known world, seducing mortals and gods with his music. He shut down the Sirens in an epic battle of the bands, saving his ship from foundering on the shoals of Scylla. Here's a news flash—guitar man freaked out the first time the Navy closed the hatches on him in the eastern Mediterranean. The slightest swells at sea and he would start to vomit. The captain had to call for his relief and the music man spent the rest of his heroic career stateside, playing in a band for high-ranking drunks at garden parties."

"Is the divorce finalized?"

"It's done. No kids. He keeps paying for the house, which is now in my name."

"The p.c. term for 'stump' is *residuum* or residual limb," said the prosthetist. People call him Joe. Months have passed since the event that took my leg. I feel that I've been underwater, or sleeping through my life since they resuscitated me. Resuscitated me twice, actually. Once in the ambulance, and again a week later when sepsis killed me. These facts are intact in my brain now that I am awake again. Just as I know his name is Joe and that his hands are warm and familiar on the residuum of my missing leg.

Denial is a powerful thing, as are the other components of the psyche that protect the ego from too much reality. They tell me that I wouldn't even look at, wouldn't touch, wouldn't bathe or care for the stump, but Joe has washed, dried, massaged coco butter into it, and is now gently, factually telling me what to expect in the future. Apparently I have a future.

Joe was working in front of me when I again became aware. Somehow I knew he was familiar, perhaps I had spent time looking at his bald spot as he measured and assessed my legs.

All of my life I was a good walker, a good runner.

"We will make your oak prosthesis similar in size to your other leg. Your muscles of your calf—extensor, peroneus, gastrocnemius, tibialis and medial and lateral malleolus—are well defined." He patted my leg and sat it down, then turned to his work table. His tools—tape measure, chisel, grinder, and sander—remind me of a painting I once saw in the Louvre, *Joseph the Carpenter*.

Mythical beings often reveal themselves to me if I look at them from a different perspective. Orpheus and Eurydice, Mnemosyne, Apollo—did you know Apollo was father to both Eurydice and Orpheus by different women? They are half siblings.

St. Joseph, I'm sure, was no stranger to the odd viewpoint—the Virgin Mary, a star in the east, this child whom he knew wasn't his. Yet, he was to function as his earthly father. Mnemosyne, Titan goddess of memory and creator of language and words, was the mother of the Muses.

"I want to begin again on this stump, rooted in oak. My namesake was an oak dryad, so it is fitting that I regain my legs and walk back into my life in this way."

The End

Katya

OLD PLASTER ON the upper half of the walls still bore earth-tone paint, a cheerful color like the inside of a ripe avocado. The lower half of the walls was exposed bargeboard.

"A fixer upper after Katrina," the FBI social worker had told Katya. "You any good with tools? The floors are good—cypress. New polyurethane. The electrical stuff's all new. The place's got plenty of outlets now."

Katya touched the line where the plaster had been knocked away. "So this is how high the water rose?" She felt the social worker looking at her stainless steel dental caps and covered her mouth with her fingers.

"That's it. They stripped out everything that had been underwater or grew mold. The house has been raised five feet on solid pilings, so it meets the new flood code. The previous owner kept seeing ghosts—people floating half way up and the rooms filled with water."

Katya's fight-or-flight response was triggered by real dangers, live people. Lizbet was her only ghost. Katya had gone to the police station morgue back in Odessa to identify her. That's how she busted out her teeth, hit the floor beside the stainless steel body drawer.

The social worker stopped toward the back of the house at a j-shaped stairs. "This is the stairs to the bedrooms. They call it a camelback. We had two bedroom sets delivered. Agent Livaudais has a debit card for you for sheets and stuff."

Katya climbed the steep, narrow stairs to the second story with the social worker behind her. The view to the south was toward the Mississippi

River. She could see outlines of warehouses, a wide space where the railroad tracks ran, metallic and concrete walkways intermittently connected strips of green with the warehouses, and the river meandered like a fat lazy water moccasin swimming in the sun.

The FBI social worker sounded like a real estate agent when she said, "It's called Crescent Park and gives people a grand view of the downtown waterfront and the twin bridges, the Crescent City Connection. New Orleans and the river has always been a popular motif."

Katya smiled at her. *That is where I washed up.*

Three weeks earlier, she had stood on a narrow ledge of deck outside the safety rail of the Ukrainian flagged rust bucket, Sevastopol, calculating the distance to the edge of the wharf. Rapid breaths sent white clouds of vapor into the unnatural blue light of a New Orleans night. As turbulent, muddy water boiled up between the freighter and the Napoleon Avenue wharf, the distance between the bollards and the ship's hull varied minute-to-minute. Katya's knuckles blanched white in a death grip on the freezing rail, "One, two, three… JUMP!" she said and gripped tighter. Mississippi River currents pulled at the ship—five feet, six feet, seven. Fat mooring lines wrapped in figure eights groaned and relaxed with the currents as whirlpools sucked at the hull and disappeared downstream. The same blue light bathed the shipping containers on the dock and shimmered across the restless surface of the water. Against a cacophony of giant blue cranes moving shipping containers at night, a passing train, and automobile traffic overhead on the two spans connecting the Eastbank and Westbank, she prayed for courage, "God help me. When it gets to five feet again I jump."

Yearning for freedom overpowered the fear of certain death. The sound of waves slapping at pilings intensified as a ship passed and the hull drew closer to the wharf—eight feet, seven, six, five… Katya leaned forward as if to jump but her shoes, greasy from weeks of working in the ship's galley, slipped and she went head first into the water where a powerful current pulled her down into blackness. No time to even scream.

Turbid, cold water rolled and raced east toward a curve in the river between Algiers Point and the Governor Nicholls Street Wharf. The river here was at its deepest, two hundred feet with a velocity equal to a hundred and sixty six freighters of muddy water passing per second. Most light is blocked out at two feet. All light has gone by eight feet.

Her lungs burned with a panicked need for air. Completely disoriented in the darkness, up and down had reversed. A bubble of coughed air floated nose to mouth, chin to chest. Floundering, she reached down, which was up, toward her ankles. Katya prayed for luck as cold air hit her wet skin and she broke the surface. "Ahhhhhhh," she screamed, and choked on muddy water that smelled like petrochemical waste as the current bore her beneath a lighted bridge, the Crescent City Connection. With an adrenaline powered scissor kick she stayed just above the currents which sucked at her shoes like monsters from the unknown deep. She inched toward lights and the dark outline of warehouses on the riverbank. As hope yielded to exhaustion and consciousness dimmed, she bumped solidly into a piling. Instinctively her body crawled onto the muddy riverbank beneath the Mandeville Street Wharf.

The morning news carried two stories about the river: A Ukrainian sailor fell overboard and disappeared at the Napoleon Avenue Wharf, and a Faubourg Marigny woman walking her dog in Crescent Park called 911 after hearing a half-drowned woman crawling out of the river screaming, "Oh my God! Oh my God! Oh my God! I am alive!" The Ukrainian sailor was presumed dead, and the woman was recovering at University Medical Center.

Delirium came with the fever. The news report sounded so final, so happy ever after, "The woman is recovering at University Medical Center."

A map of the United States, shows the Mississippi River watershed which drains runoff containing animal waste, fertilizer, insecticides and herbicides from farms and cities, and petrochemical waste from factories in thirty one states. After nearly drowning in that toxic soup one would not want to come to in a hospital bed and hear "aspiration pneumonia" from two medical students at your bedside.

Dreams came with the delirium. Katya's real mother, not Dosvedanya Mama, took Katya as a baby to a blue-domed church through cold and snow. Her baby blanket felt hot on her face, and she tried to push it away, but her swaddling cloth restricted her hands. An old priest dabbed holy water on her forehead and called her by her name. A woman? Her? Lizbet? was abducted and taken to a warehouse in Odessa where a demonic surgical team harvested her organs. She woke up in the morgue looking at herself looking down at her diminished body. She said, "Lizbet!" and broke all her teeth on the terrazzo floor. The deck of the Sevastopol was a giant waterslide from the galley hatch that led down into polluted river water. She kicked and pushed with her greasy shoes. As filthy water sucked her air, one of the demonic surgical team said, "Katya, we're suctioning your endotracheal tube. Take a deep breath. OK? OKaaaaaay?" Everything went black as a buzzer on a ventilator next to her bed signaled a dive and the submarine descended.

Katya stepped into a gondola that floated in a river that smelled of flowers. She sat on the gondola seat as her boatman, Charon, dipped his oar into the sweet-smelling water.

"What do you get out of this, Katya?" he asked her, conversation between fellow travelers on a river cruise.

Katya held a gold coin between her teeth and unscrewed the top on a bottle of vodka. She offered Charon a drink.

He wiped his parched mouth and took the coin. "This stuff is ice cold. You must have smuggled it in."

"We girls have our ways." She took a deep gulp of the cold vodka which tasted like plastic. "What is this river?" The ventilator buzzer sounded when she tried to speak, but Charon seemed to know what she meant.

"Lethe, the river of oblivion. It's one of five here," said Charon. He didn't look like a black monster at all, but was quite handsome with long dreads, tall, with smooth brown skin, and a mouth full of gold teeth. He seemed to be fond of smiling. A name tag on his shirt said, *Special Agent Beauregard Livaudais.*

By day three in the ICU of University Medical Center, antibiotics and respiratory therapy had Katya's oxygen saturation back to normal, but her confusion seemed to be getting worse. The registered nurse checked everything on her list and held Katya's hand. "I'll be back in half an hour.

Here's your call light. Press it if you need something in the meantime, I'll be right here."

Special Agent Livaudais was on second shift, guarding Katya. When the nurse left, he stood at her bedside looking down at her. She bit hard on the plastic endotracheal tube with her painful looking metal teeth. Her hair, which had been buzzed, was growing back. He imagined she would be an attractive woman if her teeth were decently capped, and she had a normal hairdo. He was startled to see her blue eyes open staring intently at him like someone who just saw a snake.

He put his hand over hers. To his touch it felt ice cold. "It's OK. I'm not here to hurt you." He left his warm hand over hers which remained in polycotton restraints. She did not take her eyes off him.

His hand felt warm and she sensed no danger from him. Touch seemed to be a universal language so she withdrew her hand and pointed to a clipboard with a writing tablet on the bedside table. She made a motion that she wanted to write him a note and turned her hand up and down in the restraint.

"I'll loosen this, but I'm holding on to the ends," he said and gave her a pencil. He held the clipboard for her.

"Cold vodka?" she wrote.

"I feel ya," he said, "but I'm fresh out."

When the nurse returned and read what Katya had written, she smiled as if a riddle had been answered. "You like cold vodka, Katya?"

"Yes. Please," Katya wrote back.

"Do you drink every day?"

"Yes. The Daddy Kat Klub gives us points for the number of drinks customers buy us."

The nurse dialed the doctor on call. "I think I've found Katya's problem, alcohol withdrawal. Maybe we could begin a detox protocol?" The nurse left the room and returned shortly with an injection of valium. "This is going to make your bad dreams go away. Do you have any allergies to downers?"

Her respiratory status rapidly improved and the endotracheal tube and ventilator were taken away the next day. She had come to trust Agent Livaudais and would tell him things she wouldn't tell others.

"What can I bring you when I come tomorrow, Katya?"

"A pizza?" she said.

So Beauregard stopped at Roma for a medium pizza and a Mediterranean salad, which they split for supper the next day.

The nurse came in with a tray from the cafeteria. She looked at the pizza and salad from Roma and said, "I think that looks so much better than this." She had several sheets of paper with discharge plans. An FBI Social Worker helped fill in the blanks.

"She's getting discharged into the witness protection program. We have her a house," said the Social Worker. When the discharge nurse left and they had some privacy, she said, "Your new name is Kat Broussard. You'll be out of here tomorrow."

When Beauregard left his shift at eleven o'clock he asked, "What can I bring you tomorrow?"

"Ice cold vodka," she said.

The FBI Social Worker drove the SUV across downtown New Orleans, by the French Quarter, across Faubourg Marigny and stopped in front of a camelback Creole cottage in the gentrifying Bywater Neighborhood.

"Your new home." said Beau. "Here's a housewarming gift," he said and handed her a fifth of vodka in a paper sack that he had bought last night and put in his freezer. "Don't let her see this or I will get in trouble."

Kat quickly put it in her freezer and kissed his cheek.

The social worker had walked through the house and checked off the newly delivered furniture and appliances. "The kitchen is the last room all the way to the back. New appliances. Your washer/dryer is installed in the utility room in the garage. Call Agent Livaudais for anything you might need. He's your handler."

Kat's first priority was to turn one of the empty rooms into a dojo. She had no illusions that Hydra would not try to kill her. She knew too much. So she caught the Marigny/Bywater bus to the French Market and began to check items off her list: torchiere lamp, bamboo stick, large shirt, hat, dummy's head, self-defense books, incense, and buddha incense burner.

At a junk store on lower Decatur Street she found a folding grocery cart on wheels.

"Is there a used book store nearby?" she asked the clerk.

"About six blocks up on Royal Street."

As Kat walked uptown she caught sight of her reflection in store windows and decided she looked too much like a homeless person. So, she turned down a narrow carriage way beneath a sign, *Thieves Market - A Treasure Chest*. Inside she bought a bandana for her head, some beaded earrings and tri-color plastic sunglasses. As she continued up Royal Street toward the used book store her reflection looked more agreeable to her, like a local hipster who had lived in the French Quarter since before Katrina.

A bewildered tourist stopped her on the street. "Could you tell me how to get to the French Market?"

Kat smiled. "You are nearly there. Four blocks as you are headed, and turn right for two more blocks. You will run right into it."

At *The Bard Antiquarian Books* Kat approached the shop owner who was lost in *The Empire of Cotton*.

"How can I help you?" he asked.

"I turn a room in my house into a dojo. Do you have any books on self defense?"

"We have some. You can leave your cart here out of the way."

He led her down narrow aisles lined to the ceiling on both sides. Smells reminded her of mice, dust mites, and cockroaches. He pushed a rolling library ladder aside and squatted down near the floor. After a minute he stood with several books and brushed off the tops with a duster. Kat saw dust motes in the slanted beams of light from the front windows. A mule-drawn carriage full of tourists passed on the street, as a liveried black man in a stove pipe hat pointed his whip toward Royal Street shops.

"I have these," he said. "The two blue books here are suited for close fighting with knives, Pekiti-Tirsia. I have standard texts for jujitsu, judo and aikido. This last one is krav maga, which is the form of defense used by the Israeli defense forces. These all have ideas on how to furnish, or rather, not furnish your dojo." He smiled at her and gestured to a seat where she could browse. "I'll be at the desk when you decide."

Kat bought all six books. "Where do I catch the bus back to Bywater?"

she asked the clerk as he handed her her change and gave back her folding grocery cart packed with all her stuff.

He pointed toward the river. "Two blocks. North Peters and St. Louis Streets."

She had tied a bamboo stick across a torchiere lamp and buttoned a shirt onto this scarecrow. A styrofoam mannequin's head wore a bowler hat. Kat focused her kicks to its throat and head. This room might have been a dining room or a bedroom before Kat turned it into her dojo and began to assault her dummy in several methods of martial arts. She hit the scarecrow's adam's apple and where its sternum might have been. Callouses had begun to grow along the sides of her hands and feet, and darkened her knuckles. As a fighter she circled her opponent, always looking for an opening.

Behind her, in the kitchen, furthermost back in the old Creole house, a shadow fell across the new refrigerator. The dark figure of a man with a stocking pulled over his head entered soundlessly through the back door. He crept toward the dojo, advancing when Kat's back was turned. As she kicked upward he grabbed her from behind, pinning her arms.

Kat leaned her weight forward. When she felt his center of gravity shift, she brought her elbow back, hard, into his ribcage over his liver.

"Oooofff," he said.

She raked his shin with the heel of her shoe as she stomped the top of his foot. She felt his arms loosen and turned with her left leg between his, then brought her knee hard up into his groin. As he slumped over she punched his sternum and his adam's apple.

"I give. I give," he said as he sank to the floor, pulled the stocking from his head, and shook out his dreads.

"Minimum effort. Maximum advantage," Kat said and straddled his muscular torso with her equally muscular legs. Seven years of pole-dancing in an erotic cabaret had left her well-toned. She sat down on his pelvis.

"I saw you when you crossed the kitchen," she said.

"You did not."

"A board creaked. You are gaining weight, Beauregard."

"I am not."

She pulled his shirt up and pinched fat at his beltline. "Muffin top," she said.

"Quit. Stop that," he said. He pushed her hands away as she felt a stirring and pressure rising in his crotch.

"I am surprised you did not grab a snack from the refrigerator."

"Well, speaking of eating—I thought we could go to Marcello's for lunch. My real reason for being here, of course, is to give you the keys to the back door that the locksmith left at the office."

She pulled his shirt up further and pinched his nipples between her thumbs and forefingers. "Do you ever wonder why men have nipples?" She felt in his pockets for the keys and found an erection.

"Stop it," he said.

Kat felt more turgor pressing between her legs. She stood and slowly pulled off her top and athletic bra. "I won this fight. I want to see you naked, fat boy."

"Kick my junk up to my throat and want to see me naked. You cold."

"Strip for me. I will strip for you," she said as Beau kicked off his remaining clothes.

Their illicit affair, she, an FBI informant, and he, her handler, was as sweet as it was dangerous. This mutual orgasm and falling onto their backs, sweat against cool cypress was, at that moment, the most valuable thing in the world to them both. They lay on the floor and interlaced their fingers to get more skin contact. She brought his dark brown hand to her face and stroked it with her calloused fingers. She sniffed the combined smells of their sex and sighed.

He brushed her shoulder a well-healed scar in a shape like an octopus.

"I've been curious," he said, "but I was hesitant to ask. What's this?"

"It is a brand. A hydra."

He rose over her and propped on one elbow. With the tips of his fingers he idly drew slow figure eights around her breasts. Then he leaned down to her face and kissed her.

"Let's go to Marcello's and split a po-boy," he said.

"Good idea, fat boy. You can start your diet afterwards." She kissed him back.

As they stood up to dress, Kat rubbed her fingers over scars crisscrossing the backs of Beau's legs on otherwise flawless skin. "As long as we are trading secrets, what are these?" she asked.

"Stepdaddy's whuppin'."

Marcello was an Italian grocer whose Spanish-looking patio was enclosed on three sides by Creole style buildings. The other wall of brick had a wrought iron gate. Language, food, and styles of building were as mixed and spicy as a bowl of gumbo. The street sign on his corner bore two names: Royal Street and *Rue Royale.* The sign on the cross street was *Franklin Street.* The neighborhood for two hundred years had been named in French, *Faubourg Marigny.* Jasmine covered one brick wall of the patio. The top of the wall gave a false assurance of safety with shards of broken glass embedded into concrete beneath broad leaves of a banana tree. A mirliton vine reached toward a ray of sunshine. The muted sounds of the city floated just over the wall—the Algiers Ferry horn, a calliope on a paddle wheeler, a slow-moving train, cranes on the docks and the sounds of a traditional jazz band toward the French Market. They split a shrimp po boy and a bag of Zapp's potato chips. Kat had come to love Barq's root beer.

Beau wiped the top of the table and checked his cell phone messages. Kat took a writing tablet and pen from her back pack. She checked a money order made out to Cafe Croissant Bakery and wrote a note to her mother.

Mamochka,

This is but a note and a money order sent through Valeria at the bakery, but it carries my heart to you. Do not begrudge Valeria her 20% for receiving this letter and cashing the money order for you. She does this at some risk—Ukraine is a devious place.

Oleksander's misfortune with jaundice is his own doing. Drinking bootleg vodka from a neighbor's illegal distillery is stupid. But he was never a smart man.

I hope he is soon dead. (Don't think bad of me).

Beau is working on getting you a passport so you can immigrate. I cannot imagine Ukraine having an interest in keeping a poor widow.

I love you, my dearest, and dream of a blue-domed church in the snow, where you took me for christening as a baby. My earliest memory, an old man saying my name and dabbing holy water on my forehead.

Love, K.

She addressed the letter to a bakery in Kiev with a good trade in international tourists. The bank would not question a money order from the U.S. The return address was a postal services store on Decatur Street. She sealed it and handed it to Beau. "Mail this?"

He put it in his pocket. "The Odessa police closed the Daddy Kat Klub," said Beau.

"That is good. I imagine Vitaly is ordering hits all over Ukraine."

"He and the suits had a meeting at the Lodge on the Dnieper."

"Good whiskey? Cohiba cigars? Strippers?"

"He wants to know 'Who's talking to the police?' Your name was prominently mentioned."

"I knew they would not just let me walk away."

"Did you think about all of this before you turned states witness?'

"The pricks should not have killed Lizbet and sold her organs online."

The Marigny/Bywater bus, with its purple, green and gold stripe, shook the alluvial dirt, Marcello's Green Market, and the wall of the Spanish patio as it rumbled past, headed back uptown. Fumes of burnt gas drifted over the patio wall mixing with scents of jasmine, fried seafood, and a coffee roasting warehouse somewhere downriver.

At Canal Street she caught the Magazine Street bus uptown to Bazaar Bizarre, a funky junktique market near the Riverbend. A display of hunting knives, left over military junk, and camping gear drew her attention into a poorly lit shop. The merchant, a fat man with a greasy stain on his shirt, eyed Kat lasciviously and tugged at his crotch.

"Can I help you?" he asked. His breath smelled of onions, cold cuts, and cheese.

"I am looking for a knife I can use for self defense," she said running her finger down a glass display case, "but none of these will do."

She wandered down aisles of junk in the cavernous room and circled a mannequin that she thought might come in handy.

The shopkeeper had not stopped staring at her. From behind the mannequin she watched him. He looked like a yard dog sniffing a bitch in heat.

She undid one button at the top of her blouse and returned to the glass top counter at the front of the store. She leaned over and rested her elbows as she looked down at the hunting and kitchen knives on display.

"I like your knives," she said, "but I do not see what I need."

"Exactly what is it you need, ma'am?"

"An out-the-front switchblade."

"Switches is illegal."

"But you can get me one, right?"

The fat merchant chewed his lips like a speed freak and rubbed his palms together.

Kat's eyes filled with crocodile tears. "You look like the kind of guy who would help a girl out if she was in trouble. You see, there is this man who has been following me. I think he means to do me harm."

The merchant motioned her to the shadowy rear of the shop and pulled a bundle of knives from a trunk. He put five blades on a table for her to look at.

"Careful. They're all pointed and sharp. This is where the blade comes out." He pressed a button on one with an ivory handle and an eight inch blade sprang out with a click.

Kat handled them all, pressed the buttons, checked their balance, and guessed whether or not they would slip in her hand if it was coated with blood.

"This one," she said and pulled out a wad of bills. "How much for the mannequin?"

With the blade in her pants pocket and the mannequin over her shoulder she caught the Magazine Street bus back downtown.

Near the Lakefront Airport at the regional headquarters of the FBI, Kat experienced a purge of emotions akin to a religious revival. With each gangster she outed she felt poison leach from her soul like a boil that had been lanced.

"This woman, Yulia Lipka, was recently arrested when they closed the Daddy Kat Klub in Odessa. Do you recognize her?"

The FBI employee flashed photos of suspected Russian/Ukrainian mob agents on the screen. It was his task to place suspects of the Hydra organization into the structure of the Zaporishya Brotherhood. It was like working a giant jigsaw puzzle.

"I knew her as Dosvedanya Mama. Seven years and I did not even know her real name. She was our 'mother' at the club, our madam. She controlled access to our identification papers, money, transportation, days off, health care."

"She is charged with prostitution and trafficking."

"She should be charged with much more—like kidnapping and conspiracy to commit murder. She set up Lizbet Dombrowski's abduction and murder."

"How do you know this, Kat?"

"She gave me and Lizbet time off together to catch the tram to Shevchenko Park. There is a transit station there where I could buy a money order for my mother. She knew where we would be and when we would be back. Mama, this woman, 'Yulia' you say, did not approve of Lizbet and me. She thought since Lizbet was thirty-years-old, her shelf life as a prostitute had expired. I was twenty-one, and she thought of me as having some good years left."

"So she gave you time off together?"

"I saw the abduction. It was a white van. I think I recognized two of the three men's voices. The third one knocked me to the sidewalk, the one who banged Lizbet's head into the van door. He never said a word." Her voice broke and tears started. "They harvested her organs and sold them just like meat."

The agent gave her a Kleenex. "Let's take a break. Would you like some coffee? I'll have some fresh sent up from the cafeteria."

"She said something that afternoon when I got back to the club that I found really terrifying. Something about 'selling organs being so barbaric.' But they use that fear to control you."

The building always seemed overly air-conditioned to Kat. She wrapped her fingers around the cup to warm them as she walked around the office and looked at framed pictures of groups of agents. "Lizbet's body did not wash up on Luzanovka Beach until a week later. How would Yulia know that on the day Lizbet was abducted?"

Kat stopped behind the desk and cocked her head to one side as she carefully scrutinized one of the pictures on the wall.

"What?" the agent asked.

Kat pointed to one of the men in a group with a soccer ball. "Who is this?"

"He's with the Kiev branch. Liason with Interpol. That was a group exercise to build esprit d' corps."

"Did you ever wonder why he has on long pants and is so covered up when you others are in shorts?"

"No. But now that you mention it."

"He was at a meeting of the suits at Lodge on the Dneiper. This must have been seven years back. I was new to Hydra. He has, or had, tattoos on his knees, stars—they do not touch the ground, meaning he does not kneel for anyone. He had epaulets tattooed on his shoulders to indicate his high rank and he had a stylized knife through his neck, advertising he was an assassin for hire. To the mob in Russia, they say each man wears his life's history on his skin."

"How do you know this?"

"Vitaly had finished with me after six months. He had given me a Mercedes and literally showered me with diamonds. He would pierce something new every week—my nose, a nipple, earlobe, lips, labia, an eyebrow—and hang a gold ring there with a tear drop diamond. I guess after six months he had grown tired of the game, or maybe he just ran out of parts to pierce, and took the Mercedes back and yanked out all the gold loops. I had more wounds than Saint Sebastian. Then he threw me to the wolves at Hydra."

The agent refilled her coffee cup.

Kat was quiet for a few minutes, remembering and arranging what she wanted to say.

"So, I was fourteen and the new girl on the auction block. This one, they called him 'The Bear' because he was so hairy, bought me for the night. His needs were specific, 'The youngest girl. Shave any pubic hair, and style her hair in puppy dog ears high on the sides of her head. Have her come to my room with a teddy bear hanging from one hand.' I was to knock on the door and say, 'Daddy, I had a bad dream.'"

The agent pulled the picture from the wall and broke the glass. He pulled out the picture and showed it to Katya. "You're absolutely sure about this?"

"Yes."

He buzzed an assistant on the intercom, "Mrs. Griffin, could you bring an evidence kit in here? I have something to enter regarding the Kiev mole."

Back at her dojo Kat had a stick in her hand and stabbed, punched, and kicked her new dummy. She had worked up quite a sweat. Red Xs over the dummy's pulse points marked where arteries would lay close to the skin. The throat on either side of the larynx, the arms at the inside of the elbows and the armpits, the top of the collar bones just in front of the shoulders, the angle of the jaw beneath the ears, base of the skull, over the heart, between the ribs, over the liver, the spleen, both sides of the groin, back of the knees, the wrists above the thumbs. She intended to spill some blood.

After an hour's hard workout Kat lit a cone of incense and placed it in Buddha's lap.

"Your dick is on fire," she said and headed to the shower. The afternoon's debriefing and her workout had left her exhausted. She went to bed early and immediately fell asleep.

Kat dreamed a fast-repeating GIF video of herself faceplanting into the terrazzo floor of the Odessa police morgue. Each replay of the video ended with a resounding "bang."

"Bang bang bang," woke her from sleep at two a.m. She rubbed her eyes and looked through the slats of the shutters.

"Who is there?" she said.

Beau stepped off the front porch and into the light.

"Kat, I love you."

"You are drunk, Beau. Go home."

"It's our anniversary—two months." He held up a paper sack. "I got some vodka."

"Then go drink it."

"I got something else." He held up a gift-wrapped box. "Vodka's cold."

"Cold?"

The buzzer on the front door sounded.

Beau entered and ran to the stairs. He climbed them two at a time as Kat pulled on a sheer lace robe.

She stood in the bedroom door, a wanton, backlit and radiant as Beau handed her the bottle of cold vodka.

"You struck out at the Bachelors Quarters?" she said.

"I could only think about you. I missed you. I wanted to see you."

"Liar. All night at the club and all you could think about was me? You liar." She grabbed his lips and chin. "Let me see your lips when you lie. I want to feel how your mouth moves." She shoved him across the landing, turned, and walked into the bedroom.

"I love you, Kat." He came into her bedroom holding the gift.

She eyed it with suspicion and took it from his hand. "What is this?" she said and unwrapped it.

"Our two month anniversary."

Kat held up a crystal heart and read the inscription, "Beau and Kat 4 Ever." She took the bottle of vodka and swallowed several mouthfuls, then threw the crystal heart against the wall. She climbed into Beau's arms and wrapped her legs around his strong torso and her arms around his neck. He was as solid as a tree. "Liar. You beautiful liar," she said.

"Don't give me shit," she said. "A man gave me a Mercedes convertible when I was fourteen, then he pierced everything on my body he could reach in his twisted mind and put gold loops with teardrop-shaped diamonds in the holes. Six months later he took the car away and ripped out all the loops, leaving me bleeding on my bedroom floor. Love is free or it is nothing."

"You should have told me before I wasted my money."

They finished the vodka sitting on her bed. Their lips collided like magnet and steel—her metal temporary caps and his gold grill. She pulled off her lingerie and threw it aside as he ripped at his clothes. Their mouths tasted of liquor, spit and blood.

"How did I get hooked up with a crazy woman like you?"

"You violated your professional code of ethics and seduced a client."

Beau had suggested to Kat that her mail would be safer in a post office box from a mail services store. "You don't want your letters and bills setting out on the porch."

So she had rented a box from Vieux Carre Postal Services on Decatur Street. At the door of the shop she dropped the junk mail into the trash and stepped outside into a French Quarter morning. Smells rose from the street where merchants swept and scrubbed cocktail waste and vomit from the sidewalks into the gutters where it mingled with the aroma of mule dung from rental carriages and other leftover waste from the previous night's bacchanal. The Morning Call added more optimistic smells of cafe au lait and beignets to the mix. St. Louis Cathedral bells summoned the faithful to mass. Church bells always reminded Kat of her mother in Ukraine. *I miss Mamochka.* She stepped off the sidewalk toward the French Market.

"Look out!" screamed a woman.

Kat jumped back by reflex onto the sidewalk as a car, a rental car from the airport, jumped the curb blowing out a tire and colliding with the base of a cast metal balcony support. The collision left stunned silence and a deep V crushed into the car's front end. From the driver's side a man with tattoos on his face emerged focused on Kat. He covered the distance from the car to her in an instant and pulled a hunting knife as he did.

Kat recognized him—Mikelo, a mid-level assassin from Hydra. She knew him from the Daddy Kat Klub. Sexually impotent from an old back injury, he was fond of snuffing prostitutes with a knife. Kat had once talked with him when he was very drunk and he said, "I like to kill up close and personal. When I stick them I like to watch the lights go out in their eyes." She instantly knew Vitaly had sent him to cut her throat and to cut out her tongue as a warning to others in Hydra who might have occasion to talk to the authorities. He was likely expecting someone untrained in martial arts and unarmed, "a washed-up whore" was something else he had once said to her. So Kat knew she had an advantage and flicked open her switchblade behind her as Mikelo said, "Come to papa."

He slashed at her throat as she dodged and circled. He came closer to her and stabbed for her chest. As she turned slightly to let his momentum slip by she thought of her knife dance from Pekiti-Tirsia and began. She slid her blade into his rib cage on the right slicing his liver and danced in a graceful arc behind him where she sliced the arteries to both his kidneys. Reaching over his right shoulder she sank her blade again just behind his clavicle slicing his subclavian artery. As he looked for her over his shoulder she cut his eyeball.

For a moment he looked like he regretted getting out of bed this morning, and he regretted having drunk so much at the bars on Bourbon Street the night before. He again slashed wildly at her throat when he caught sight of her with his good left eye, but she ducked down low into a squat and stabbed his femoral arteries. As his arterial blood ran into the gutter to mix with the fragrances of the morning, Kat said, "Your dick is in the dirt."

He crumpled to his knees as the bells of St. Louis sounded the last of their call to worship. Shortly he fell face down into the gutter.

The police arrived within four minutes. One of the officers searched his pockets as another searched his rental car.

A tourist who saw the whole thing said, "He tried to run over her with his car, then he came after her with a knife."

Another officer read from a plane ticket. "Odessa. I don't think that's in Texas."

Agent Livaudais arrived shortly after the police. He showed the officer in charge his identification and spoke quietly into his ear. Then he put Kat into his car and drove her home.

"He is Mikelo, one of Vitaly's assassins," she said. "I have to put an end to this or I will never have any peace. I need to get Mamochka out of Kiev."

"How can I help?"

"Get her a plane ticket and a passport. We have to work quickly, or they will kill her." It wasn't exactly a lie, but she left Beau with the impression she was going to Kiev.

For Katya, de-planing in Odessa seemed both a homecoming and a return to bondage. Passengers could still smoke here, she hated the stench of cigarettes. Her Mamochka, newly widowed, still lived in Kiev and expected Katya to visit in three days. Her following *EuropCar* signs through a cyrillic maze after months of English was a detour back into trafficking hell. She left the EuropCar desk, accessed her rental SUV, and headed for Arcadia Beach. There were only two reasons young women stay in the Rischeliyevskaya Hotel: It's near the train station, and its status as a sex carnival on the northshore of the Black Sea. For her it was where she hoped to find Vitaly, the pimp who had turned her out seven years before. When she found him she had a rough idea of what she would do.

With short spikes of moussed platinum hair and metal caps on her teeth she let it be known without speaking a word that she had no interest in attracting anyone. Indeed, her black jeans and black pullover (three of each in her suitcase) lent themselves only to work. Her severe appearance belied the allure and beauty that only a few months before had had her starring with Lizbet in *Duo* at the Daddy Kat Klub. She had commanded $1,000 per night for her sexual favors. Her years of pole dancing had left her taut, lean and beautiful. The beautiful part had changed with her faceplant onto the morgue floor.

The recently closed club had been the anchor for revitalizing a rundown area of delapidated Soviet era limestone buildings. Her testimony to the FBI and their sharing information with Interpol had brought about its closure, and brought down many powerful gangsters. Another, less wanted result, was that again it set in motion the slow creep of blight into the neighborhood. What had been a rejuvenated business district now lay fallow and wasting. She parked the SUV out of sight in an empty parking lot behind the club.

A studio apartment upstairs had been her home for seven years so she knew which boarded up windows were the kitchen. She felt the nails in the boards and counted eight of them as she wrote a list of supplies she would need. Her "rough idea of what she would do" took shape with the detailed list of items.

EpiCentre K is Ukraine's version of the big box hardware store. She looked like a stereotypical lesbian pushing her oversized shopping cart down the wide aisles. She gathered things: a crowbar, hammer, tiny nails, big nails, nylon rope, a box cutter, a plastic five gallon fuel container, a carton of paper matches, cans of acetone, a battery powered flashlight, and duct tape. At checkout she added replacement batteries and paid the clerk.

Back at the Risheliyevskaya Hotel she hauled the stuff in two large plastic shopping bags up to her room, and returned to the clerk at the desk.

"I am being followed. Someone wants to hurt me. I wonder if you could tell me where I could buy a taser?"

The clerk looked behind her and to both sides, "I do not see anyone following you. Are you sure?"

"They are not here now, but when I go out in the street I catch a glimpse of them fairly frequently. What I need has two electrodes, an X 2 Defender. It shoots twice without having to recharge."

"Tasers are fairly easy to find in Ukraine. All weapons, in fact, if you know where to look." He rested his hand palm up on the desk.

Katya slipped money into it.

The clerk dialed the phone and briefly spoke into it. Then hung up.

"There is a tobacco kiosk just down the street. Go there in an hour and ask for a basket of cherries. She will charge you $200. Have correct change."

"Do you also know of a veterinarian? I need medication for my horse. We are moving him in a trailer tomorrow."

The clerk entered a search term into his computer. "ExcelVet. Here is the address on Troitskaya Street." He handed her a piece of paper.

"Thank you," said Katya.

"Enjoy your stay at Arcadia Beach. If I can be of further assistance…" He pocketed the cash.

Katya took the tram to Troitskaya Street and found the vet. A spring operated bell chimed as she entered.

A man in a dirty lab coat covered in animal hairs and spatters of blood appeared behind the counter and impatiently asked, "How can I help you?"

"We are moving my gelding tomorrow and he needs to be sedated before we try to put him in the trailer."

"I see. It seems like everybody is moving horses this week." He went to the back of the shop and returned with several syringes and two vials. "These are xylazine and acepromazine, "ace" and "X." Used together they act quickly and should keep the animal sedated for an hour or two. It is calming, so they wake up without terrors. I call it a 'smooth landing.' Follow directions on the package for dosing by weight. Anything else?"

Katya paid the vet and took the bag.

Outside, she took a deep breath and exhaled. She could feel sweat had dampened the back of her pullover.

The tram let her off near the tobacco kiosk. As she approached, an obese woman looked over the top of a movie magazine.

"Gauloises. No filter," said Katya. She didn't smoke, but wanted a cigarette that would completely burn up leaving no filter residue behind.

The merchant put a blue pack of cigarettes on the counter and raised her eyebrows.

"A friend called earlier and said you might have a basket of cherries…?"

"Two-electrode X 2 Defender." She put the cigarettes into a brown bag with the other merchandise. "Two hundred, plus the cigarettes. A girl can not be too careful on these streets."

Katya gave her money plus a large tip. "Thank you. Keep the change."

Back at the hotel she took all the stuff out of its packaging and bundled the trash into the garbage chute. She guessed Vitaly's weight might be around a hundred eighty pounds and, calculating the dosage, she drew up two syringes of ace and X and put the cap back on the needles. She put batteries into the flashlight and arranged all the equipment and supplies into one plastic bag.

She dialed 504 and a number, New Orleans area code. A man answered on the second ring.

"Beau, it is Katya. I am in Ukraine."

"How was your flight to Kiev?"

"I am tired and about to turn in."

"How's your mom?"

"That is what is up. I am not in Kiev. I am back in Odessa."

"Katya, don't be foolish. You know these are dangerous people and you've stirred up some real shit."

"Yes, I know. But I have a big score to settle. I may not make it out of this, so listen up. Mamochka needs her visa and plane ticket tomorrow morning. They will come after her out of pure hate for me."

"It's at the Kiev embassy. I'll call and have them send a car tomorrow morning."

"I will call her and tell her to get a small suitcase packed."

A heavy silence fell between them. Beau was the next to speak.

"It can't end like this, Kat. I love you too much."

"Did they not tell you at Quantico not to fall in love with your stool pigeons?"

Another silence. Then Katya spoke.

"I have to call her. Tomorrow I put an end to this madness one way or another. Do not send the cavalry, Beau. You will just fuck things up. Anyway, they would get here too late. It is already going down."

The line went dead.

Katya dialed her mother in Kiev.

"Mamochka?"

"Babochka!" Sobs and wailing on the line. "Oleksander is dead. Liver failure. We got him buried."

"I am sorry for your loss. Oley was never more than forty watts. Who drinks bootleg vodka from a patched-together still?"

"You do not know how that man suffered over the last two months. I finally took him to the hospital, but there was nothing they could do but keep him comfortable and clean."

"At least you did not have to break your back on that. We will talk about it soon, Mama."

"Yes, day after tomorrow. No?"

"That is why I called you, Mama. Plans have changed. You are getting out tomorrow morning, so pack a small bag. Just the essential stuff. A couple changes of clothes. If you take pictures, remove them from the frames. Your prayer book. A rosary... Leave everything else as if you are returning right after mass."

"This sounds so strange, Katya. Like something on TV."

"A car will come for you very early. The driver will give you your visa and take you to the airport. Tell no one. I repeat to you, tell no one. Your safety, your life, and mine depend on absolute secrecy."

"Oh, Katya..."

"I love you, Mamochka. I will see you in a couple of days. Now go pack."

She made a kiss-kiss sound into the phone and hung up.

The next morning Katya scoped out the area around Cafe Petrograd. It was not long before Vitaly's BMW arrived and he got out. He had always had his breakfast there, even when they were together and she was so young and dumb. Behind him an overdressed girl of about fourteen, platinum blond and very pretty followed in his wake. *His taste in girls hasn't changed.*

Katya drove to the now closed Daddy Kat Klub and parked out of sight at the rear. She used the crowbar to pry the nails loose from the board over the kitchen window, then hauled her equipment inside. From the S&M playroom she dragged a heavy wooden chair into the bar which was decorated a deep red. The carpet and drapery looked like they would burn, and the furniture was all of pressed wood with laminate. She nailed the chair to the floor and tied lengths of nylon rope to the legs and arms.

Early the next morning she returned to Cafe Petrograd and parked near the rear exit. She attached the taser to her belt and hid it with her loose pullover. Inside she requested a table in the back with a clear view of Vitaly's favorite dining spot—overlooking the Potemkin Stairs with a view of the lighthouse and the Black Sea beyond. Katya felt a great weight lift off her shoulders. *One way or another, it ends today.*

Vitaly entered shortly and took his usual seat. The girl wasn't with him. Katya waited until his breakfast was in front of him and he had tucked into it, then slowly walked by his table and toward the restroom at the back. He took a few seconds to recognize her with the short hair and the metal teeth. When he did his face turned an angry red and the veins and cords of muscle in his neck bulged out. She flashed a metallic smile at his recognition of her and quickly walked down the hallway. She stepped into a janitor's closet opposite the doors to the toilets and pulled out her taser.

"Bitch!" he hissed between clenched teeth and dropped his knife and fork onto his plate. He pulled his gun from his coat and outside the toilet, he paused to chamber a round. From her hiding place behind him, Katya aimed her taser at his neck and fired. Vitaly sank to his knees and she fired again. He went limp onto the linoleum floor that smelled like pine cleaner and urine.

Katya worked quickly to drag him through the back exit and into the SUV where she injected one of the syringes into his shoulder. She tied his ankles together, and did the same to his wrists.

"A little kinder takedown than you gave Lizbet, you son of a bitch." She slid into the driver's seat and shortly parked at the utility entrance to the bar of the Daddy Kat Klub. She dragged Vitaly by his ankles inside and tied him to the big wooden chair. Then she took a scissors from her bag of equipment and cut off all of his clothes.

"God has come, Vitaly," she said and took out the hammer and a big nail. She stretched his dick until it looked like about six inches of a Polish sausage, or half of a pork tenderloin, and she drove the nail into the head of his penis, pinning it securely to the wooden seat. When she began to fillet the tenderloin in a style of genito-torture called *gates of hell* and to drive tiny nails into the various strips of meat Vitaly began to moan. She tried to remember the diagram from an anatomy textbook, and concentrated to miss major blood vessels, but to follow where the nerves ran.

When he came to, Vitaly thrashed and flipped like a landed trout. He screamed in pain, "What the fuck have you done?"

"It is called justice, Vitaly. You cut Lizbet up alive, and sold her organs online, like meat by the pound. Now you know what a rape feels like."

"You will curse your mother. You will hate the day you were born…"

"Think of something else, Vitaly. We played that little game when I was fourteen."

Katya poured fuel and acetone all around the bar. She walked just outside the door, broke a Gauloises in half, and splayed a book of paper matches out into a fan shape. She tucked the lit cigarette inside the match book cover and set it near the edge of the fuel soaked carpet.

"I am not exactly sure, but I think that should burn about two minutes before it gets to the matches."

She turned on the flashlight which she had taped just above and in front of him. Then cut one strand of rope from his left wrist. Finally she placed the box cutter on a butler's table in the circle of light and poured the last of the acetone onto what was left of his crotch. He screamed like a slaughtered pig.

"I hate to cut and run, Vitaly," she said as she headed for the exit, "I will see you in hell."

Katya cranked the SUV and was two blocks away when a sonic wave rocked the neighborhood. Through the rearview mirror she saw an orange fireball lick at the L-shaped Daddy Kat Klub sign as she headed toward the airport.

The End

Alice Silver-Blue Hair and the Saints

ALICE SILVER-BLUE HAIR awoke with high vibrations that day, so she folded a bandana into a triangle and tied up the parts of her head front-to-back and sides. The flap over the top she tucked under the knot in back. All of this kept her head together so the parts did not fly off on the bus. She put orange ear buds in place and cranked up the Queen of the Night aria.

People have said the queen is a villain in this opera, but Alice did not believe it. Her motives were pure, to steal the Circle of the Sun, that is the power of the patriarchy that has messed everything up. Alice went to the opera once and got a ticket to lean on the rail to see it for herself. The Queen of the Night just wanted to reclaim what was once hers, but when you go up against the patriarchy it ends badly.

Alice's case worker had got her a bus pass so she could get to where she needed to be. Her first stop was the Church of St. Dymphna for her supply of holy water. It was for free and set out in a marble bird bath just inside the front door. She had learned to make the sign of the cross to stop people from staring as she filled her palm-sized sprayer bottle and put it inside the pocket of her hoodie.

Alice used to like St. Dymphna. It fit her spiritual needs, but not anymore. Now it smelled like urine and winos were passed out on the pews. Alice herself was always meticulously clean. Number two stop was by the bathroom of the Burger Barn to wash herself and, if she had been able to score some toothpaste, to smear it onto her teeth with her finger and swish up a lather.

The vibrations of places modified her own vibrations to either bring her up or bring her down. She preferred high vibrations, like today, because she had an intense sense of purpose. This purpose came to her in a clear message through her ear buds: "Bless the Trumpeter Saint Don of the Wall with holy water."

She could, as always, choose to obey or ignore these messages but this one seemed good. Trumpeter Saint Don is an advocate of slamming people into the wall—people who go by vibrations, people who are displaced, people who sleep in pews and stink up churches, people who bathe in public places, people like herself who resource what they need from public utilities like the marble bird bath at St. Dymphna.

She used to find comfort and solace at St. John of God Church over by the Blameless Eve Mission. She could get a scoop each of scrambled eggs, grits or hash brown potatoes with a biscuit or pancakes. The nuns and social workers there were cool. One once pinned a scapular on her blouse. It had a picture of St. John of God that said, "I confess that I know of no bad person in my hospital, except myself alone, who am indeed unworthy to eat the bread of the poor." The yuppies who moved into the neighborhood and bought up all the old houses then flipped them to rentals, preferred gentrification to serving bread of the poor. They turned Blameless Eve into daycare and the church into condos. So Alice was stuck with sourcing food from dumpsters behind the supermarket and restaurants on the drag downtown.

The message that Alice received through her ear buds said that St. Don would be speaking that day. Admission was free but a ticket was required and could be obtained from various businesses downtown. After dumpster diving for breakfast behind the Shambala Bakery, she walked up the street past the Sports Bar and there on the sidewalk was a free ticket to the St. Don of the Wall rally. She made a note of the time, noon, and of the place, the auditorium at the community college. The topic of his lecture: "The Divine Right of Capitalism." Alice slid her handicap go card through the slot by the bus driver and took a seat. A straw hat with a red, white and blue band had been left on the seat beside her.

"God provides," she said and put it on her head over her bandana.

At the auditorium as people crowded in she talked with a Central American boy who sat to one side with a housekeeping cart.

"You clean up afterwards?" Alice asked.

"My mother is undocumented, so she asked me to fill in for her. She was afraid to come."

"Are you an 'anchor baby?'"

The boy bristled at the words, but kept his composure and dignity.

"No 'del anclo.' Mi madre me llama 'hijo.' Me llama Oscar Romero Ortega."

"Si, hijo," said Alice.

As the Sousa music died down Trumpeter of the Wall began to speak, and Alice's ear buds said, "Do it now."

She stood and aimed her squirt bottle of holy water from St. Dymphna.

"She's got a gun," shouted a voice over a walkie talkie.

"Shoot. Shoot now," said another voice.

"Squirt now. Squirt him now," said the ear bud voice.

Alice squirted holy water as the hat flew off her head. Pink mist blew out of holes in the back and sides of her bandana.

A long, silver-blue streak of hair with a fragment of bone, blood and cranial tissue attached to one end floated down into the refugee boy's lap.

"Estas son reliquias sagradas," said a voice. It sounded like melted silver written across a night sky.

Oscar Romero Ortega put the hair and bone fragments into a ziplock bag and put them in his coat pocket over his heart.

The End

Elysian Fields Next Exit

CHANTAL AND STACIE were guided into Gentilly Funeral Home, past a pedestal bearing an urn of cremains. A card—Jocasta Williams—was placed there.

"Excuse me," said their mother, Angelina, to a thin young man standing in the doorway. He wore a tuxedo, which appeared by smell, dirt, and wrinkles to have been worn for several days. The little group gave him a wide berth as they walked to the front pews marked by white flowers and black bows. "Family" read cards posted on the aisle.

The thin young man appeared older than his years. He leaned on crutches and frequently adjusted his weight side-to-side as if he were in pain, or undecided about where to sit. He leaned close to the cremains and squinted to read the writing on the card.

An usher approached him and gestured to the back pew.

"Service is about to start," said the usher.

The man, hobbled by a blue plastic cast on his right leg, entered the pew, knelt with some difficulty, and made a sign of the cross. He removed a backpack which appeared as dirty as his tux.

Chantal and Stacie were Protestant children dressed in scratchy black dresses to attend their Aunt Jocasta's Catholic funeral.

"What's this for?" asked Stacie as she pulled on a kneeler which came down with a bang.

"Shhhh," said Angelina. "Leave it down. It's to kneel on to pray. Ya'll follow my lead. When I kneel, you kneel. When I stand, you stand. Okay?"

"Okay."

The girls knelt, following their mother's example. They awkwardly crossed themselves and settled into the pew. Stained glass windows offered them inspiration. Stacie looked toward the back of the auditorium at a round window high up toward the ceiling. A stylized dove with an olive branch perpetually descended. She saw below it the stinky man on the last row. He was crying.

The last person to enter, just before the start of the processional, was Athena Williams, their Baptist grandmother. She made her regal way to the front pew and sat down without kneeling. She did not cross herself. A large gold cross prominently hung from her neck against black fabric. No crucified Jesus there—her spiritual roots proudly on display. In her hand she carried a King James Bible. As she sat in front of the girls, they caught two smells: a cloying floral perfume, and whiskey.

"Aunt Jocasta died because she was so black," said Stacie, who at five-years-old was the younger.

"No, she didn't," said Chantal.

"Yes, she did. I heard Mama Athena say so, 'Black as Aunt Tarnell.'"

"She was upset. Aunt Jocasta was her daughter, Mama's sister."

"Mama Athena said she was 'a liquor-drinking, club crazy road ho. Just like Tarnell.'"

"Don't say 'ho,' it's not nice."

"They didn't love her. That's why she killed herself."

"Who's Aunt Tarnell?"

"Another one of Mama Athena's daughters."

Chantal heard whispering and rustling of garments from the back of the chapel and turned to see incensers being lit and people lining up.

"The man in the green and gold dress is the new priest. The old one wouldn't say mass."

"Aunt Jocasta always sent birthday and Christmas presents," said Stacie. Drops of childhood grief stung her eyes. "Aunt Jocasta had a baby."

"That would be another cousin," said Chantal.

"Ya'll hush. You're talking too big," said their mother.

The organ sounded and the people stood.

Chantal leaned and whispered into Stacie's ear, "Boy or girl?"

"Boy," said Stacie.

"I don't believe you. Where's the baby at?"

"Mama Athena says the nuns took it. Heaven I guess."

"Shhhh," said Angelina. "Don't make me take you out of here."

Stacie waited until the processional was in front of them, and leaned close to Chantal, "You ought to listen to Mama Athena when she's drinking. She says plenty."

The funeral service was brief, a mixture of Catholic and new age beliefs. During communion the ushers moved to the front of the gathering and row-by-row the faithful stood before the priest to receive their wafer and sip of wine before returning to their pew.

Meanwhile, at the rear of the chapel, the thin man in the tuxedo stood on his crutches to leave. He stopped beside the pedestal bearing the funeral urn, tucked the urn into his backpack, and slipped silently away.

Five weeks earlier, Jocasta had answered her cell phone.

"Jocasta Williams, Krewe of Gentilliers Twenty Year Coming Home Queen," she said.

"Hey, grrrrrrrl. It's Serena."

"I feel old."

"You are old, what thirty-eight?"

"Leroy's coming back."

"The baby's daddy?"

"He will think I'm an old maid, standing around for twenty years carrying a torch."

"Marry me. I could wear my tux and we could fly to Gay Las Vegas for a civil ceremony."

"Serena, you're my best friend. I've loved you since grammar school, but there's not a sapphic bone in my body."

"Damn. Always a bridesmaid. Look, I've found a king cake for the Twelfth Night party."

"Black baby?"

"Yeah, I had to go all the way to Magazine Street."

"You'd think bakers would get it that there's a market for other colors than pink plastic, white babies."

"You'd think."

"How many people are coming?"

"A mob. I lost count at a hundred."

"I'm making fish courtbouillion as well as bringing the king cake."

"Showing pescatarian love?"

"I'm a vegan Jew. You put pork in everything you cook."

"I'm a southern girl. I cook with bacon grease."

"Gotta run. A client's calling."

"I love you, meshuga."

"Bye, sweetness. Let me know if you need anything from Schwegmann's."

In the background of Jocasta's house a radio broadcast the news headlines, "A series of carjackings have N.O.P.D. hopping. At the Read Boulevard interchange of I-10 yesterday, a Slidell man was forced at gunpoint to give up his Honda Accord. A man disguised in a yellow wig and dress pointed a gun…"

She turned off the radio. In the bathroom she removed a bottle of antidepressants from the medicine cabinet and poured the last one into her palm. The label said no refills were available. *I need to see the shrink.* In the living room, she poured herself a drink from the bar and washed down the pill.

Recently a recurring dream had disturbed her sleep. In it a young man whose face she couldn't see stood before her. A nun in a brown habit brought a crying baby and laid it on a changing board. As the nun changed the baby's diaper Jocasta noticed an hour glass shaped birthmark on its butt. As the young man approached her, her nipples leaked milk. She unbuttoned her blouse and gave him her breast.

At the Twelfth Night feast Jocasta gathered the crowd around the banquet table. She sliced the king cake into tiny slivers.

"This cake has a black baby. We had to go all the way uptown to Magazine Street to find it. The selection of this year's Lord of Misrule is purely up to fate. Whoever gets the baby will be it."

She passed around the king cake.

"Laissez les bon temps rouler," she said to her guests.

"Hail the Returning Queen," and "Wassail," they said and bit into their slivers of cake.

"I got it," said a handsome young man whom Jocasta did not know. *Who is he? With that accent he isn't from here.*

"A toast," he said and raised his glass. "Let the servants rule the master. Tonight we turn the world order upside down. Let loose the dogs of Misrule until Carnival is done."

"Wassail," the guests said to "The Lord of Misrule," also known as the Queen's Consort, as they slapped his back and poured him drinks.

Jocasta's confidants, courtesans and ladies-in-waiting gathered around her and speculated about the mysterious guest.

"North Louisiana," said one.

"I've heard people from the Delta talk like that," said another.

"Memphis," said Serena. "Mid-south."

"Definitely not from here," said another.

Jocasta poured punch into a goblet and approached the young man. She placed the goblet in his hand and crowned him with a coronet.

"Lord of Misrule, walk with me and we will grace the garden with our royal presence."

"In all things delightful and bawdy, I obey my queen."

"I don't believe we've met. It is fate—pure chance—that has brought you here and turned the world order upside down."

"My name is Eddie Azizel."

"You sound like Elvis."

"Tupelo honey, Elvis Presley, and me. Three of the sweetest things that ever came out of Mississippi."

"Tupelo? Serena's right."

"Corinth actually. Community college at Itawamba."

"Did you graduate?"

Eddie's cell phone buzzed.

"Barely. Excuse me, my queen. I gotta take this."

He turned aside.

"This is Eddie. Uh huh. I see. Mona's at two. Show me some green."

He turned back to Jocasta.

"I got an associate degree. Liberal arts."

Eddie offered his hand to her and they danced around the patio. A guest offered them a joint.

"What do you do, Eddie?"

"Imports and exports."

"Do you specialize?"

"Nah. Whatever the market demands. The mouth of the Mississippi is the gateway to the Carribean and Latin America. Right now, used luxury vehicles. I get them on the cheap and move them to a middle man. He sells them down there, whole or in parts, for five times what they'd fetch here."

"What do you import?"

"Whatever people need."

His phone rang again.

"Excuse me, please. This thing is an aggravation, but it's my life line."

He walked to the edge of the garden.

"This is Eddie. I can get you some tits or a kilo. Yeah, Mona's at two. Show me the money."

Late the following morning, Epiphany 2005, Serena knocked on Jocasta's door. It was fortunate that they had been pals since they were children because a hangover like Jocasta's could end a friendship.

"Have you accepted Jesus as your personal savior?" said Serena to Jocasta's tormented face as she answered her door.

"Get off my porch, Christer bitch," said Jocasta.

"Bloody Mary?" asked Serena.

In the kitchen, Jocasta sat on a stool and covered her eyes with her hands.

Serena closed the venetian blinds against daggers of light.

She put two aspirin in front of Jocasta and mixed them each a drink.

As Serena drank she placed dishes into the dishwasher and put trash into a large bag.

"Who's Eddie Azizel?" she asked as she worked.

"No one seems to know. He's from north Mississippi, so you were right about his accent."

"Your Lord of Misrule's a complete stranger?"

"Pure chance. He got the slice with the baby."

"You should be more careful about your guest list."

"I think he's kind of cute. Talks like Elvis."

"Sociopaths are usually endearing."

"He makes a good toast. I liked the references to medieval England."

"Endearing. My point."

"He's a good kisser."

"You didn't. Tell me you did not."

"OK. I won't tell you."

"I'll bet you can't remember half of what happened last night."

Jocasta's cell phone chirped. It was her mother, Athena. She put it on speaker.

"Wishing you a blessed Epiphany, mother dearest."

"I heard on the police radio that law enforcement had to be called to your place."

"Some of the guests were propped against the yuppie neighbor's car."

"I heard they were smoking dope."

"They were a little drunk. The officers checked their IDs and told them to go back inside. They told us to turn the stereo down. That was it."

"You're back to your old ways, running wild in the streets with those Mardi Gras folks?"

"They're old friends, Mama."

"You're just like your Aunt Tarnell."

"It's Epiphany. Shouldn't you be radiating the love of Jesus or something?"

"Don't tell me how to act, I'm Baptist. You were lost the minute those nuns got their claws into you. Your daddy and I should have never sent you to the Carmelites."

"Athena, we've already discussed this. I've gotta go. You have a blessed day."

She clicked off the cell.

Serena put a fresh Bloody Mary in front of her.

"Athena would curdle yogurt," said Serena.

Later that day, at The Inn On Rampart, Jocasta met with Estelle Theriot, secretary of the krewe.

"Leroy's coming back," said Estelle.

A pain low in her abdomen caused Jocasta to take a deep breath and rub her hand in a slow circle.

"You OK?" asked Estelle.

"Too much Twelfth Night." said Jocasta. "Can you believe twenty years?"

"He's living in Chicago. Got a catering business."

"Leroy was always ambitious. He's a hard worker."

"We all thought you two would hook up."

"No. Just friends."

Jocasta remembered the last time she saw Leroy. He was reading the *Times Picayune* sports page. She could remember the headline: "Jim Moro Saints Coach." She had been cooking his breakfast and pouring his coffee.

Or, perhaps that was confabulation. She remembered morning sickness, throwing up in the bathroom as Leroy packed for his get away. He thought it was just another of her hangovers—they partied a lot. Whatever, she pulled it together enough to drive him to the airport.

"So, Estelle, we have a party to plan, this Gentilliers Ball?"

"We already have a plan, Fated Follies is the theme. Invitations go out in the mail today. You and I just have to make a place to party."

The hotel manager pushed aside wall panels to open two large suites into one cavernous hall.

Jocasta took a deep breath. *I can deal with this.*

Next day over chicken and jambalaya at Popeye's, Eddie shined with what Jocasta had come to see as an inner light. Serena said it was social deviance. Most of the other women in the krewe wished it shined on them, a handsome beau half their age—or so Jocasta thought.

"Krewe du Flambeaux parade is Monday night. Would you like to go?"

"Are you asking me out on a date?"

"Would that be so awful? After all, what is this?"

He rubbed her ankle with his shoe and lowered his chin in that way that he had come to realize people regarded as sexy.

"Only if you will come to the ball as my Queen's Consort."

"I am your Lord of Misrule, I obey my queen in all things."

"It will let me off the hook with Leroy."

After midnight, in the Ninth Ward a blue neon sign hung over the sidewalk beneath a balcony, *Mona's*. Inside the front entrance a community bulletin board held notices of importance. Tonight was a drag show and free HIV testing by volunteers from the NO/AIDS Task Force.

Upstairs in her apartment Mona daubed heavy make up over a lesion on her cheek. Her perch before the three mirrors of a large vanity was her favorite place. Eddie stood behind her and massaged the illusionist's neck as she adjusted her wig. She turned her back covered in a rhinestone gown toward him and said, "Zip." She pulled gloves over her bony, spotted hands. They reached above her thin biceps hiding Kaposi's sarcoma lesions on her arms and leaving only elaborately glossed nails visible at their open tips. She pulled away from Eddie's hands as she attached jewelry to her ears. Her fabulocity was complete. She was ready for her show.

"Come on, Mona. I need the money for a tux and some shoes," said Eddie.

"You're sitting on a gold mine, Sweets. Cash it in," Mona said.

"You know I don't bottom."

"Tell that to one of your straight buddies."

"I got invited to a ball out in Gentilly."

Mona looked at herself in the mirror and surveyed the reflected image of the room like a railroad car with all her stuff collected over the years, costumes, feathered headdresses, massive antiques. The memorabilia of a festive life now gathering dust and throwing shade.

"I need your stuff out of here. I want the space for a craft room," she said.

"You're not crafty."

"Then I need it for a library to write my memoirs."

"You're not a writer, and you don't read anything but the weekly bar rag."

"No, and a TV lounge is also out of the question since you stole the plasma screen and Bose to support your crack habit."

Mona, I'm sorry. I just got a little crazy, that's all. It was The Ninthz Boyz that made me do it. You know I'm good for the money. I'll repay you."

He bent down as if to kiss her neck.

She pulled away from him. Moana preferred the illusions she saw in her mirror, but she was not afraid to look reality squarely in the eye.

"You may have recently fallen off the turnip truck from Corinth— dust still in your hair. I, on the other hand, have been around and I know a user when I see one. You need to make other arrangements for a place to stay."

"Come on, Moana. You don't need to be so cold."

"Pretty boy, we're way past all of this. Pack your shit, and git."

Jocasta helped set up the hospitality suite at the Inn On Rampart as Serena checked and filed text messages.

"You've lost your mind over Eddie."

"You don't like Eddie. You looked at him like a snake in the parlor the moment you were introduced."

"I have no opinion about him, except you're spending a great deal of time with him."

She frowned at a text message and deleted it.

"You're jealous. That's it. Because I'm not lesbian, you take that as rejection, and you've displaced that anger onto Eddie."

"Jocasta, I'll forgive that once, but you don't want to go there again."

On her cell phone she selected "archive."

"You're sounding more like Athena everyday. Judgmental. Bossy," said Jocasta.

"Athena squandered her moral capital with you a long time ago. She internalized the racist value of light and dark skin. She held that close and took it with her into a whiskey bottle and pulled the cork in behind herself. Nonetheless, due diligence when it comes to one's lovers is a good idea."

"Serena, this has gone too far. You should leave now."

Serena walked to the door and opened it. Then she turned back to her friend.

"I'm going, but I'm not giving up on this friendship. If you won't vet Eddie Azizel, I will."

Then she left the hotel.

It was dicey that rapprochement was even possible. Perhaps Jocasta could have changed things if she had not chosen to ignore signs that urged caution and instead rushed headlong into carnival, a hedonistic season named after flesh.

Serena parked her beemer in front of a rundown commercial building in the Irish Channel. A sign with peeling paint advertised suites for lease. If gentrification were enroute, Serena had preceeded it. She pressed the button marked A Knowes, P.I. and pushed on the door at the sound of a buzzer.

Aaron Knowes had nearly graduated from Tulane. He talked fast and used big words which affected people in either of two ways: It instilled confidence in his intelligence and abilities, or it made him sound like a wind bag.

A sign on his receptionist/assistant's desk said, "Girl Friday." She acted as a buffer to the wind bag effect. Her twinkling brown eyes and easy warmth set people at ease.

"I need to check someone's background," said Serena.

"Knowes Agency can do that," said Friday.

She walked toward a kitchenette and returned with a carafe of coffee and a plate of pastries.

"I find that the brain works better on sugar and caffeine. Would you like some?"

She smiled at Serena and served coffee.

"Do you know the name of the subject of the check?"

"Eddie Azizel. He says he's from Corinth, Mississippi. And he has attached himself to my oldest friend."

Girl Friday entered the name and some search terms into her computer then pushed "enter."

"His last known address is in Corinth, Mississippi. Back in September he dropped out of Itawamba Community College as soon as his student loan check arrived. No known address here. Police have watched him around a bar called "Mona's" in the lower Ninth Ward for several months now. They believe he is a street level drug dealer, and that he is fencing stolen vehicles as well."

She refined her search and looked puzzled.

"There's some kind of code attached to his birth information. I'll have to work on unsealing that."

Fog swirled beneath the orange lights of the Airport Auto Rental. One last luxury car was driven from the maintenance garage and certified roadworthy by the manager. In the background, classic Carnival music: The Meters' "They All Asked For You."

Leroy King stepped off the shuttle from the airport and signed for the access card to the Lincoln Navigator.

"I love me a Lincoln," said the rental agent. He wiped moisture from the side mirror as Leroy handed back the clipboard.

Leroy headed east on Airline Highway and turned toward the entrance of I-10. In the rearview mirror the lights of Airport Auto Rental went dark.

At the same moment at the exit ramp to Elysian Fields Avenue a man in a yellow wig and dress sat in the tall grass near the signal light and watched traffic. Heavy fog muffled sounds and refracted blue halogen lights, and the changing green, yellow and red from the intersection.

Leroy signaled to take the Orleans Avenue/Vieux Carre exit, but a car full of drunk revellers cut him off. He swerved back into traffic.

"Idiots," he said.

A traffic sign indicated Elysian Fields Next Exit. As he approached he signaled the turn. Ahead at the intersection the traffic light went yellow and then red. A sign with an arrow pointed to the right towards the Mississippi River warehouses and the French Market.

The disguised man stood up and ran across the exit ramp to Leroy's rented Navigator. He jumped onto the running board and tapped the window with the butt of his gun.

"Out of the car, bitch," said the carjacker and pointed the gun toward Leroy's head.

Leroy hit the gas. A shot blew glass across the intersection and the gunman fell to the pavement. A wheel ran over his right foot. The Navigator burned rubber toward the median and made a complete circle before it came to a stop.

"You should have gave it up," shouted the carjacker.

He hopped to the median and pulled open the driver's side door. Leroy's brains and half of his face were stuck to the glove box. Blood covered the passenger side floor. The shooter pulled Leroy's body from the vehicle and raced the Navigator south toward the river.

Jocasta and Eddie slung quart-sized wineskins around their necks. They were in Lafayette Square across from Gallier Hall. Predictable standards like "Mardi Gras Mambo," as well as Cajun and Zydeco music blasted from giant speakers. The festive crowd pushed toward Camp Street as the Krewe du Flambeaux parade rolled past and turned up the night. Eddie's pain medication topped off with alcohol, and the presence of a blue walking cast cooled his zeal for celebration.

During the parade they made their way toward the French Quarter and the hospitality suite at the Inn On Rampart Street. Jocasta had taken a room for the week, so she wouldn't have to drive.

In the hospitality suite, a strange quiet had settled over the krewe. Estelle made her way to Jocasta and placed a supportive hand on her shoulder.

"Leroy is dead," Estelle said. "Killed in a carjacking last night on his way from the airport. He panicked and tried to drive off."

Jocasta turned to Eddie's arms and found comfort as readily as she had found excitement and joy earlier.

Jocasta rested among pillows on an opium couch in her shrink's office. It was on Prytania Street across from Touro Infirmary. Jocasta was medicated on something that made her talkative and uninhibited. In the distance she heard a streetcar pass on St. Charles Avenue.

"I need a new prescription," said Jocasta.

"Let's give this one time to work, then we'll see," said the doctor. "I'll write you a refill when you leave."

"Everything goes by so fast. One minute I'm Queen of the Mardi Gras ball, the next I'm Twenty Year Returning Queen. I look at Athena, a once beautiful woman, then I turn around and she's a bitter old alcoholic. My nieces, it seems, are babies in spring and by fall they're starting school and asking me judgmental questions."

"Is this about time passing, Jocasta? Or is it about your perception of loss?"

"Either. Neither. Maybe something else? I can't believe Leroy's dead."

"You said you had not seen Leroy in twenty years, yet he had fathered your child."

"'Fathered' would be the wrong word. He was little more than a sperm donor. I never told him about the pregnancy. He had graduated chef school at Delgado and had dreams of Chicago. If I had snared him into a marriage, how long would it have been before he looked at me and the baby as the killers of his dreams?"

"You said you stopped throwing up long enough to drive him to the airport."

"It's like a room in my mind that I locked away. Mama and Daddy dropped me off with the Carmelite Sisters. I got pre-natal care, learned a trade, and at the end of the year I woke up from the dream. The baby was adopted and I was a Catholic. Life moved forward."

On Lundi Gras or Fat Monday, a courier in an olive green uniform located Serena and handed her a manila envelope from the Knowes Agency. Fat Monday is the day when Carnival season's gumbo pot is readied. All the savory ingredients of debauchery are gathered in the pot and the last sinful stew with meat is prepared for consumption on Fat Tuesday. It is inevitable that Ash Wednesday comes as a shock to the system.

"Oh my God! No!" said Serena as she opened the envelope and read.

She speed dialed Jocasta's number, but it went straight to message.

"Answer. Answer it," she said.

Even though she did not believe in God she prayed, "Please. Oh please, dear God."

She grabbed the access card to her Beemer and made her way through a sea of drunk drivers and disbanding carnival floats. Kids in high school band uniforms, policemen mounted on horses, revelers laden with plastic beads and turned out in fantastic costumes—in the surreal landscape, all conspired to keep her from Jocasta.

"It's a fucking Fellini film!" she screamed, and slammed her palm into the BMW's horn.

It was a trek getting to Gentilly. Jocasta's next door neighbor waved to Serena from her porch.

"Jocasta's not home," said the neighbor. "She got a hotel room in the quarter so she wouldn't have to drive."

Serena traveled her own Via Dolorosa south on Orleans Avenue. When she reached the Casino and Armstrong Park she pulled onto the sidewalk and abandoned her car. She took the manila envelope and ran to The Inn On Rampart. She marked the envelope "Urgent: For Your Eyes Only."

At the registration desk she addressed the clerk.

"Is Jocasta Williams here?" she said.

"I believe I saw Miss Williams leave earlier with that cute young man of hers."

"Do you know where she went?"

"To a parade, maybe?"

Serena pushed the envelope at the clerk but pulled it back when he reached for it.

"Jocasta has to get this as soon as she comes back."

"Yes ma'am."

"It's life-or-death, vitally important. The consequences are dire."

Tears started down Serena's cheeks.

"I'll give it to her myself. I'll place it in her hands the moment she comes back. I promise."

Serena let go of the envelope and left.

To the elite of New Orleans at their balls, when Rex and Comus meet and drink a toast, Carnival ends. In the streets mounted policemen precede a cruiser with flashing lights. Those are followed immediately by tractor sized street sweepers.

"Move off the streets. Get into the bars or go home. Mardi Gras is over."

Eddie leaned into Jocasta, shoulder to shoulder, his arm heavy around her neck. His walking cast and one shoe were coated with muck from the streets. They used the service entrance and made their way to the nearest elevator before the clerk waved to them.

"Miss Williams, I have a message. It's urgent."

The elevator doors closed and the car ascended. The clerk looked at the envelope and placed it into the box above her room number.

Jocasta awoke on Ash Wednesday hungover, naked and cold. Eddie was passed out on his stomach with all the cover on his side of the bed and on the floor. As she reached across her young lover to retrieve a blanket she noticed in the morning light how thin he appeared, how parts of his body she had not seen before had purple spots. His hair looked dry and thin, and there was that nasty walking cast on his leg. What really socked her in the guts was an hour glass shaped birthmark on his butt.

Jocasta walked around the bed and picked up a blanket. Wrapping herself in it she backed up until she felt the wall and then sank to the floor.

When Eddie woke up he found her there, crouched and trembling in spite of springlike weather.

"Are you OK?" he asked.

"No. You need to go," she said.

"I don't understand. What's wrong?"

"You can't be here."

"I'll get a shower and go," said Eddie as he walked into the bathroom.

Jocasta pulled on jeans and a shirt and left the room.

Downstairs in the lobby the new clerk called to her.

"Miss Williams, I was told to give this to you the minute I saw you. The night clerk couldn't get your attention when you came in."

He placed the envelope in her hands and she went into the restaurant where a waitress put coffee in front of her.

Jocasta looked at the writing and frowned as she took out the contents of the dossier. After a few minutes reading she shuffled back through the papers and picked up her coffee cup. It seemed to vibrate with the intensity of the information and crashed onto the saucer.

Jocasta stood and ran from the hotel into Rampart Street. As she turned in circles on the median the bells of St. Jude sounded the hour and she walked in that direction.

Eddie came into the dining room a few minutes later. The waitress was picking up shards of pottery and wiping up spilled coffee.

"Miss Williams?" he said to the waitress.

"She left this," said the waitress and handed him the contents of the manila envelope.

He read it quickly and said, "Oh my God." He then ran into the street. He looked east and west and turned around, but Jocasta was gone.

Inside St. Jude a light on the nearest confessional stall indicated the priest was ready for his next penitent, so Jocasta entered.

"I have sinned a great sin, Father. It has been years since my last confession."

Her confession came out as screams and sobs, a word salad. This kind of speech is a sign of a deranged mind. People withdrew from the pews nearby and fled through the doors of the church. The crazy woman ran into traffic on Rampart Street.

She walked like a zombie to a hardware store and made a purchase.

The clerk looked into the cash drawer as she made change and asked, "Are you okay?" but when she turned to hand the money to the customer, the woman had gone.

Back in her hotel room Jocasta pulled a chair to the middle of the room and climbed onto it. She tapped on the ceiling until she located a beam and screwed a sturdy hook into it. She then looped a length of rope around her neck and fastened the loose end to it.

She looked for a long moment at the bed she had so recently shared with her lover and kicked the chair from beneath herself. Her body alternated between decorticate and decerebrate posturing before flipping like a fish out of water. Then it became still.

A few days after Jocasta's funeral the moon became full. Eddie stumbled along the outer walls of St. Roch's Cemetery until he found an old section where the bricks and plaster had crumbled. He waved a cane in front of himself and felt with his other hand. His raised forehead and upward nose were indicative of a newly blind person.

He felt tombstones and names on the front of family crypts until, after midnight, with the moon high overhead, he located one that said "Williams." He knelt and took the urn of cremains from his backpack.

"Jocasta, I think this is it. The doctors at Charity say I'm blind from HIV/AIDS, but I think this is the right place. The priest wouldn't bury a suicide here, but I'm making things as right as I can."

He opened the bag and poured the cremains onto the ground.

"I love you, Mama. Rest in peace."

The End

Mnemosyne's Daughters

To stop her hands from shaking, Mnemosyne squeezed her fingers together until her nailbeds blanched white.

"Amyloid plaques," said the neurologist. "The MRI and PET scans show senile plaques throughout the cerebral cortex. Your brain size is shrinking."

"I've been losing it for some time. I left the spa's money pouch at the bank last week. I leave notes on the mirror in the bathroom, on the fridge, stickies stuck to the front door. And sometimes I still can't remember."

"Losing memory of recent events is often an early sign. Your forgetting to do basic hygiene, loss of competency in familiar, habitual tasks, and the recent getting lost downtown, where you've gone all your life, are signs of advancing Alzheimer's."

"How long do I have before I'm completely dotty?"

"It varies with each person. Ten years of slow decline usually precedes loss of organ and system function, which is what ultimately causes death. Your disease is moderately advanced. We don't know when it began. This stage in an average patient, if there is such a thing, could last at your current level of functioning from one to five years. There are a number of medicines now available which show promise…"

Mnemosyne, in a soiled duster, answered the doorbell. Her eldest daughter, Calliope, stood there with a bottle of wine and a bouquet of flowers.

"Calliope, what a surprise," said Mnemosyne.

"Why aren't you ready?" said Callie. "And you know to call me Callie, everyone else does."

"Ready? For what?"

"Mom, dinner? We've had this planned for weeks. You said you needed to talk to me about something?"

"Oh my god. It slipped my mind. Of course. Come in."

They walked to the kitchen. No dinner had been prepared.

Callie put the bouquet in a vase—tea roses, zinnias, Gerber daisies, forget-me-nots, with sprigs of periwinkle, myrtle and lilac, all surrounded by fragrant green branches of rosemary.

Callie removed glasses and dishes from the sink and put them in the dishwasher. She dried her hands and turned to her mother, "The maid quit?"

Mnemosyne searched notes stuck to the refrigerator door.

"Here it is. I found it," she said holding up a yellow post-it. *Calliope. Dinner @ 7. New will.*

Seated side-by-side at the kitchen table, they held hands.

"My first born."

"Don't get all sappy, Mom."

"Well, I miss you girls. It's too quiet in this big, empty house. All those loud, noisy years crammed full of nine girls—two to a bedroom."

"We weren't that loud and noisy, were we?"

"It was like a transportation hub every morning. Somebody wanted to borrow someone's camisole. The middle girls were braiding the youngest's hair. You would help them with their homework. What would we have done without a cook?"

"Mrs. Tucker."

"God bless Mrs. Tucker. She passed away last year, you know?"

"It was two years ago. We sent flowers, remember? We couldn't have done without a cook. Eating out would have bankrupted us."

"This house is too quiet."

Callie got a hair brush and walked behind her mother. She took the pins from her hair and began to brush. *Look at the gray.* She added and subtracted years in her head. *She's nearly sixty.*

As Mnemosyne's eyes closed and she leaned into the rhythm of the brush strokes, she grew thoughtful.

"Calliope… Callie, did I put too much responsibility on you too young?"

"No, dear. You delivered me from my own lifetime of mommy-dom. I learned early on that I never wanted children."

"Oh, Callie, you sound so sterile. And bitter."

"Stop. The guilt and responsible-older-daughter thing doesn't work with me. You installed that emotional motherboard but I rewired it, expensively and carefully on Dr. Mather's opium couch. Besides, schlepping brats to volleyball would interfere with my softball."

"It bothers me that you never had children."

"It doesn't bother me. I don't need the ethos of personal immortality through offspring. There are way too many people on this small planet. What—eight or nine billion now? Who needs that? They just grow up to resent you and blame you anyway."

"See. I knew it. I did ruin you by laying so much on you too young."

Callie braided her mother's hair and pinned it into a neat bun, then kissed the top of her head.

"I'm not ruined. I'm fine. Me and the flutist got corgis. Let's get you changed and go out for supper."

They walked down a long hall, past five bedrooms with doors closed, past two bathrooms, into the master suite.

"I met with Abe Fisher last week. He's drafting me a new will."

Mnemosyne took off her duster and went into the bathroom.

"Should I be worried? I'm still not having a baby—you can disinherit me if you want."

"No, nothing like that."

"You already have plenty of grands. How many more do you need?"

"Stop it. I just wanted you to know. You'll help me tell the other girls? I'm looking at fifty in the rearview. You start to feel the weight."

Callie took her mother's shoulders.

"What are you not telling me?"

"Nothing. It's nothing."

"It's something, or there would be no 'it.'"

"Seriously, things should be ready in case of eventualities. I mean we all die. I don't want to worry about loose ends. There's a lot of property and wealth and I want it divided equally among you girls. And I want to take care of the business partners—to keep things going, if they want. He said he could have it all done in a couple of months. I want it all straightened out by winter."

Mnemosyne stood in her clothes closet looking at rows of things to wear as if she couldn't make up her mind.

Callie took a dress from the bunch and held it up to her mother's shoulders.

"This one looks pretty. With your lacey blue jacket?" she said.

"Yes, that."

"If you're driving, I've got the check. Where do you want to eat?"

"Olympia? Greek. No… There's a new Chinese place downtown. Let's do Chinese."

They stood outside Mnemosyne's SUV. She studied it like she wondered who it could belong to.

"Ready, Mom? The remote?"

"The remote, yes."

She dug in her purse, and searched some more. But came up empty-handed.

"It's a fob," said Callie.

"I know it's a fob."

"Let's take mine."

They drove until they reached the Veterans Memorial.

"Which way?" asked Callie.

"Olympia is the other way," said Mnemosyne.

"Olympia now? Are you OK?"

In the eighth century B.C.E. the old Etruscan gods produced a slew of divine offspring. Uranus and Gaia were the first parents—one was the sky and the other was the earth. Their children were various things to the creation myth of the day, which explained natural phenomena. Her namesake was among a race of Titans, Mnemosyne. It means memory. Some wanted to call her a titaness, but she didn't care for diminutive titles. She stood as a giant among the other giants, not a giantess.

In-breeding or line-breeding is a way to produce show stoppers and champions. Close relatives should not try this. Participants should be at least five generations removed from each other's forebears. The idea is to select the desired traits and hope they show up in the whelps, or foals, or kittens. Whatever. These might be speed, or coloring, length of legs, strength, intelligence, etc. You get the idea. There are mathematical probability tables, actuarial guesstimates of the likelihood of sperm and egg, genetic predisposition influenced by environment, to produce divine children, or freaks. The downside of it is, undesirable traits also become more likely the closer the parents are to each other's origins. Things like weak eyes, blood dyscrasias, organs incompatible with life, or insanity.

This story tickled Mnemosyne every time she read it: "For nine nights did wise Zeus lie with Mnemosyne, entering her holy bed remote from the immortals. And when a year was past and the seasons came round as the months waned, she bore nine daughters, all of one mind, whose hearts are set upon song and their spirits free from care, a little way from the topmost peak of snowy Olympus."

That last phrase means low born. Obviously the writer had not raised a family of girls, and his ideas of bearing children, length of gestation and number of siblings per birth were also skewed. Perhaps if they had cavorted closer to the immortals, their kin, someone would have thrown a bucket of cold water on them both and said, "Knock it off, you two."

You can tell that was written by a man, right? Rugged, manly type who didn't engage in parenting, or husbandry to his woman? Likely out in the mountains, maybe raising some livestock. Goats, perhaps. Or maybe hunting dogs. Something mammalian that gestates quickly and has multiple offspring. Do you imagine this man drinking beer and celebrating sports with his buddies? Can you see the decals on his truck: Zeus Sports Equipment, Olympic Bows and Arrows, Club Parthenon? He got his brains a little scrambled over time with booze and sorting out sires and dams.

She was a single mom, with nine talented, beautiful daughters, who wanted to put her affairs in order, and they were messy affairs indeed. She wanted this done by winter, so hired a psychiatrist, Dr. Mather, to help her with her forgetfulness, especially around recent events.

"Don't tell the girls, but I'm rich. Rich beyond belief. I started as an herbalist, helping women with aches and pains. A sprained wrist, an abrasion, a yeast infection. I had a boy bring in ice from the mountain top, and I bought herbs and essential oils from the bazaar by the bay. Sometimes a solution of vinegar water was all that was needed. The traders went all over the Mediterranean, as far as Spain and Africa. The merchants from the orient who had traveled the Silk Road were always interesting. They had otherworldly things that removed pain and brought on a most dreamy sleep. Upon waking, the patient did not even remember having had discomfort. Unfortunates who were abused, some by fathers, some by brothers, who had got them in a family way, came to me for help. At the risk of being called a witch, I helped them. Mostly I helped by listening to their stories while I brewed a cup of tea and held their hands. They didn't want to hear me talk, they wanted me to listen. That was my job," Mnemosyne said. "Do you think a tea of Asian ginseng, or ginkgo biloba would help?"

"I doubt that they could hurt. If you feel empowered to take charge of improving your health, I recommend that. I'll give you a couple of scripts. One helps the chemistry in your brain. The other is vitamin E in a strong dose."

Mnemosyne took a pen and notepad from her bag and wrote a note to herself. She tore the note loose and pinned it with a safety pin to the flap of her handbag.

"You tell an interesting story, but perhaps parts of it are confabulation. Can you tell me about things closer to the present?" said the psychiatrist.

"I bought a building and turned it into a gymnasium for women. It was a public bath house for women, where they could go for solace and healing among like minds. You've heard of the Venus de Milo? That famous statue of the beautiful woman with missing arms? She was my advertising campaign—my shingle hanging over the sidewalk. 'Open for business,' she proclaimed as she tossed golden apples. Or, did she carry a vase of olive oil on her shoulder? Somebody broke off her arms so it's difficult to tell. She was of classic proportions, the ideal of feminine health. I opened the original spa, and after that I opened more in other cities. As my brand spread, my wealth grew. I am worth tens of millions, if not hundreds of millions of dollars. But, don't tell the girls. I don't want them to become greedy."

"Mnemosyne, some of the things you say are a little… um, far-fetched. Reality checking: snow from the mountaintop, Mediterranean, North Africa, the Venus de Milo. This is the U.S. We're in North America."

"All my life, even while I endured all those pregnancies, I was scheming, saving, investing, working, managing and expanding my businesses. After all, I had nine girls, one after the other, to look after. All as headstrong as their parents."

"You chose not to marry and you chose to have nine daughters out of wedlock."

"Out of wedlock sounds so Victorian. My choice of a man was not exactly primordial. He was, in my eyes at least, a god of the second order. As much as I loved him, Hera had him first. I may have been his whore, but I was not a home wrecker. For years we were hot for each other, and I was as fertile as the Nile Delta. It was later that we came to realize that I was his aunt, and he was my nephew. So, you see, even if we had wanted to get married, we probably could not have got a license or a health permit."

She stuck the next appointment slip to the visor of her SUV and concentrated on driving to the pharmacy. She had two scripts: one for a cholinesterase inhibitor, and one for a large dose of vitamin E.

At the front door of her house she turned the key in the lock, and pulled a notice from the front door. She clicked the light switch on and off, with no response from the foyer light. A strange silence emanated from the whole house. No appliances, no climate control. She stepped back onto the front porch for the light and read the notice from the electric company: "Service temporarily suspended for non-payment. Contact us to arrange for a deposit of $200 and to pay your current bill. A $50 reconnection fee will be imposed."

Her business associates wouldn't have recognized the disheveled elderly woman. She'd tugged her hair back into a careless ponytail. Loose strands were pushed from her face and tucked behind her ears. She scrolled through messages on an expensive smartphone, which seemed incongruous with her questionable hygiene. WiFi was free in the coffee house. If you could look beneath the wrinkles, stains, and musty odors of her clothes, you might see that they bore designer labels. She stopped at "message from Clio" and listened.

"Clio," she said, and stroked her hand across the face of the smartphone.

"Hello, Mummy. It's your youngest, although even our long-gone daddy couldn't swear to our birth order. He thought we all came out at once in a litter like puppies. How many tits do you really have? I'm Clio, the keeper and proclaimer of history, and your family's is sordid indeed."

"Callie called to tell me about your new will. Like I care. Did you ever wonder, or were you even aware, that all of your daughters wound up crazy at some point and sought mental health therapy on Dr. Mather's couch? Our chaotic household, your satyr and maenad relatives who came and went at will, remember those, Mum? Did it ever occur to you, after you whelped so many little bastards on the world, that pedophiles would descend like flies on carrion? With that tantalizing bit I'll leave you to imagine the details."

"What really got me pissed at you was your comment about my husband after I moved halfway down the world to Chile: 'Llama herder' you said. I was throwing myself away on a llama herder. Urania is down here with me. They named an observatory in Berlin after her. Actually, her namesake, but it gives her some bullshit for the locker room. She introduced me to him—they work together at A.L.M.A. He comes from indigenous people here, and he has multiple degrees in astronomy and mathematics. His head is literally in the stars, observing celestial births and deaths, when he isn't jetting off to Berlin, or Australia, or some other observatory's scholarly group who values his opinion. I stay here most times with our three lovely children, a big percentage of your grandchildren, whom you will never see. I don't give a damn about your will. I hate you from the bottom of my heart. If you want to do something for your grands, send money."

"Callie tells me you're rapidly losing it, so I want you to have this information while you can still process it. I hope it torments you like scorpions in your coffin. Wishing you godspeed on your journey into the void of dementia."

An electronic note sounded on the smartphone. "End of message. Next message," it said.

Mnemosyne clicked off her cell phone. She dropped her ceramic coffee cup in the trash can at the door and, in the parking lot, wandered right past her SUV.

Erato had taped an interview an hour before at the studio of the public radio station. As she sped toward Mnemosyne's house she listened to it through earbuds beneath her mirror-black crash helmet. Her Suzuki C90 purred a throaty growl between her legs as, in her head, she outlined her next erotic novel.

"I've never followed rules," she had told Dee Jay Drivetime. She checked her speed on the crosstown freeway and gave the Suzuki more gas.

"You'll say anything, won't you?" said Dee Jay.

"Mostly the truth."

"Are your erotic stories actually true?"

"It's fiction. This stuff is almost never done. Well, not done as well as my stories tell it."

"How do you come up with characters?"

"They're grafted onto people I knew growing up in my mother's household. Her relatives are a wild bunch of Greeks."

"One of your characters is a dominatrix. How did you come up with her?"

"Mistress Midnight titillates your imagination, does she, Drivetime?"

"Well, I have a certain fascination for a woman in severe leather and stilettoes."

"Mistress Midnight spanks her bare-bottom supplicants with her shoe, a fetish object. Our cook when I grew up was her root, I guess, in my creative subconscious. I won't call her name. She would give us kids a sharp whack across the back of our legs with a wooden cooking spoon."

"Ouch!" said Drivetime.

"There were nine of us kids. Mom was a single mother and worked. She was a business woman who owned gyms, spas. Mrs. Tucker…oops, I said her name. She had to keep order in an almost industrial kitchen. She cooked in large pots for a dozen people. She could not safely work in chaos, an element that felt comfortable to all of us girls."

"Nine girls."

"Nine of us. All talented: musicians, singers, one opera diva. One's an astronomer in Chile. We have an actress, two study religious hymns of the Smoky Mountain region for Juilliard. I'm a writer of erotic fiction. We have a poet. And there's one more…oh yes, a dancer. So we're a pretty creative bunch."

"Wow, you must have had a wild household."

"Don't spray your shorts, Drivetime. I write fiction. It wouldn't do to try to pin the tail on that donkey."

She had winked at him and he couldn't think of his next remark.

"They're hanky-spanky books. Nothing too kinky. I try to dig to the bottom of various paraphilias for the plots."

The program cut to a commercial break. Erato signaled her exit: Parnassus Estates Boulevard.

Mnemosyne heard Erato gun the engine coming down the street and slow to turn into the driveway.

The neighbor's dog started barking.

"Got him started," said Mnemosyne.

Erato let herself in the front door.

She flipped the light switch in the foyer.

No light came on.

She walked into the living room, and flipped the switch.

No light.

The lack of climate control left the room dank and heavy with still, exhausted air.

"Your electric's out?" she asked her mother.

"They cut the power." She handed Erato the notice.

"We need to get this turned back on. You don't need money. You have lots of money. What's up with that?"

"I have a notice…somewhere."

"Right here. You just showed it to me."

Terpsichore had traveled to Chile to visit Clio.

"Do you think they will ever sort out our lineage?" asked Terpsichore.

"Not likely, Terpie," said Clio.

"Don't call me that. I hate my name, but I hate 'Terpie' worse—it sounds like a turtle, a terrapin."

"What shall I call you, then?"

"Galatea, maybe? Elysia? I'll think of something."

"Until you do, I'm calling you 'Terpie.' It's what I remember as a child. Like I was saying, old storytellers, like from 3,000 B.C.E., said that we were really primordial, that Gaia and Uranus were our parents."

"Personally, as a dancer, I like the idea of Pegasus 'touching his hoofs' to the ground on Mt. Helicon. Four sacred springs came forth and we muses were born there from the union of the earth and sky through water. I could dance that—horses' hoofs and springs of water." She danced in half circles, lifting her legs high like a Tennessee Walker.

"Twenty-three hundred years later in 700 B.C.E., Hesiod laid it on us like we heard it, Mnemosyne and Zeus."

"Romans called us 'water nymphs' who drowned our lovers, or blinded them, or ruined their voices," said Terpie.

"Romans were degenerate."

"I could dance to the one, or dance to the other. After busking we could count the money in the hat from each. Consider it a poll."

She danced *Pegasus*, then *Four Springs*. Terpie then sat down and stretched.

Clio slumped and sighed.

"Callie and Rato saw Mom," Clio said.

"She still crazy?"

"As a shit house rat. Only now she has Alzheimer's."

Terpsichore became still. Rare for her to be so still. "I hadn't heard that."

"My fate to bring you the news."

"That big old house must be awfully quiet."

"Which bedroom was yours?" asked Clio.

"I never felt I belonged more to one than the other. Seems like I slept in all five of them."

"Safety in numbers. I remember we used to group together four to a bed."

"Remember that night when Aunt Gertrude came to get Polly and Thalia? 'I'll take these back to their beds,' she said and started to pick them up from where they were sleeping."

"She procured girls for Uncle Gus," said Clio.

"You jumped up in her face."

"I scratched her eyes out and knocked her back into the edge of the door."

"She was in I.C.U. for a week. They had her eyes taped shut and said she had a cracked skull with a concussion."

"I remember her sorry ass up there in the hospital bed telling me I couldn't tell Mama. I told her the only way I wasn't telling Mama was if she agreed right there to never come back to our house to visit again. I told her to swear, or I would get the social worker right then and she would spend the rest of her hospital stay handcuffed to the bedrail."

"I remember her laid out on the floor in the doorway of the bedroom. You were all over her! I jumped up and down on her chest," said Terpie.

"That would explain the broken ribs. Show me that pony dance again, Sister Woman."

Terpie stepped high like an Irish dancer, or a Tennessee Walker. "Trainers hit the backs of the horses' legs to make them step higher."

"No pain, no gain. Girl, you got some fine legs on you."

Terpie finished her dance and took a deep curtsy.

"She has made a new will," said Clio.

"I hope she gives away my share to dance scholarships or something. I don't want her guilt money."

"I want cash," said Clio.

Her three children came in from school. "Somos hambre, mama."

Melpomene and Polymnia studied sacred music of the Smoky Mountains in eastern Tennessee for traces of Irish and Scots influence, possibly left behind by pioneers moving westward.

Melly stood at an open window in an ancient church looking over a valley. She fanned herself with a manila file folder and pushed a sweat-slick strand of hair from her eyes.

"What do you think happened to them?" asked Polly.

"Banjos and fiddles," said Melly.

"That doesn't explain anything. Those are just musical instruments."

"Maybe joy was squeezed out of their lives along with any passion and sin. Life was hard for pioneers."

Polly entered search terms in her computer and scrolled through results.

"The goal of the Restoration Movement was to recreate first century Christianity as much as possible in the new world, here in America," said Polly.

"Sad," said Melly. "Even the degenerate Romans hated them and tried to feed them to the lions."

"It seems like mental illness to me when you put all your eggs of joy into a future-world-in-heaven basket. No dancing. No makeup. No sexy clothes. They made lousy citizens of Rome too."

"No lust. No fun. Just shoot me."

"How would anyone know what first century Christianity looked like anyway? It wasn't even written down until nearly three hundred years later."

"Can you imagine anything being accurate after three hundred years of an oral tradition?"

"They certainly preserved joylessness intact," said Polly.

"I read that at the Coliseum they recently restored the elevators that carried Christians and lions to the arena floor."

"There's a start."

Melly alphabetized files and placed them in a box. "Shultz called. He said our funding is good until fall."

"Is he any more enthusiastic? I don't think he gets it," said Polly.

"He's clueless. Juilliard's his universe."

"And here we are in the Smoky Mountains. Mrs. Campbell must have footed the bill for another semester's research."

"Do you think we can finish this by August?"

"The research, yes. The writing? Well…" Polly said.

"I write better back in New York. Educated people stimulate me to use polysyllabic words in compound sentences to describe complex phenomena."

"Mama's getting worse."

"I should stop by for a visit on the way back."

"Do you think she would recognize you?"

"Last time, she didn't remember me, or even that I had visited. About fifteen minutes into the ordeal, she asked me who I was."

"Maybe that's what has kept these fundamentalists going all these years—duty and guilt," said Polly.

"Maybe their God has Alzheimers too?" said Melly.

"That would explain the last century."

Melly put the cardboard box next to her purse and dug for her keys.

"There's a revival in Plowshares. It's fundamentalist, a Primitive Baptist Church."

"Snakes?"

"Rattlers, but the Rev has a cell phone so that's a good sign. He says we can record without participating—no hands on."

Melly dropped her keys and shivered, in spite of the heat, as she blindly reached beneath a pew to retrieve them.

"Grateful for that. Probably no air conditioning?"

"No. The Rev says it makes his rattlers sleepy."

"And that's a bad thing?"

Mnemosyne had chosen to be cremated. Thalia carried the cremains in an urn tucked under her arm. Twilight calmed the nerves of day.

Most of the nine daughters gathered at the Unitarian Church that Thalia had made arrangements to use. She had been the least protected of the girls, perhaps that's why her sense of humor was so strong: coping.

Clio and Urania had stayed in Chile.

"I figured it was the least offensive to the most people. Mama had a diverse bunch of friends," said Thalia, explaining why she had chosen a Unitarian chapel for the service.

Euterpe had always been the most quiet. Perhaps that's why she had chosen the flute, and let it speak for her. "I'm starved. They didn't feed us on the plane."

Thalia led her towards the social hall. "We have a ton of food. The Rev says they have several shelters that can use the leftovers. Casseroles and funerals. Like anybody eats."

"I thought gaming at the tables of the Casino of Life went on forever, then last week all the slots and games of chance shut down," said Euterpe.

"You see life as a casino?" asked Thalia.

"Like one of those classy, surreal places in the Netherlands. Then all of it shuts down, like the Puritans are back in vogue. And we line up at the cash out window to divvy up what's left."

"Abe Fisher said she left us all rich."

"I don't feel rich. I feel empty," said Thalia.

They hugged each other for comfort.

"We girls did this for each other growing up—comfort."

"Mnemosyne wasn't there. She dropped us like an old cow that has pushed out so many calves, then wandered away. Maybe it was pain in her tits that brought her round for an occasional look at us," said Thalia.

"I don't feel sad over her death. I feel empty from the absence of things that never were. Filial relationships with her. She dressed for business right out of the labor and delivery suite."

"She had daughters to support. She had to work."

"I wonder how I'm failing my own daughters, not having any instincts or examples of mothering to give them," said Euterpe. "Do they have remedial classes for that sort of thing?"

Thalia scooped food onto Euterpe's plate—everything she pointed at—and said, "That. Some of that." She put down the urn and scooped brownie fudge pie onto a saucer.

"Don't leave the urn there. Someone might think it's a condiment."

Thalia said, "Yours seem to be fine. No social deviants. Glad I had a choice. None. No offspring. Raising you guys was enough."

"They're popular, and poised. Acceptance by one's peers is the most important thing. Parents are the force to be resisted. Rebellion and walking away from them is natural. I think the absence of something strong to push against is where trouble starts. It leaves them uncertain, insecure."

"I don't think I've ever heard you say so much." Thalia held up a glass. "Wine? Tea?"

"Wine. Red."

"Thank God for Unitarians," said Thalia.

Terpie and Mellie, in silky dancing dresses, stood at the back of the auditorium. Thalia had handed off the urn to Mellie. They looked over the gathering as night descended.

"Are there any religious here?" asked Terpie.

"Mrs. Tucker's kids. Two of them. Christians," said Mellie.

"'Profane Blessing' danced at a religious gathering is sure to offend."

"They don't seem too judgmental. Their late mama probably filled them in regarding Mnemosyne's daughters."

"I would hate to disappoint them."

"You're dancing your goodbye? Your mourning? Your grief?"

"Something like that. The funeral urn with cremains represents a void, an empty space. Someone was there, now they're gone. Or maybe, in our case, that someone was never there? The dance is a ritual of mourning that questions how to say farewell to something that never really was. Perhaps the mourning can facilitate the grief."

"You think Mama was absent?" asked Mellie.

"Pretty much, yes. She provided a house, a cook, things we needed. Otherwise she was like some kind of livestock with depleted genes and exhausted instincts. Dropped her offspring and wandered away."

"Still, her death caught me by surprise. It seems odd that I didn't see the warning signs. Perhaps because we always saw so little of her."

The minister and others lined up in their vestments. They lit incensors and raised their banners of faith.

Mellie put on her mask of tragedy and held the cremains aloft.

Euterpe led the processional playing on her flute, Jethro Tull's *Living in the Past*.

Terpsichore, her face painted like a mime, leapt high into the air. She scattered white rose petals from a basket as she danced jetes, pirouettes, and plies down the center aisle. As Mellie placed the urn on a pedestal, and the processional circled into a sacred space, the dancer's body defied gravity with a tour in l'air into a vole that quickened mourning into grief. The holes in the network of memory became as incandescent as stars in the night sky.

The End

Layla And The Rage

LAYLA WIPED THE glass table top with a napkin before setting her teapot on it. She pulled more napkins from the Bevnap and wiped the seat. Unhappy with this she took a section of newspaper and folded it on the seat. Then she sat down because the big, red-faced guy at the next table had noticed her.

He noticed her cleanliness, her manicure, her darker skin, her high round bottom, her tight black curls and her eyes which radiated distress—her otherness. It made her uncomfortable that she had caused him to notice her.

An old voice, teacher-in-her-head, "Muslim women do not draw attention to themselves." It seemed perverse to Layla that merely being a Muslim in Palms, California drew unwanted attention from a white guy little removed from his own immigrant roots. *His cheap shoes aren't shined. His shirt is wrinkled and that pot gut.*

"Layla, sweetie," said an ebullient brunette who approached and kissed Layla's cheek. Both women were dressed in snappy casual with designer shoes. The energy changed with words between friends and the blank spaces between words.

They talked over tea as the red-faced man glared at them, then turned away. He gave his newspaper a snap. The women's words, a succubus, drifted into Red's tufted ears.

"I want Fatima to come with me on Hajj, but she can only think of boys," said Layla.

"Teenagers are meant to torment us," said the brunette.

"I don't want to go. Saudi Arabia's full of Sunnis, but Hajj is required, right?"

"Take Zakariyya, you won't have to worry about driving."

"He's afraid they'll cut off his head or throw him off the roof of the hotel."

The brunette touched Layla's hand. "I didn't mean that. Our children are a blessing, not a torture."

Layla faced a choice between tradition and the new world. *What to keep for my children, what to leave behind?*

The man had grown florid as his neck pushed heat into his hairline. He stood to leave with fire in his eyes, threw his paper onto the table, and kicked his wrought iron chair.

"Ignorant superstitious camel jockeys, if you don't like America then get out! Go back to where you came from."

"Fresno?" said Layla.

He spat and lunged toward the door. His unbalanced rage, like his gut hanging over his belt, proved too much for his thin legs to support. His shins contacted the iron chair and for a moment he looked like a penitent kneeling on a prei-dieu then flailed into thin air.

Inertia loves the top heavy, that moment when gravity faceplants hubris into the cold reality of a terrazzo floor.

The two women sidled toward the door.

"Mercy," said the brunette.

"Good heavens." said Layla.

As they reached the sidewalk their pace quickened to a dead run even though Muslim women do not like to draw attention to themselves.

The End

The Crab

"No, I AM Marie," Mrs. Lafourche could have been heard to say had anyone been close enough to hear. Andy, the reservations clerk, watched her from the patio where he sorted supplies into storage. He had noticed the elderly guest talked to a familiar spirit. She pointed to the bed, held out her hand, and dropped something. Then she returned to reading the April 10th *Times Picayune* on her private balcony.

He thought it odd that she talked to herself. No one else was with her. She was a woman of a certain age who vacationed alone at the bed and breakfast on Royal Street at Esplanade. Andy felt somewhat parental towards her, in spite of her crotchety ways.

She walked into the bedroom and shortly reappeared on the balcony as if looking for someone. In a gesture of territoriality that filled the space of the open French doors with arms and elbows, she put her hands on her hips and turned again towards the bed as if puzzled. Then she picked up the breakfast service and walked back inside.

He locked the storage closet and stopped at the utility sink to wash his hands and fasten his black bow tie to his shirt collar. Inside the lobby, he overheard the ancient gate of the elevator open and Mrs. Lafourche approach the lobby desk. She had the accent of a south Louisiana Cajun. Maybe one from Terrebonne Parish.

"I asked her to just spread up the bed. Not even to change all the linens, just spread it up. And she didn't even do that," Mrs. Lafourche said. She sounded like somebody who was used to giving orders and getting her way. "That burned smell? Did the cook burn something?"

"Our housekeeper is still working on the first floor rooms. She should get upstairs in about an hour," said the night clerk, who then locked her cash register drawer and waved to Andy. As the maid pushed her cart toward the elevator, the clerk called to her, "Soledad, did you not hear Mrs. Lafourche ask to have her bed made up with the same sheets?"

"No, not her. The other one. The black one, a little girl," said Mrs. Lafourche. She selected two pamphlets from the concierge rack: *April In The French Quarter* and *Ghosts of the Vieux Carre*. "She asked me if I was with Delphine. She seemed afraid of something." Mrs. Lafourche dabbed sweat from her forehead as she sat on the nearest chair.

"Tres es proximo. I do three… um, third floor next," said Soledad as she pushed her cart onto the elevator. The doors rattled closed and the car jerked heavenward.

The clerk looked puzzled. "Soledad is our only housekeeper. She will do your room first when she gets upstairs." As a diversionary tactic, she asked, "Did you enjoy your fruit and pastry? We get them fresh from Marcel every morning."

"Yes, very good." The old lady wouldn't let it go. "Something was burning."

"Probably you smell one of the coffee roasting warehouses down the river."

"It wasn't roasting coffee. It was burning wood, like a house burning, and if you don't have a black girl cleaning rooms, who was that barefoot child in a long dress and maid's cap in my room?"

"We don't employ any children. I'll ask security to watch for such a child. Did anything come up missing?"

"No. She was rail thin. I gave her a ten dollar bill to go get something to eat. This is all very odd. I didn't come to New Orleans to be bothered by foolishness. I have that at home."

Her family, a care-taking daughter and extended kin along Bayou Terrebonne had all pitched in to get the old lady out from under foot. They sent her for a week's holiday in the city. She fretted their nerves, and worked her own, but would have sworn no malice. It was, after all, April and the world renewed itself in every opening leaf and every new lengthening day. A dozen Cajuns had lined up along the station platform to see her onto the Sunset Limited and waved in relief as the porter hollered, "All aboooooaaaaard."

As she turned to leave the lobby, Mrs Lafourche mounted the bottom step, paused as if judging the distance to the third floor, and turned to the elevator. She stuck the two pamphlets into her dress pocket and pressed the up arrow. "I want a report filed with your security. This is not right," she called back to the desk before the door closed and the car ascended.

Andy stood beside the night clerk who rolled her eyes. "What a pill," she said and handed him a large ring of keys.

It was noon when their peevish guest caught the Vieux Carre trolley toward Canal Street. She made her way back through the antique shops of Royal Street and the junk shops on Decatur, and felt her strength ebb by the time she got to the French Market. Standing before a large vat of crabs, pink boiled shrimp, crawfish, and oysters on the half shell laid out on a bed of ice, she had a craving for seafood. At an open air cafe, a waiter in a dirty apron with dark crescents under his fingernails seated her at a table with a red checkered cloth blowing in the spring breeze. She quickly chose a large bowl of seafood gumbo and gratefully drowned her hot thirst in the foaming white head of a mug of beer.

At about four o'clock Mrs. Lafourche re-entered the lobby from Royal Street. She was sweating under a load of shopping bags. A damp strand of hair which might have been a curl that morning was plastered straight across her forehead. Andy watched in concern as she sank into the sofa nearest the entrance. He locked the cash register and got a cold bottle of water.

"Good day shopping?" he said. He twisted the plastic cap from the water bottle and handed it to her.

She took a long drink and mopped her forehead and throat with a handkerchief. With effort she focused on the voice as Andy came into view.

She looked done in.

"Yes. I got a couple of dresses and had lunch at the French Market, one of those little open air cafes. The seafood gumbo was delicious, but I think the crabs may have been off." She placed her hand over her stomach and whispered, "My digestion is not right."

"Let me help you with the bags. We'll get you upstairs."

He gathered her bags in one arm and supported her with the other.

Her touch shocked him: she was ice cold.

The elevator klunked to the third floor.

She got to the bed and lay down, barely pausing to kick off her shoes. "I'm so tired. I need to rest a bit. Amazing how fast seafood goes off," she said, and seemed to fade with the words.

"Would you like me to call a doctor? You don't look well," Andy said.

No response from Mrs. Lafourche who softly snored.

Andy pulled the door shut and returned to the front desk.

Sometime during the evening Marie Lafourche awoke with a sense of dread. The smell of burning wood made it difficult to breathe. She struggled to sit up and was startled to find the same little girl in maid's cap and long dress standing at the foot of her bed. Her cheek had a gash like a whip mark washed by her tears.

"What on earth?" said the elderly woman. She stood on weak legs and reached out to the child.

The girl withdrew to the middle of the room. Orange light flickered in her eyes as she looked out the balcony doors and returned her gaze to the hotel room.

The source of the smoke and strange light could be seen as Marie pulled open the French doors and stepped onto the balcony. A building in the other half of the block was on fire. People in a line hauled buckets of water arm over arm. She thought it odd that there were no fire engines, just people shouting and sweating and throwing water.

On the third floor of the burning building she saw a giant crab climb a drain pipe to the attic. It scuttled across the side of the building and entered a window near the top. A closer look revealed it to be a horribly deformed man, a black man so twisted in his arms and legs, he was barely three feet tall.

The girl pushed past the old lady to get to the rail of the balcony and screamed, "Run, Jonah. Run!" She stood on tip toe to see the progress of the crab man toward the attic. Windows along the upper floors began to open and men emerged in clouds of smoke.

As the child jumped up and down, Marie noticed she had a wound around her ankle, a massive sore completely encircling her leg and bleeding onto the balcony floor.

"Here, let me see your leg. What has happened to you?"

The girl clutched at something under her dress. Wide-eyed she pulled away from the white lady's touch.

"I got to run away. Tonight! I'll get north and buy my freedom."

"Buy your freedom?" Mrs. Lafourche sat on a chair near the open balcony doors. Her head reeled from the smoke and excitement just across the patio. She felt like she was underwater. She could feel it in her lungs. "What do you mean, buy your freedom?"

The girl reached beneath her long dress into the folds and unpinned a brooch. She held it out for Marie to see.

"I stole this from that devil woman, Madame LaLaurie. Delphine!" She spat the name like a curse word.

The antique brooch was a clever, detailed piece, a rose gold crab encrusted in precious stones. Marquise diamonds formed the legs, sapphires the body, and two pigeon's blood rubies stuck up on tiny golden stalks to form the eyes. It looked so much like a real crab one expected it to pinch and scoot toward the river.

"I will sell it and buy my freedom," said the girl.

Her hand closed around it and she reached beneath her dress to secure her treasure.

Shouts, whistling, and the crack of a whip from the alley separating the patio from the LaLaurie Mansion yanked their attention. A black cabriolet pulled by a massive horse shot from the stable and careened on one wheel onto Royal Street.

"There goes the Devil's bitch. Get her!" shouted one of the men fighting the fire. A glimpse of a woman's face, shockingly white and framed by a wild mane of black hair, peered from a window of the buggy. Its wide, evil eyes fastened on the girl by Marie's side. Long white fingers clawed at the glass and the mouth and face contorted into a mask of rage as the carriage disappeared into the night.

The next morning, Mrs. Lafourche jerked awake from a restless sleep and gasped for air. She heaved herself to her feet and tottered to the bathroom, leaning heavily on furniture and the wall as she went. In the mirror her gray face stared back at her in the unflattering light. After a shower she felt a little revived, so dressed and went downstairs. The breakfast service looked unappealing.

She tested her legs with a short walk to the pharmacy on Royal Street and made a purchase, then walked on Ursulines Street to Croissant Patisserie. The entrances into the cafe, marked one for ladies and one for gentlemen, were separated by a bay window that displayed a carousel pony. She ordered coffee, fresh fruit and a croissant. As she lingered over her breakfast a Vieux Carre Ghost Tour paused just outside the window so the guide could speak.

"How do I buy a ticket for the tour?" Mrs. Lafourche asked the server.

"Just join in. The tour guide will take your money."

So Marie walked with the group and listened to tales of spirits, voodoo, orbs and hauntings. As the group rounded the corner from the French Market onto Governor Nicholls Street at Royal, she recognized the three story house she had watched burn the night before. Her tenuous feelings of well-being sank when the tour stopped in front of the LaLaurie Mansion.

"Delphine McCarty-LaLaurie was a late eighteenth century socialite, twice widowed, who later married a physician, Dr. Louis LaLaurie. Their A-list social status and their reputation for fantastic *bals masque* among the Creole elite was jeopardized by her sadism. Her cruelty to her slaves resulted in the authorities removing them from her house and selling them at auction where her relatives purchased them and returned them to her."

The guide gestured with a prop, a buggy whip, toward the third floor. "In 1833 neighbors witnessed Delphine chase a slave girl onto the balcony, and so mercilessly beat the child that she climbed toward the roof and fell to her death onto the patio below. Her body was quickly taken inside and disposed of. Rumors flew and grew among the aristocrats. The following year on April tenth a fire in the kitchen behind the house drew a bucket brigade to the mansion. The fire was set by two slaves who were chained to the stove. The men entered to put out the fire and they were pointed to a locked door on the third floor. They rammed the door to gain entrance and found a chamber of horrors."

The guide paused for effect, closed his eyes, and placed his hand over his heart. "Medical experiments: slaves, disemboweled and with their guts sewn to the outside of their abdomens, so their digestion could be observed while they lived. One man so deformed and twisted by his broken limbs that he looked like a crab and was forced to sleep in a square wooden box, and one early sex change operation. Most of the victims had already perished. Twelve people were found there in the charnel house. Those who were alive begged the fire fighters to put them out of their agony."

Marie felt her fruit and pastry begin to rise into her throat. She left the tour and walked quickly back to the bed and breakfast on Royal Street. She took the elevator to her room without speaking to the clerk at the reception desk.

After the nausea and vomiting had subsided she succumbed to a fitful nap which left her unrefreshed. Upright in the chair by the open balcony doors she felt less able to draw a deep breath with each minute that passed. She fanned her face with a page of newspaper. The shadows from the LaLaurie Mansion lengthened across the alley and across the brick wall of the patio to incorporate the bed and breakfast hotel in its maw of evil. Night again brought the stench of burning wood and carrion as Marie checked her bag of supplies from the pharmacy. She watched the shadows lengthen as the moon chased its reflection across the Mississippi River. The silver light touched her swollen ankles. Her hands waited in her lap to staunch the bleeding and pain of a nine-year-old girl enslaved by a sadistic mistress.

Her head tilted to one side as if listening for a footstep on the balcony. The wide blue eyes, irises ringed by arcus senilis, glossed over like blue marbles and focused on nothing. The moonlight touched her chest as her breath paused and did not rise again.

The following day in the mournful room, the coroner removed Marie's body in a bag. A smell of antiseptic hung in the air from the disinfectant the maid had used in the bathroom. The bed had been stripped to the mattress. On the end table, still in a bag with a sales ticket attached, Andy found a can of spray antiseptic, antibiotic and lidocaine salve, gauze, tape, and bandage scissors, all unopened. He unhooked the drapery from the balcony doors. Then pushed the armchair and tea table aside and straightened to look at the LaLaurie Mansion as it glowed in the morning sun. Perpetual fire seemed to leap from the upper windows facing east. The current owner of the building sat on a balcony having coffee and smoking a cigarette. The ferry to Algiers crossed the river into the sunlight.

At Andy's feet something glittered bright red in the pile of the carpet He bent to see what it was and lifted in his hand a tiny antique brooch: a rose gold crab, crusted in jewels, diamonds on its legs, sapphires on its body, two pigeon's blood rubies for eyes. He turned it over and squinted at the inscription on the back—"Delphine." Beside it lay a folded ten dollar bill.

The End

Medea Royal

MEDEA ROYAL, THE diva, costumed in fierce black and silver for her role as Queen of the Night sat before her mirror, backstage at the opera house in New York, and repaired a tiny makeup flaw at the corner of her eye. She had just concluded her first aria to a standing ovation. The showrunner stuck his head into her dressing room.

"What's up?" asked Medea.

"Your understudy is taking over," he said.

"But my voice has never been better."

"You're done here." He shut the door.

A hard knock on the door immediately followed. A uniformed policeman strode through the door and announced, "Medea, we have a warrant for your arrest for the murder of your husband's mistress, Dixie DeKalb, and for questioning regarding the disappearance of your twins, Paul and Mark." Behind the first officer was another from the NYPD and, finally, like the vindicated wrath of God, red-faced, scratching his neck and wiping his nose—Detective Erinye.

"Medea," he said, "You can't just run around killing people."

He chuckled as he blew his nose and stuck his handkerchief back into his trousers pocket.

"It'll be good seeing you in these bracelets." He turned to the NYPD officers and said, "Cuff her, and tell her about Miranda."

"You have the right to remain silent. You have the right to a lawyer…" the NYPD officer said as he led her on a backstage walk of shame past her colleagues, out the stage door, and placed her into a waiting police cruiser.

At the precinct headquarters she was put in line for booking behind four desperate-looking characters. They stank and they looked sick.

"Hey, Red. Where's the party?" a man with pinpoint pupils and jaundiced skin asked her.

"I love your dress—can I wear it?" asked another who looked like he was chewing off his own teeth.

"Your hair is werkin'. Who does it?" asked a third man, pulling imaginary bugs off his face.

"X?" whispered the nastiest smelling one of them all. "Spliff, crack, pot? What chu want is what I got." Medea recoiled from the odor as he leaned toward her. "I cater to the needs of theater people," he said and grinned over brown nubs of teeth, his breath a miasma like that over a medieval plague city. She could see track marks from his wrists to his elbows.

A policewoman behind a glass window asked her the necessary questions and another took her into a room with only a table. Latex gloves, lubricant, and a sack with her name on it sat on top of the table.

"Remove your clothes and put them in this bag," said the officer as she snapped on latex gloves and squirted clear lubricant on her finger. Another officer stood by the door. After the strip search the policewoman led her down a long white corridor with heavy green doors every ten feet, and finally locked her in a six-by-eight foot cell. Fluorescent lighting behind a hard plastic square in the ceiling provided harsh blue light. There was a tiny metal desk attached to one wall. A stool and a narrow bunk were fixed to the other. There was no window she could see out of. A small metal toilet with no seat, and a cold water sink completed the furnishings. A silver ball appeared to be stuck in the ceiling.

"The eye of God," she said and stood a long time in the center of the room as if waiting for room service to bring her sheets and unfold the mattress. When no one came and she grew tired of standing she straightened the thin mattress and looked closely for bugs. Finding none she sat down. After eight impossibly long minutes of ennui she curled into fetal position and began to sob.

After two days of this she was glad to hear a court-appointed psychiatrist would come to interview her. This would give Medea a chance to reflect on how she had risen to diva heights and fallen so low. The shrink appeared a disappointment at first. She was fat, frumpy and skittish.

"I don't do this for the money, but to give something back. I like your voice. My real practice is on the upper East Side." She scratched her nose, touched her lips, rubbed her eyebrows and scratched her neck. She looked around the room as if the walls and ceiling were starting to close in on her. Medea noticed brown stains on the middle and index fingers of her right hand.

"Are you a smoker? If you need a cigarette you can slip the guard a bill and she'll let you smoke up a forest fire."

"I would kill…".

"Don't say that. That's how I got started," said Medea and laughed. The shrink looked puzzled. "It's a joke," said Medea.

The psychiatrist found some money in her briefcase and gave it to the guard for a light. Medea made a gesture with her fingers as well and said, "Props." The shrink gave her a cigarette.

"Two," said Medea and the interview began.

"Think back in your life, as far back as you can go. What is your earliest memory?" she said. A small voice recorder was running.

"My name on my birth certificate is Medea Cobb. My mother is, or was, Tiffany Cobb. Her occupation is listed as waitress, but I want to set that straight right now. She was a prostitute," said Medea. "I changed my name to Medea Royal when I started singing professionally."

"My first memory is dumping my mother's purse onto the vanity at the Magnolia Suites Inn. I was about five-years-old. There was a cellophane package about two inches square, clear on one side with something round, slippery and red inside. The end of the thing had a nipple, and 'strawberry flavored' was written on the other side along with 'pre-lubed.'" In her mind, Medea slipped out of the present and went back in time.

"What's this?" she asked her mother who was deep into her beauty routine at the mirror.

"Rain hat for squirrels. Your mama believes in preserving wildlife." She fiercely massaged the corners of her eyes and mouth with beauty fluid. The fine lines there bothered her more than anyone else. She was obsessed with them.

Medea pulled out a wooden handle wrought with metal, with a button on one side. She asked, "What's this?" and pushed the button. A long silver blade flicked out the end as quick as a snake's tongue and caught the light from the vanity. Medea dropped the switchblade and looked up at her mother.

"That's sharp. You'll cut yourself," said her mother and gathered the condom and the switchblade back into her bag. Medea sat on the edge of the tub and watched her mother fix her face. She examined the shimmering dress that caught the light and moved it around.

"When I'm grown will I be as pretty as you?" Medea asked.

Tiffany put a dollop of cream on Medea's elbow and knee. "You'll do all right," she said. "Rub that in. You want to stay young and beautiful as long as possible. Just take what nature gave you and improve it any way you can." She pulled on black tights with silver sparkles, and pushed her feet into impossibly high heels. "Don't open the door for anybody but me. I'll call ahead when I want you two to go stay in the car." She checked her stuff: makeup travel kit, blade, condoms, cigarettes and lighter. One last critical glance in the mirror and she kissed the two kids, Medea and Morris, and stepped into the neon lit night. *Magnolia Suites Inn* and *No Vacancy* signs proclaimed for a half mile in either direction as the taillights of their mother's car faded toward whatever roadhouse she was currently working.

Medea massaged the beauty cream into the rough ashy skin of her elbows and knees. She and her half brother, Morris, who was three years older than her, had their own checklist of things to get through the night.

"Pillows and blankets," said Medea.

"Check," said Morris.

"Cookies and chips."

"Check."

"Change for the Coke machine."

"Check."

"Flashlight."

"Check."

"What's on TV?" said Medea.

"Movie classics, sports, news. Here's something, 'Friday Night Frights,'" said Morris.

"That," said Medea. "Got your tablet?"

"Check," said Morris.

Later Medea had fallen asleep and Morris was still in front of the TV when the phone rang. It was Mama.

"What are ya'll doing?" she asked.

"Nothing. Hanging out. Watching TV," said Morris.

"Take your stuff outside to the picnic area. I'll be in with a client in a few minutes. I'll leave the car unlocked."

Medea the sleepyhead watched her mother and a john get out of the car and walk to the motel room. From the picnic area by the chlorine-smelling, blue pool they waited until they saw her subtle wave. Then they made their way to the car where they tucked themselves in. Morris powered up his tablet to the WiFi. Medea was back asleep in minutes.

The following evening the motel owner lit the *No Vacancy* sign and slipped into comfortable house shoes and the wasteland of TV. His nosey wife watched the two children out by the pool. Under a large oak tree where picnic tables had been set up, and at the back of the property where a creek ran, were the children's favorite hangouts. The creek was a ditch full of polluted water, runoff from the highway, factories, and industrial farms, and full of excrement. Chemicals nourished a plethora of salamanders, snakes, frogs, and crawfish—one of which had split Medea's fingernail. She retaliated in anger and pain by pulling off both its pinchers and throwing it back into the ditch.

"Die mudbug," she said.

Back at the picnic table of the motel she wrapped her bleeding finger in a napkin from the Bevnap dispenser.

The nosey wife checked her kitchen pantry and invited the two inside for supper.

They had only seen a glimpse of the rooms behind the motel office counter, but at the table of the small kitchenette, with the living room and its TV and a bedroom off from that, it looked like a home. Their hostess wasted no time in pumping them for information.

"Does ya'll's mama entertain a lot of men in that room?" she asked as she poured them Coke and set plates of food on the kitchenette table.

Medea looked at Morris across the table. *Ready?* "Oh no ma'am. She's a recruiter. She interviews them for jobs."

Their hostess looked closely at Morris's African-American features and Medea's red hair and skin like freckled cream and remarked, "Ya'll had different daddies."

"Yes'm." little Medea said. "Mama's divorced and remarried."

"Well, where's ya'll's daddy?"

"He's in the Middle East. Mama gets by as best she can on his military pay."

"Can I have a piece of that coconut pie?" Morris asked.

The woman wanted to get some juicy gossip out of the children. What she failed to understand was that such children only took what life put before them but gave nothing away. Morris and Medea had been as carefully coached in fibs for proper occasions as they had in not to talk with your mouth full, to say "Please," "Yes'm," and "Thank you," and to always smile when dealing with small-minded, small town people. A dysfunctional family's survival depends on carefully guarding their secrets. That their mom currently worked the Red Hills Hideaway, a lounge by a truckstop down the highway, and brought her tricks to their motel room was the succulent bit of gossip the motel wife wanted but the kids weren't givng it up.

When their hostess gathered the dishes, the motel owner turned his attention from the TV. He opened the fridge for a beer and said to her, "You don't need to go spreading all that gossip around town. Folks'll think we're running a hot sheets motel out here."

Both Morris and Medea's young lives were elaborate fictions which they could reinvent every few weeks with each new move to a new town where their mother was not known by local gossips or law enforcement.

They sat in the picnic area at dusk and watched as fireflies lit up the creek bottom with their luminous mating calls. They reviewed their performances at supper.

"I want to tell the next one my daddy's a singer in a band that plays on Rampart Street in New Orleans," said Morris.

"What's his name?" asked Medea.

"Zoots. Zoots and the Blue Notes," said Morris.

"That's good," said Medea. "I want to tell the next one my daddy's a engineer at NASA, who works on the Space Shuttle."

"You ever wonder what people get out of gossip?" asked Morris.

"Naw. Like Mama says, we got a more interesting life and we ain't stooping that low."

Two nights later Mama came back without calling first. She had blood dripping from her nose and a swollen black eye. She emptied the water from the ice bucket.

"Morris, go get me some ice," she said.

Medea stood frozen to her spot beside the bed until her mother shook her shoulder.

"Pack your stuff quick." She handed her a suitcase from the closet.

"Mama, what happened?" asked Medea, panic rising in her voice.

"Be quiet and pack. Do it now," said her mother. She examined her eye and hissed at the mirror. "Oh my God!" she moaned.

Medea saw blood on the handle and the blade of her mother's knife as Tiffany took a toothbrush and soap and cleaned it in the sink.

Seeing her daughter staring at her, "Pack, girl. We got to go."

Morris came back with the ice bucket full. "Mama, you want me to go beat him up?"

"Just pack your stuff." She kissed the top of his head. "I think he may already be dead."

She made an ice pack out of a facecloth and held it to her eye with one hand, as she threw her clothes into her suitcase.

It was the middle of the night when the little trio quietly slipped away from the outskirts of Atlanta headed southeast. The lights from the motel rapidly faded. Medea lay awake and watched through the rear window as a million stars spread across the narrow strip of sky between the tops of pine trees.

They awoke to the smell of breakfast in a strange house. The two children followed their noses to the kitchen where they found their mother, wearing an apron and pouring coffee, with a black man.

"This is Mr. Eshu Carter," she said to the children, and put biscuits, bacon and eggs along with juice and milk in front of them. They were not used to seeing her so domestic. "Cat got your tongue?" she asked. "Say hello."

"Hi, Mr. Carter. I'm Medea." She shook his hand and sat down to eat.

"I'm Morris." He did the same.

Eshu Carter glanced at red-headed, freckled Medea, and then fastened his attention on Morris. He studied closely the child's features, bone structure, face, eyes, hair and hands. Medea watched her half-brother smear preserves on a biscuit and bite into it. As he did he glanced uncomfortably at Mr. Carter staring at him then to Medea and rolled his eyes.

Tiffany Cobb slid an affectionate arm around Mr. Carter's neck and patted his chest. She looked at her two kids who looked back at her. *Wassup?*

"Morris is your son," she said to all at the table.

Medea's biscuit felt suddenly dry in her throat and she coughed. She reached for her milk and knocked over her orange juice. Morris went slack-jawed staring at Mr. Carter.

"Don't be clumsy, Medea," said Tiffany.

"My daddy?" said Morris. "How come I never seen you before?"

"Are you my daddy too?" asked Medea.

"No, you had a different father," said Tiffany as she wiped up the spilled juice.

Medea had seen her mother dressed for some roles with clients: black leotards and a leather bustier, cheerleader complete with pom poms and knee socks, flapper from the 1920s, and pink waitress. The white apron could be adapted to naughty French maid, and now apparently Georgia housewife. Her mama's secrets lay in a small flexible wardrobe, some skill with improvised dialogue, and talent with hair and makeup. One would imagine trunks full of clothes and accessories but it all fit into two big suitcases in the trunk, along with two smaller suitcases for two fellow travelers. Suddenly their years long arrangement seemed threatened; the next installment of their elaborate fiction dubious.

They cleared the table of dishes and Eshu Carter asked the two children, "Ya'll wanna help me plant peanuts?" He could have said they were going to a fairyland theme park and the two children would have been no less excited.

"What'll I wear, Mr. Carter?" asked Medea.

"Jeans and a t-shirt will be fine, and a straw hat," said Eshu Carter. "Ya'll call me Daddy Carter."

The three stopped at the barn door. "This is a work area, not for play. You can get hurt in a barn if you're not careful." The two children waited and listened to the sounds of equipment hitching to equipment and an engine being cranked. To their amazement the largest tractor they had ever seen emerged from the barn.

"Claim a seat," said Daddy Carter. He gestured to Morris to stand to his right side and lean against that fender, and Medea he gestured to his left. "Get a firm grip," he said and they headed into heat mirages, dust devils and waiting rows of newly cultivated dirt.

As he drove, Daddy Carter magnanimously gestured to the left and to the right. "From Singing Water Creek to over those hills and all the way to the sunset this land been in my family for five generations. Since before 1838. My great-great-great-granddaddy wasn't no slave. He was a free man married to a Injun woman."

That night was the last time Medea observed her mama's intense attention to her beauty routine. She seemed as transfixed in massaging beauty cream into the fine lines of her eyes and mouth as she had ever been. But something was different. Gone were the sparkle and high heels, and gone was the razzle dazzle, dressed up for the night. Instead she dressed in a mauve and green gown that suited

her red hair and freckled skin. Her hair was down and pulled into a side ponytail. Her perfume smelled different—less sexy, but Medea lacked words for that. Tiffany cooked supper and set the table with Daddy Carter's good china and flatware. Medea had never seen her do that for anyone.

"Long time since anybody's warmed them pots and pans 'cept me," Daddy Carter said when the four of them were seated. "Bring your hands together and bow your heads." Medea started to clap, but Morris grabbed her arm as God was invoked. "Father, bless this meal and the hands that prepared it."

That night Medea and Morris both got a bedroom of their own. Their mother went down the hall into Daddy Carter's bedroom and shut the door.

Medea heard it out by the barn, like in a dream, when Daddy Carter cranked the tractor. Lines of morning sun streamed in through her window as the sound of the tractor faded toward distant fields. Downstairs she heard the sounds of a washing machine and dryer, and smelled coffee and clean laundry from the direction of the kitchen. Tiffany Cobb worked at a folding table on the glass enclosed back porch off the kitchen. Her large suitcases lay open as she packed her stuff with the efficiency of a seasoned traveler. Medea's and Morris's clothes were arranged in stacks.

"Take these up to your room, and give Morris these to put away," she said and handed Medea two stacks of folded clothes. "There's milk and juice and pop up pastry you can warm for breakfast."

Morris followed Medea back downstairs to the kitchen and poured some coffee. He rubbed sleep from his eyes and looked at his Mama, "What're we gonna do today?"

Medea smeared butter on her pastry and poured orange juice.

"I'm going job hunting over on the coast," said their mama.

"Which coast?" asked Morris, "Atlantic or Gulf?"

"Both," said Tiffany. "You guys will stay here with Daddy Carter until I come back." She quickly inventoried the contents of her suitcases and closed the lids.

Their two stacks of clothes put away in chests of drawers, separate from her two suitcases ready to travel, seemed odd. Morris and Medea frowned at her and at each other. They had never been left behind like this.

"Both of you mind what Daddy Carter says and don't give him any sass, or I'll tear your butt up when I come back."

"How long you gonna be gone?" asked Medea.

"Awhile," said Tiffany. "These applications can take some time." She carried her two suitcases to the front door.

"Ya'll eat. Your food's getting cold."

After breakfast the two kids dressed in jeans and t-shirts. From her bedroom window Medea watched her mother load the two suitcases into the trunk of her car. She unfolded a map across the roof.

"You two see what you can find to play with around here, but stay out of the barn. That's a work area. You should only go there with Daddy Carter." She sat at the kitchen table and wrote a note to Eshu Carter:

"Eshu,

Here's their birth certificates and vaccination records from the Atlanta Health Department. If you take them to the county health department here the nurse will get their shots up to date in time for school.

If you notice Morris's name is Carter on his birth certificate, and Eshu Carter is the name of his father. As I said, he is your son. Medea has my last name and unknown for father. I'm not proud of that but things are what they are and we move forward, baggage and all.

With this letter I give you legal guardianship. You can get a lawyer and get yourself appointed guardian ad litem so there will be no problems with school or any health agency.

I love you. I'm sorry our lives can't be together right now, but perhaps that's for the best. When I return from Seattle to get the kids, things will be different.

Affectionately,

Tiffany Cobb

The police psychiatrist cleared her throat to bring Medea back to the present and asked, "What do you imagine went through your mother's mind as she left you and your brother?"

The psychiatrist seemed less anxious on this second visit to the correctional center because she had permission from the guard to smoke. She had brought Medea a couple of packs, as requested. "To help jar my memory," Medea had said.

To this day Medea could only guess why their mother left without even a hug and a kiss. Perhaps she had believed that the shortest goodbyes were the best. Perhaps she had steeled her nerves for what lay ahead and had resolved to move forward and let nothing stand in her way.

Or, maybe, Medea herself had run her mother off. She was bad, always dumping out her mother's purse to see what was inside. She ate a lot of food and wanted a lot of clothes and shoes that she grew out of so fast they were scarcely even worn.

"That's what I believed—that it was my fault. But she never intended to come back and she never intended to be found. That's why she told me and Morris that she was going 'to the coast-Atlantic and Gulf,' and she told Daddy Carter, 'Seattle.' She dropped off the baggage (that would be us) and covered her tracks with lies."

"Ya'll go play," said Tiffany on the day she sat down at the kitchen table to write Eshu Carter a note. Medea and Morris had known asphalt and concrete motel parking lots, chlorinated pools, picnic areas and idealized play equipment all their young lives. Their serendipitous favorite things were drainage ditches, and ponds or creeks near the motels where they spent days or weeks before moving on. So Daddy Carter's frog pond, full of algae green water, and the nitrogenous run off from fertilizer and manure, held them fascinated. Large gold and brown eyes surfaced to observe them and then disappeared beneath ripples and tiny whirlpools as the kids crept closer and knelt at the edge of muck and water. They scarcely noticed the sounds of the trunk and doors on their mama's car opening and closing. A large pair of golden eyes opened and peered out through slits in a head of green slick skin wider than Medea's hand. It surfaced right in front of her. She lunged and came up with two hands full of a bullfrog whose legs kicked past her elbows as she held it up for her mother to see.

"Medea got one!" screamed Morris. "Medea caught a big one." He jumped up and ran around the pond. "That a girl," he hollered.

Medea looked for her mother but her sunglasses had slipped and she looked right into the sun as she heard the car engine start and shift into gear. She caught one last glimpse of her mother, who did not take her eyes from the gravel driveway or the asphalt road ahead. Medea could see her mother's ponytail, too young for a woman her age, and the big round sunglasses hiding her eyes, which were set on the future. She did not even look back at her children as she drove away.

Medea's jaw fell slack and she began a low pitched scream like an animal in pain. Turning away from the sight of her mother's leaving she threw the bullfrog against the trunk of an oak tree. It tumbled down the rough bark and landed on the ground. One side of it kicked trying to get aright as the other side sprawled flaccidly. One eye had popped out of its head and its tongue lapped at dust.

"What'd you do that for?" asked Morris with some disgust, but Medea had no words for her betrayal, loss and rage. So she jumped up and down on the frog. It made a flatulent sound like air trapped in a twisted bladder, then it popped. Medea ran into the vast green of Daddy Carter's peanut field and kept screaming until she grew hoarse.

Daddy Carter heard her screaming over sounds of the tractor, and he came running. Medea had gone limp and fallen face down between rows. He scooped her up and carried her on his shoulder like a sack of grain into the house where he washed the dirt off her face and laid her down on her bed. It was then that he found the note from Tiffany.

Eshu Carter pulled a rocking chair into the room and tuned a radio into the classical music station. After he read the note he wiped his eyes with a Kleenex and stared a long time at Medea. She slept all day, all night and most of the following day. Her eyes moved beneath fluttering lids and she occasionally moaned before falling back into unresponsiveness. Eshu picked her up every couple of hours and took her to the bathroom from which she walked like a zombie back to her bed. Eshu did not leave the house.

"Let her sleep," he said when Morris came to check on his sister. Mid-morning of the second day Eshu awoke to the sound of "La Mama Morte," from the opera *Andrea Chenier* on the radio, and little Medea trilling lovely Italian vowels along with the music. Perfect pitch and on key. Tears ran down her face and she appeared transfixed by the depth of loss and tragedy in the music.

"What are you listening to?" he asked and handed her a tissue.

"Radio. It's an 'opera,'" she said.

"What are they saying?"

"I don't know. The radio man said it was Italian."

"Why are you crying?"

"Because it's so beautiful and so sad."

"How do you know?"

"The music."

Daddy Carter studied her for a long minute as if he had finally seen something of worth.

"You haven't eaten in two days, are you hungry?"

"Starving."

About two weeks after Tiffany Cobb headed out, a Detective Erinye showed up at the farm. It was the first of several encounters Medea would have with him. Both Medea and Morris were stood up in front of him and expected to answer questions about what happened between their mother and a man she was supposed to have stuck a knife into. That man was in the intensive care unit at Emory.

"I don't know," was all he got from either of them. They had sucked in their liar status with their mother's milk. No matter. If they had been telling the truth the answer would have still been the same, "I don't know." Because they didn't.

Medea watched Detective Erinye wipe his eyes and blow his nose on a handkerchief that he put back into his pocket. She thought he must have a lot of snot in there. His skin was so red it looked burned and raised, not blistered, but covered in large bumps. He never stopped scratching the whole time he asked questions.

He soon grew tired of grilling the children and turned his laser-like stare to Eshu Carter.

"Did anything seem unusual about Tiffany Cobb when she came here?"

"It all seem unusual. I ain't seen Tiffany in about nine…ten years."

"Did she appear upset in any way?"

"She had a black eye on the left side, and a busted nose and lip."

"Any other wounds that you noticed?"

"Big bruise over the left rib. Look like somebody fond of punching women with they right fist."

"Punched her?"

"With his fist. She say she got her hand on her blade and 'cut him up.'"

She say she didn't know if he dead or alive, but when he hit the ground, she beat feet."

"Is Miss Cobb here now?"

"No. She spend two nights here then leave. Say she had some friends in Seattle could help her get re-settle and maybe find a job."

Medea and Morris exchanged looks at the mention of Seattle. She had most certainly said "the coast" to them.

"Do you know the names of these friends?"

"I don't believe she say."

"Do you know how she knows them?"

"I don't know. Like I say, she show up here and drop her two kids off after nine years…ten, I guess, since I see her."

"Why did she drop off her kids with you?"

"Because she say the boy mine. Look here, it's on his birth certificate— Morris Carter. Eshu Carter my name. Birth date's on the line by where it say 'father.' Nearly exact nine months since we…uh…" He cut his eyes toward the children and grew silent.

"I see," said Detective Erinye. "What about the girl?"

"What about her?"

"You her daddy too?"

"I don't know who her daddy is. On her birth certificate it say 'unknown.'"

"You sure it's not you?"

"Look at them children. Morris look like me, he half African roots and look a little like his mother too. Medea look like her mother. Nothing like me. It wouldn't do for me to claim parent on her. Any fool can see she as Irish as whiskey."

Detective Erinye had developed a wheeze Medea could hear from her perch, ten feet away.

"I'll be in touch. Goddamn peanuts," he said. He handed them each a copy of an old mug shot of Tiffany. "Call me if she shows up again. It would be aiding and abetting a fugitive if you did not."

"I'd hate to be charge with 'aiding and abetting.' That sound serious," said Daddy Carter.

The children wondered at Daddy Carter whose English was usually very good. "How come you sound so stupid, talking to that detective?" Morris asked after Detective Erinye had hit a deep breath off an inhaler, cranked his car, and left.

"It don't pay to sound smart when you a black man talking to the police in Georgia."

The next day Eshu Carter was surprised and touched to find that the Wanted for Questioning poster of Tiffany had been trimmed of any indication it was from the police, and stood framed on Medea's chest of drawers.

Medea had learned to read from Morris but both would start school behind their peers because of their irregular lifestyle. Neither wanted to think of going to school or of the necessary trip to the health department. So when Daddy Carter said their appointment for shots was today, there was no option but to go.

"Let's talk about this," said Morris.

"We already got our shots," said Medea.

Daddy Carter took out the Atlanta Health Department record that Tiffany had left him. They knew there was no other solution than to shut up and drop trou for the nurse.

"Get in the truck," said Daddy Carter.

The envelope lay on the seat beneath Medea's butt so she pulled it out as soon as they were underway and let it lay in her lap. "Eshu" was written in Mama's cursive script across the front. As Daddy Carter's attention settled on driving she opened it and studied the records, the two birth certificates, and the sad but stoic letter Tiffany had written Eshu on the day she left. "I'm not proud of that, but things are what they are and we move forward, baggage and all." Reading it clarified things for Medea, and brought both past and future into focus. Although she could not say how it would take shape, she knew the word "baggage" was pivotal.

The nurse looked at their records and said, "Good job, Mr. Carter. You would not believe the mess some of these women come in here with. They both need one shot today and bring them back in a month and we'll give them the flu vaccine. After that they're cool for school."

When they arrived back at the farm Medea hurt in a lot of ways. She chose to walk to Singing Water Creek and further west than she had ever gone exploring. She found the abandoned ruins of a water-powered cotton gin that, she would learn later, had seen the farm through Reconstruction. She went inside to rest and think. She stood in the quiet green light and listened to the sounds of water and tried to calm herself. A breeze cooled her face so she shut her eyes and tried to think of what "baggage" meant. A pounding of wind and a loud honking brought her up short. She squinted into the fury of the noise and wind like one would squint into traffic beside a busy highway. There she saw a giant drake honking and running towards her with its wings spread. Her heart kicked into overdrive and she could not catch her breath. The strength of a drake's wings can break an arm, and there are spurs as hard as horn on their wings. When they attack they frequently go for the face. When it leapt above her to strike, Medea grabbed its throat and squeezed until she felt the bird go from attack mode to escape mode. She struggled in front of the bird as it stretched its wings upwards, reaching, called by the safety of the sky. It had chosen her as surely as the ram in the Bible story, caught by its horns in a bush, had chosen Abraham to save his child.

The drake stood five feet tall and it's wingspan was fully seven feet as it hissed through it's nearly closed airway. Medea could imagine it bullying smaller drakes and female geese and leading a V-shaped flock to Canada. God knows how it got separated and lost in the ruins of a cotton gin. She squeezed harder. She found a piece of rope and tied the animal to the boards that remained in the wall and picked up a rock. The corners of the eyes and the stretched mouth sucking for air radiated distress and Medea's psyche went back in time to her mother's concern with the cracks in the foundation of her beauty. She tried to pull together the pieces of her mother's face in her panic but no image came as she raised the stone and smashed it into the drake's head again and again. "Why did you leave me?" she screamed to God or her long gone mother, and the mighty wings weakened and grew still.

When her heart slowed and her breathing again approached normal, she washed the avian blood off her face and hands. She untied the bird and took it outside where she threw it into the creek and watched as it floated out of sight.

Months passed and grew into years. On the seventh anniversary of their mother's leaving the children on his doorstep Eshu Carter noticed some odd things. As a farmer with St. Francis as his Christian patron, he was aware of nature and animals on his farm. He pointed out a mockingbird's nest to Medea and when she stood on a ladder to look inside at the hatchlings the adult birds dived at her head. She scrambled down the ladder, waving her arms and hands at the fiercely defensive birds.

"Get away! Get away from me," she said.

Medea had also taken to feeding kitchen scraps to a fat tabby that belonged to their neighbor on the next farm. A couple of days later, "Heeeeere kitty," said Medea, kitchen scraps in her hands. She stood at the back door off the laundry room. The fat tabby came running and followed her into the field. From the barn door, Eshu watched them wander toward the creek.

Daddy Carter caught Medea by the arm as she got off the school bus later in the week. He walked with her to the tree where the mockingbird nest had been. The nest lay in ruins on the ground. The adult birds screeched their distress over their squashed offspring. The tiny birds, all beak and eyes, had had their eyes stabbed with a knife. The corners of their mouths had been sliced open.

"What's this?" he asked her.

"Cat got 'em?" she said. She wouldn't meet his eyes.

"Cat would've eat 'em up. These was stepped on." She still wouldn't meet his eyes.

"That cat's dead anyway," she said.

"Yes, I know. It was hanged from a sapling with some baling twine tied in a granny knot," he said as he walked in front of her, caught her shoulders, and tried to make her look at him. "I found its body down by the creek after Mrs. Stevenson came over here looking for it. Its eyes and mouth were cut in the same way."

Medea put her hands behind her back.

"What are you hiding? Show me your hands and arms." He pulled her arms forward to reveal deep scratches that covered both arms and hands.

"How did you get these?"

"Briars," said Medea as she looked away, down the road her mother had traveled. She tried to remember what her mother looked like but none of her features came together in her mind—just the tiny wrinkles at the corner of her eyes and her mouth. Instead of an image of her mother, the word "baggage" stuck in her head. *I don't even have a proper picture of her.*

Eshu grabbed her by her shirt front. "Look at me when I talk to you."

Tears started down Medea's cheeks.

"I'll give you reason to cry. Girl, you're not gonna live here and tell lies. You're not gonna live under my roof and mistreat animals. How do you think those helpless creatures feel when you stab their eyes and slice their mouths?" He shook her hard. "If you wanna know what mistreatment feels like you gonna find out in foster care. You only here because Morris is your brother and my son, and I love your mama. Your mama gave me this responsibility to raise you and I'm gonna do it, but you're not gonna tell me lies and you're not gonna torture animals. Do you hear me?" He shook her until her teeth rattled and she feared her neck would snap under the weight of her whipsawing head.

"You do anything like this again and you're gone into foster care. Morris is going away. Bedroom by yourself is going away. Free groceries is going away. School is going away. Do I make myself clear?"

Medea sniffled and sobbed.

"Come with me," said Eshu Carter. He led her by the arm to her bedroom where he placed a pillow on the floor by the window. He placed a framed picture of St. Francis in front of Medea on the window sill.

"Kneel. I'll tell you when you can get up," he said. "Look at this picture of St. Francis of Assisi, patron saint of animals, and think about what you've done. Think about the distress of those mockingbirds, their grief over losing their children. Think about the pain and suffering you inflict on innocent animals when you cut their eyes and mouths, and hang them. Takes a long time to strangle to death."

On the edge of adolescence, errant, misbehaving Medea was left kneeling in her bedroom in front of a Christian icon of St. Francis. Eshu Carter imagined her a Christian, but in reality she was naive to any religious instruction. He had tried to force her and Morris to attend his church for a few Sundays, but it was no good. They felt the other children were simple-minded and believed nonsense, so the two of them slipped away to play in the creek as soon as his back was turned. Looking back, Medea knew what she had learned, though she had no words for it then, was what an amazing, frightful and angry man Daddy Carter was.

Was the religious icon Eshu Carter had set in front of her meant to punish or to instruct? Why was it so dear to his heart that he kept it framed in his house? On two levels she could imagine a connection: His middle Christian name was "Francis" after his patron whose name he had taken. Medea had seen this on Morris's birth certificate. Second, as a bachelor farmer most of his life, he must love animals more than people. Why else would he not be married?

She had heard Daddy Carter talk of his roots all the way back to the Yoruba of west Africa. His first name "Eshu" was after the orisha of chance, an animistic deity who lives in the crossroads of life. He said the orisha was a trickster god. Maybe that's what he was about now, having her kneel on a pillow and look at this stupid picture.

Medea was neither idle nor lazy as she looked upon the parts of the icon. "St Francis" and "As-sisi" were written beside his oddly shaved head. A radiant, holy light burned down from above. Medea thought of her straw hat. *Maybe the sun's radiation had burned off his hair on top.* He wore a rusty red tunic the color of old blood, and a rope around his waist which was tied in an elaborate knot. At the end of the rope a tau cross hung over his crotch. Green and gold leaves from two trees framed the saint on opposite sides. A menagerie surrounded him: birds in the trees and at his feet, various other animals—a cow, a donkey, rabbits, a goat, ducks, and a dog, or maybe it was a wolf—populated the portraiture space.

"He must be feeding them," she said aloud, "before he dresses and cooks them."

When Daddy Carter reappeared he was dressed in a Yoruba ceremonial hat and robe. The robe was two colored, red on one side and black on the other. "A trickster god whose parishioners wondered after he had gone was he red, or black, and asked each other what did he mean by that lesson," he said.

"Come with me," he said to Medea.

He had changed the arrangement of the living room into a temple.

The curtains were drawn against the afternoon light which l⟨
bathing the prie dieu, altar table, candelabra and an odd cabin⟨.
closed doors she had never seen before. He lit incense and a candle, poured
holy water into a cobalt blue bowl, and pointed her to the prie dieu.

Morris opened the living room door and stepped inside. "The
fuck…?" he said.

"You watch your language. Come in and sit. It's time you learned,"
said Daddy Carter.

"Kneel," he said to Medea. She looked to Morris like she'd rather be
swimming in the creek.

Three books were opened before Daddy Carter and he read from each
of them. From the Christian Bible: "In the book of Proverbs, God tells us,
a righteous man cares for the needs of his animals. In the New Testament,
God reminds us his eye is on the sparrow. In the Muslim book, the Quran,
Allah tells us anyone who kills a sparrow or anything bigger than that
without a just cause shall be held accountable on the day of judgment.
Killing is only for food and should be so merciful that the animal to be
slaughtered should not even see the knife. A good deed done to an animal
is like a good deed done to a human, while an act of cruelty done to an
animal is as bad as an act of cruelty to another human being." Finally
he read from the Yoruba holy words: "The breath of god is in us all. We
celebrate the oneness that exists between the creator and all creatures." He
held up the three books one atop the other. "Words of gods and prophets,
light to our feet and hands," he said.

Eshu had cleverly hidden a razor blade between his fingers, which
would open a vein when he clapped his hands. This he did seven times
in sets of three before the strange cabinet. After each of the three sets he
said in a loud voice, "Ellegua, open to us your secrets." He fell to his knees
before the cabinet and hit it three times, leaving bloody handprints on the
door. It opened.

From the cabinet he took a bundle wrapped in soft goat leather. It
contained stones from Africa carved in the shape of orishas, a vial of
sacred dirt from Nigeria, and a small bottle of 151 proof rum.

"Ellegua, guardian of the crossroads we respect you. We invoke your
presence." He sprinkled a pinch of dirt into the candle flame. He poured a

shot of the rum and set it away from the candelabra. He washed his hands in the bowl of holy water and drank from the carmine liquid, then gave it to Medea. "Drink," he said. She took a small sip of the metallic tasting liquid and tried not to throw up.

When Eshu held it out to Morris the boy pushed it away with both his hands. Morris was so scared his legs quivered like a sprinter's in the blocks, ready for the starting gun.

"The mysteries need to be smelled, tasted, and shared. We need to feel the heat of fire and see sacrificial blood. That is why father Abraham offered a male goat instead of his son. One day soon you will also need to control your women. Listen and learn," said Eshu to Morris.

When he saw Medea's eyes close after she swallowed a little of the red water, he set down the bowl and poured the shot of rum into his own mouth. He lifted the candalabra to his face and pursed his lips. When he saw Medea's eyes open again he sprayed the rum across the flame where it burst into a blue and orange fireball over her head. He pushed on her forehead as her eyes rolled upward. Medea felt she was falling through a tunnel of white light into darkness. She screamed and lost consciousness.

Like a released spring Morris, in two powerful strides, covered the distance of the living room and put all of his one hundred sixty five pounds, behind a roundhouse right. Daddy Carter hit the floor.

"What do you intend to do next, old man? Cut her genitals?"

Morris hit him again and Daddy Carter put his hands up, palms out.

"I'm not going to hurt your sister. You need to learn to control your women. Soon enough you'll have a wife and some kids. If you don't earn their respect, you'll have no peace in your house."

When Medea came to she did not know how much time had passed. Seconds? Minutes? Hours? In the distance she heard the creaking of the barn door, then the cranking of a tractor. She opened her eyes and felt her panties and jeans were wet. She lay on her back in a rapidly cooling puddle of her own urine. All the religious trappings were gone. She got a towel from the bathroom and some disinfectant and cleaned the pee off the floor. She did not want to leave the scent of her own fear in Daddy Carter's living room. From the kitchen she heard the sound of Mahalia Jackson from the stereo, "His Eye Is On The Sparrow." She walked to the laundry room where she stripped out of her wet clothes and placed them into the washer.

The court-appointed psychiatrist listened therapeutically and blew smoke. Occasionally, when Medea said something of interest, she jotted a note in her notebook. When Medea described the Yoruba ceremony and commented, "Fathers are set on drilling into their children patriarchal beliefs, which I believe are quite harmful, especially to girls," she thought the shrink's head would explode as she scribbled several pages.

"You got another cigarette?" asked Medea.

Medea and Morris were the offspring of a woman who worked nights. They were accustomed by years of habit to sleep in. Five a.m. on the Carter farm was an abomination in their young minds. The smell of brewing coffee, bacon, eggs, and biscuits would sweeten all. If they had no opinion of southern black gospel music it would soon become hateful to them. The volume increased by 6:00 a.m. with African drums, woodwinds and bells urging all to rise and rejoice.

"What is the meaning of all that?" screamed Medea from her bedroom and pulled her pillow over her head.

From the kitchen Daddy Carter answered, "There is no 'meaning.' It enters through the heart." He danced from the refrigerator to the stove with a carton of eggs.

Medea reinforced the pillow with the bedspread. "Sort of like parasitic worms." They had read about those in freshman science class at school.

"You miss that school bus and you walkin'. You ain't hangin' around here all day doin' nothin'. Idle hands is the devil's workers, and the devil got plenty invested in you."

Medea knew what would come next—Daddy Carter through her bedroom door, grabbing her mattress and dumping her onto the floor. "Now get your ass up."

"Morris, you up? You got ACT prep and you got to meet with the senior counselor," he hollered up the stairs. Medea heard Morris's feet hit the pine boards.

"Yeah, Daddy, I'm up." Not a complete lie as he weaved forward and back, tottering between the sunlight calling him into consciousness of a rural morning and the seduction of adolescent dreams pulling him back to the bed.

"I'm up." Medea stomped to the bathroom. She looked at herself in the mirror and blew morning breath onto her palm and sniffed. A frown and she squirted toothpaste onto her brush. "What did Mama ever see in him?" she wondered aloud and scrubbed her teeth. "Probably just the rent." she spit into the sink.

At times Eshu Carter cursed Tiffany Cobb but always he came back to a bachelor farmer's idea of love. Medea felt it like a chemical messenger. From the day the two kids were dropped on his door step he regarded Morris as a gift from God. His barren bachelor existence had been given an heir, a shoot of flesh-and-blood immortality sprung from his loins over a decade ago—wild seed spilled in a night of drunken lust with a white prostitute. When he looked in the mirror at himself and Morris (he liked to shave with Morris, a manly father-son thing he thought, whereas the adolescent scion found it embarrassing to be half naked in the presence of such an old man) he saw the resemblance. He even got another mirror so he could see both their eyes, the shape of the ears, their noses and their mouths at the same time. He rubbed his hand over his own chin as he looked closely at Morris's image, like he was trying to find a physical connection. He had never looked at her like that.

What Medea sensed from Eshu was absence or cold dislike. The girl looked only like her mother, at best a painful memory for Eshu. From the first she had been the tare in the field, the briar that grew with the bean vine, the crabgrass in the flowers. She suspected all of this had something to do with the word: *baggage.*

"Never was nothin' to me but trouble," Eshu muttered into eggs he scrambled in an iron skillet. "Girl, don't make me climb them stairs," he hollered.

"I'm up," she hollered down the stairs and pulled a pair of black jeans from beneath her mattress. She sniffed them, checked the leg crease, and squirted perfume into the crotch.

"Bus's here in fifteen minutes," said Eshu as he plated the food and set it on the table.

Five minutes later Medea set her backpack on a chair and poured coffee into her go mug. A kiss on Daddy Carter's cheek, "Props," she said and headed for the door.

"You gotta eat," said Daddy Carter.

"I got chorus today—can't sing around all that grease and milk."

She ran toward the bus.

Morris bolted down the stairs pulling out a flat spot in his hair. He made a biscuit sandwich, poured coffee into his go mug and headed for the door.

"Where's my kiss?" said Daddy Carter.

Agony on the boy's face, "Can't we just fist bump like normal people?" He held up knuckles and tapped Eshu's fist as the bus honked from the road. He grabbed his backpack.

"We got to plant peanuts this afternoon. One more crop before frost."

"I know. I know. I won't hang out after school. I'll come straight home," saying all the proper things, against his nature. His job at this time in his life was to fit in with his peers.

"Morris," hollered Medea from the door of the bus. "You're making us all late."

"Coming," he yelled and sprinted to the road from the kitchen door. Daddy Carter watched from the door with a cup of coffee in his hand. He waved to the bus.

Medea had saved Morris a seat.

"He's pathetic," said Morris as he sat beside her.

"He thinks you're made of gold."

"'Where's my kiss?' Yuck."

"Has he tried to see your dick yet?"

"Old dude creeps me out."

Medea watched as acres of farm country rolled by, rows of green chopped clear of weeds. The straight lines from the roadside ditch to the horizon seemed to her like spokes on some giant wheel. She could imagine the bus not moving at all; instead the giant wheel rolled out their lives. She tried to see ahead to what was coming but could not. She looked behind but what was gone was lost. She stared out the window at the eternal present until the field was interrupted by a farmhouse with a cardboard sign, *Free To Good Home*. A little girl held up a kitten by its front paws, its back legs clawing the air. "Free," she mouthed. Medea put her hand to the window and as they passed the house she turned in her seat and watched until it disappeared around a turn in the road.

"Why are you crying?" asked Morris.

"Shut up," said Medea and wiped her eyes on her sleeve. She felt something wet and warm at the crotch of her jeans. She felt to see what it was and found blood on her fingers.

The International Baccalaureate courses in music kept Medea sane during her public school years. She had a 4.0 grade point but like most gifted kids she was bored and likely to drop out before graduation.

"The relationship between Maddalena (the lead soprano), an aristocrat by birth, and her servant, Bersi (the mezzo soprano), struck me as complex and a little unbelievable. That Bersi would prostitute herself to save her mistress's life...well, I think she would have taken advantage of the chaos after the French Revolution and escaped," Medea thought aloud to Miss Alma, her music teacher.

"That's perceptive, Medea," said Miss Alma Williams, who had to work overtime to keep up with her I.B. students. "Upon what do you base this assumption?"

"Family history," said Medea. "The same things that brought me to the title: *Woe To Those Who Love Me Well*."

"Let's continue with our aria," said Miss Williams. "From *Tutto intorno e sangre*." She nodded to the pianist.

Medea sang:

> *Tutto intorno e sangre e fango?*
> *Io son divino! Io son l'oblio!*
> *Io sono il dio che sovra il mondo*
> *scendo da l' empireo, fa della terra*
> *un ciel! Ah!*
> *Io son l'amore, io son l'amore...*

At this point in the aria Medea's voice broke and she fell to her knees and began to cry. Her sobs were so violent they seemed capable of breaking her in two. The pianist stopped playing and stared with her mouth open. Miss Williams knelt beside Medea and placed her arm around Medea's shoulders.

"What in the world?" she asked.

"She's dead. She's never coming back. It's too much. I can't! I just can't anymore," said Medea.

"It's a difficult and sad opera. The French Revolution has come to Maddalena's door. Her house is burned. Her mother is killed before her eyes. Her lover is in prison… *La Mama Morta* is a lament in a violent opera that has always broken opera fans' hearts." She rubbed Medea's back and handed her a Kleenex.

"I read the translation. It's not Maddalena's mother. It's my mother. Mine! I believe she's dead. We never even got to say goodbye."

"Let's take a break," said Miss Williams. "I'm going to call the counselor." She sent the pianist to get a glass of water and paged the guidance counselor.

A flood of pent up emotions rushed out of Medea as she talked to the counselor, "I've been swelling. I gained five pounds last week, and now I'm bleeding…down there."

"You've got your menstrual period," said the counselor. She got Medea a sanitary napkin from her supply cabinet.

"Maybe that's it. I cried on the bus. Morris was so embarrassed and I told him to shut up."

"You say you think your mother is dead?"

"She abandoned Morris and me nearly ten years ago. Morris, my half brother. Different fathers. My stepfather is my brother's biological father. It's complicated. My mother was a prostitute who dropped us off on his doorstep and never came back. I believe she's dead…" Medea's voice broke and she began to cry again.

The court-appointed psychiatrist gave Medea her bribe to cooperate, a pack of cigarettes. "You were quite open with your high school voice teacher and with the guidance counselor."

"I was a freshman when I got my menses. No one had prepared me.

My step dad was a bachelor farmer. In a way, Miss Alma was a surrogate mother, I guess. I always put a lot on her."

"Your notes from your high school counselor say your mother abandoned you when you were five-years-old. Can you recall any of your feelings about that at the time you started school?"

"Maybe 'abandoned' isn't the right word. Both of us, Morris and I, hoped Mama would come back and claim us. Well, I hoped it more than Morris. He had his biological father and they eventually bonded in spite of a rocky start. But Daddy Carter and I never had much chance."

She lit a cigarette and gathered her thoughts.

"Daddy Carter got a letter from Mama a few weeks after she left. She said she had found a job."

"How did you feel about that?"

"Boy, it made me feel good. I thought she was coming back. I started putting my things in my suitcase instead of in my chest of drawers." *Baggage* drifted at the edge of her consciousness.

"Did any more letters come?"

"No. Daddy Carter would always shake his head at me as he took the mail out of the box by the road. I don't think she abandoned us. I think she must have crossed paths with a serial killer or something. Lots of prostitutes wind up in shallow graves down on the Gulf Coast."

Medea withdrew into herself. She crossed her arms over her chest and seemed to sink into the metal chair.

"You mentioned 'things,' plural—that you remembered about your mother," the psychiatrist gently prodded.

"Tiny lines in her face. They must have been like cracks in the foundation of a house to a woman who traded on her looks. They worried her, so she concentrated on them with her beauty products. A really vivid memory: I dumped her purse out on a motel vanity. It must have been at the Magnolia Inn Suites. She had a small kit that had everything she needed. I'm amazed now that I know what it meant—she had an American Express card. She had a small bottle of vodka, some breath drops, cigarettes, a lighter, condoms, and a switchblade. I remember the night we ran for our lives to Daddy Carter's—she cleaned blood off the knife in the sink. It was covered in blood."

The shrink scribbled furiously while Medea studied her. Then she asked Medea, "What else do you remember feeling right after your mother left you?"

"It hurt like hell when she didn't come back. I didn't have a picture of her, not a real picture. I had a wanted poster from Detective Erinye that I had trimmed and framed, but over time it faded. I couldn't recall what she looked like. Just the corners of her mouth and her eyes, the rest wouldn't come together."

"While an International Baccalaureate student she collapsed in music class," Medea's lawyer said and submitted to the judge copies of the psychiatrist's findings, and the high school counselor's report from years before. The lawyer was a friend of the shrink, and both were opera fans as well as advocates for disadvantaged women.

"I'm grateful to have a competent lawyer," Medea whispered to her attorney.

The attorney spoke to the judge. "Survivors of loved ones who have disappeared without a trace often tell of being driven to the brink of insanity, like it's some door to a room in their psyche. They never have closure to their grief hence they only partially move on with their life and, more often than not, they've progressed inadequately. They objectively describe themselves in the second or third person as someone they've observed—they've separated their self from their self. 'Driven *nearly* to the brink of insanity' or 'I nearly lost my mind' they say, unaware and therefore inattentive, to the cryptic, obscure language of the heart— denial. They are not still standing at that portal but long ago transgressed into that forbidden room and pulled the door shut behind themselves."

Two minutes ahead of the start of 3rd period Medea dashed up the L-shaped hall toward the chemistry lab, as Jason Carpenter ran down the hall toward Business Club, where he was president and about to start the meeting. His mind was on his notes as he hurried on the right side of the hall. Medea checked her cell phone as she cut around the corner of the L and knocked Jason flat, spilled her chemistry homework, and strewed her sheet music across the tile floor.

"Why don't you watch where you're going?" she screamed.

"Why don't you walk on the right side of the hall?" said Jason.

"Just because you're an upperclassman doesn't…"

"I am an upperclassman, therefore I know which side of the hall to walk on. You, on the other hand, are obviously a freshman…" He stopped talking and his mouth formed an O. "You're Medea," he said.

"Last time I checked. Help me get these together," she said as she scrambled after chemistry homework and loose sheet music.

"I'm Jason, I can't believe I'm actually meeting you."

"Please don't ask for my autograph, Jacob, I'm late."

"It's Jason. Jason Carpenter. Business Club President? Most Likely To Succeed?"

Jason gathered her chemistry papers and put them in order. "You're taking Baccalaureate classes?"

"Yes, and I'm late." She took the handful of papers from Jason and turned to go.

"Don't I get a 'sorry'? You did knock me down. I'm a huge fan of yours, you know?"

"Don't spray your shorts, Jacob." She turned back to Jason. "Look, I'm sorry. Is it better now?"

"It's Jason, damn it. You have a terriffic voice. Would you go out with me?"

"I'm a freshman. I don't date, Jason."

"Maybe we could eat lunch together?"

"Freshman/senior? That always ends badly. I have to go. I'm late." She turned and ran down the hall.

"I have a car," Jason hollered after her. "My dad's old—"

"Good for you," she said without looking back.

Later that day Medea warmed up her voice in the music lab and practiced her piece for competition. Jason searched the practice studios until he found her and propped himself against the wall, outside in the hall, to listen. "Musetta's Waltz" from *La Boheme* was what she had chosen for All State. The role of the vain flirt was not natural to Medea. She had little self-esteem at this point in her life.

Cuando men vo soletta per la via
La gente sosta e mira
E la belleza mia tutta ricera en me
da capo a pie…

The hall security monitor approached Jason. "Hall pass?" she asked.

"Umm… I don't have one."

"Do you have a place to be?"

"Study hall."

"That way." The monitor pointed down the hall.

Medea concentrated on sheet music and waltzed while she sang those beautiful Italian vowels. She caught a glimpse of Jason and the hall cop through the long narrow glass in the studio door. She sang and smiled.

Cosi l'effluvio del desio tutta m'aggira
felice mi fa!

Medea waited for her bus to arrive after school. It was already fifteen minutes late when Jason drove past in his father's old car. He waved to her as he passed. She waved back. He turned around and parked across the street. She unbuttoned one button of her blouse and walked over.

"Hey," he said.

"What's up?" She leaned over.

"Wanna go to the truckstop for a burger, somethin' to drink?"

"Bus's late. Sure." She got into the old Toyota, obviously a handed-down family car. Jason had tried his best to trick it out with decals and rims. He had put in a good sound system. It was well-vacuumed and smelled like the floral woodsy air freshener hanging from the mirror. There was a quilt folded in the back seat.

At the Three Roads Truckstop on the highway they blended with the interstate commerce crowd, no longer merely locals from Cheatham, Georgia. Alice, a timeless fixture behind the counter, took their order.

"Got your girlfriend today?'

"Hi, Alice. This is Medea."

"School friend. Not a girlfriend. Pleased to meetcha."

"Beef tips in gravy's the special."

"I'd like a cheeseburger, no onions, with fries and a chocolate shake," Medea said.

"Same for me, Dr. Pepper."

"So, Jason, you're hanging out in the hall while I sing. Then you're at my bus stop. What's up with that? You a stalker, or what?"

"You've stolen my heart. I can't help it."

"Cleptomaniac of hearts. They're dried and mounted in shadow boxes by my piano."

"Word on the street at school is you outed Miss Fulton and the coach."

"Where did you hear that?"

"It's all over. You're the most cool girl in school."

"I was just smokin' up in the rigging behind the auditorium stage. There's a skylight window I open to blow smoke out."

"Were they really doin' it? Coach and Miss Fulton? Who would've thought—those two holier-than-thous?"

"They'd been at it for a couple of weeks. They pulled the stage curtain shut. It's kind of cozy back there and they'd have a props bed."

"How'd you catch them?"

"Well, they've made me late a couple of times because I can't climb down with them bonking on stage. So I heard the principal come in with a contractor, to do some repairs."

"So they just drop trou? ...and fuck right there?"

"Panties hit the stage floor. Mormon shorts are made funny. He's LDS you know, but I don't think Miss Fulton is the one he married in the temple."

"What do they look like?"

"Long boxers. T-shirt. White. Boring. Miss Bonnie Baptist got a camisole and drawers by Victoria's Secret. Probably drove all the way to Atlanta. Or maybe she got it online. Neither of 'em nothin' special but they wanted their money's worth out of those fancy drawers—tryin' hard on the props bed. Didn't hear the principal and contractor come in. So I just flipped the switch to open the curtain."

"You are bad."

"I'm tired of their holiness. He got to teach creationism over science, and she got to put Jesus up in the middle of everything in the art department. Christers!"

"So the principal seen 'em?"

"Full monty. Full moon. Up an' down and up an' down. Miss Fulton clutched at her dignity best she could—that black lace camisole. But everybody done seen the cat, it was outta the bag."

"I hear they're both leavin' at the end of the semester."

"Good riddance. Small town hypocrites and homemade sin—ain't nothin' uglier."

As they passed the Feed and Seed store coming back into town, Medea saw Daddy Carter's Ford F-150 parked outside.

"Stop!" she hollered.

Jason threw on brakes. "What?" he asked.

"I gotta get out here. Something I forgot." She opened the door, grabbed her backpack, and stepped away from the car. "See ya tomorrow at school," she said and waved to him from the side of the road.

When Jason's car was out of sight, she walked back up the road to the Feed and Seed and found Daddy Carter.

"I missed my bus," she said.

Morris stood before the mirror in his room in his mortarboard and gown for high school graduation. Medea knelt in front of him pinning the hem of his gown. As she measured she looked at the marks on the edge of the closet door. The earliest one, marked "Morris Carter," stood at about four feet, and now Morris was more than six feet tall.

"Do you remember when we first came here?" she asked.

"Yeah, we thought Daddy Carter was weird as shit."

"He used to stare at you like you were some exotic pastry and he wanted to eat you up with his eyes."

"I thought he was queer or something."

"Did he ever try to compare dicks? He compared everything else."

"No. He turned out to be alright though."

Medea continued to stick pins into the hem of the gown, then instructed Morris to pull it off so she could sew it.

"He believes you're his blood son. His real offspring."

"I am. It's on my birth certificate. I stand to inherit this farm."

"And then there's me. He says he agreed to raise me because he loves Mama. Ten years in between a piece of her ass (the first one paid for) and the last was the last. She finally gave something away for free."

"How come you always go so hateful on him? He took us in and raised us after Mama dropped us off and never came back."

"He says he loves Mama, but he doesn't even know her. He slept with her, what three nights and got stuck with raising two kids? He's delusional—can't see her, or us, for his own dick."

"I ain't bad mouthin' him. He's done all right by me."

"Yeah, you stand to inherit the farm. I'm just 'baggage.'"

"You done?" Morris pulled the gown over his head. "I got work to do in the barn."

Medea took the sewing to her room and pulled the portable Singer from the bottom of her closet. She rubbed the marks on the door frame. They were about three feet from the floor. She had to stoop to read the name above the marks, "Medea Cobb" beside the first date, ten years before.

May is hot in Georgia. The shingles on the roof made soft whispery sounds as the boards of the roof expanded. The floor did the same with soft pops. In hot weather the floor boards let in a little ventilation from beneath the house. It rises from the floor through fourteen foot tall rooms. Ceiling fans, installed as the Tennessee Valley Authority brought electricity to rural residents, helped cool a little. Medea's head was a cauldron that did nothing to vent her inexplicable anger as she sat before the sewing machine, hemming her brother's academic robe. The sun bore down on the roof like the wings of a fallen angel who'd stopped just short of hitting the ground. The hot breeze drifted across acres of peanuts, vegetables and hay into the shade of the farm house yard.

The angel's longing for home and his coupled anger at God might have found something like sanctuary as he rode the latest wave of heat through the opened window. He hovered just above the hair that waved like flames emanating from Medea's seething brain. Perhaps this is how evil enters.

Father-to-son, father-to-son, father-to-son all the way back to

Abraham-to-Isaac. When did the girls ever get a break? This great green farm, green from algae to pecans, wet from well water to creek that turned a wheel to gin cotton after Sherman's march to the sea. This farm just out of the general's reach. Too remote. Of little importance except to the poor farmers who depended on fair treatment from its black owners, fair treatment of white and black alike through those dark years of war and reconstruction—commerce among men. What they had in common was their spent sweat and toil under the sun and over crops that prospered or failed. The land and the water that turned the wheel would not even have been in the Carter family had it not been for the "Injun woman," as Daddy Carter called her: Hepsie Mary Singing Water.

Medea found the records in the basement of the courthouse, records all the way back to the Indian Land Act of 1838—descendants of some Indians could keep their ancestral lands and not go on the Trail of Tears. It was through a woman, she thought, that this land had come down to the Carters, despite the War, Reconstruction, and Jim Crow. Even the name of Singing Water was lost to history. By the goddess Hecate, Medea, a woman dispossessed of any patriarchal name, would take it back. Daddy Carter said he and all his forefathers (always the men) had dealt fairly with both white and black. But where was their commerce with women, other than household expenses, and child care? Debits on a balance sheet, or entertainment expenses—the fee for an hour of my mother's time? Fate gave you back your son, my half brother, like a windfall crop, but I was the briar in the bale of hay, the tare that grew with the beanstalk, the crabgrass in the flowers. It's complicated, more complicated than you've ever cared to explore, she reckoned as the needle darted a seam into the cloth. As she worked Medea keened her lament to a lady god, *Ave Maria*.

Miss Alma and Medea met for a faculty/student conference which was required at the end of the school year.

"Good news. I've heard that Reverend Whiteacre wants to hold a revival this summer, and he really needs help with the choir. It's a protestant fundamentalist church, Faith Tabernacle Church. He needs a lead soprano."

"So?"

"I've suggested he meet with you."

"Why? I'm not a Christian."

"It's not required. He needs your voice. The pay is $100 per performance."

"Per week? Wow! When's the gig?"

"It's no gig, it's a weekly paycheck. You sing with the choir, and you sing a solo each Sunday during worship."

"And I get $100 for that?"

"For that you should get $200. It's two jobs. Don't let him bamboozle you. Reverend Whiteacre is desperate for a good strong voice like yours. Without it his plans are toast."

"I could break the poverty ceiling with that."

"The money would come in handy for a girl like you. Give you a good start towards what you need for college. It would also look really good on your resume."

"I'll give him a call."

MissAlma wrote down the number and gave it to her.

"Miss Alma, you remember the trouble I had when I got my first period? My first menstrual period, I mean."

"Yes, you were pretty unprepared."

"No mother to guide me. You stepped in."

"I'd think Eshu had worked with large mammals enough to know to get you some information ahead of time."

"Daddy Carter had no experience with raising children. A bachelor farmer. No talent for it. I guess he thought nature took care of those things."

"Glad to have helped."

"I'd like to start a club for high school girls to explore women's health issues."

"That's an interesting idea. Maybe you could coordinate with the school nurse."

"I was thinking maybe you could be our faculty sponsor?"

"I'm pretty busy. Ten baccalaureate students and I already sponsor the Mousai Club."

"Thinking of a possible name, at least at the beginning, something like 'The Goddess Club.'"

"Some Christian fundamentalists might have a problem with that."

"Then they have a problem. I think the old goddesses might have some wisdom to share. And we might also look at folkways and folk medicine."

"I like the idea of the school nurse being in on this."

"Maybe the science teachers too, for talks, or whatever they want to contribute. I'd hate for other girls to get to puberty with as little information as I had."

"Start by putting a request into the principal's office. You'll need to inform the Student Council by letter as well. Include the Superintendent and Board, and maybe the Mayor. Just in case all of this goes south. Copy me on all of it. I'll act as your faculty liason until you find someone permanent. It sounds like a good idea to me."

"What do you think of 'Hecate' in the name?'"

"Isn't she the goddess of witchcraft?"

"No, those are Wiccans. They're all tangled up in patriarchy. You know, worship the Devil, male gods and all that. Hecate was pre-Christian by thousands of years. She was a feminist before it was trendy."

"For now don't mention that. Let's get it okayed as a Women's Health Issues Club, or something. Once we get it up and running, the students can decide what they want to be called."

If Medea hated the small-minded, small-town southern citizens of Cheatham, it was because she saw through the veneer of sweetness and Christian piety right into their evil hearts. What she gave she got back: most hated her in return. If her resentment of Daddy Carter had grown large during her kneeling before the icon of St. Francis, it turned ugly and festered during the next few weeks at school. The hateful boil on her character finally popped when Miss Fulton assigned a paper and work of art based on iconography. *Just like that hypocrite to fornicate her drawers off and still force her Christian views on her students.*

Jason developed a habit of finding Medea in the public library and sitting at her table to study. She sketched ideas about the iconography project, and he stared at her over his Principles of Business textbook. Medea had several images of St. Francis open on her laptop and a sketch pad open on the table.

"I'm going to move to a study carrel downstairs if you don't stop staring at me." She didn't look up from her sketch, which was in the form of the St. Francis icon Daddy Carter forced her to meditate upon. "You're one step away from drooling."

Jason closed his mouth and scratched his lip. "I'm not."

Medea looked at him after a few minutes of concentration and sketching, and held up a picture she had titled *Frank's Butcher Shop*. "What do you think?" she asked.

"It's cool. Looks kind of like a portrait of a saint, but it's a shop really. A butcher shop?"

She pulled up a traditional icon on her laptop, holding both images side-by-side. "See any similarities?"

He looked them over. "Compositions are similar. Portraits. Objects are arranged in the same places. The trees in one are store shelves in the other. Birds on the limbs of two trees are hanging on a meat rack in the other. Ewwww, they're corpses. Well, poultry for sale. Chickens and geese. The animals in the foreground are—yuck! They're skinned."

"Dressed. What do you think about the central figure?"

"He's St. Francis in one, and Frank the Butcher in the other? The bowl-over-the-head haircut gives it away."

"The robe is interesting, I think. I want them to both be similar colors like dried blood. Carmine or some reddish brown. Only Frank has on a white apron. That should make the color of the fresh blood really pop."

"The dog, or is that a wolf? It has been skinned. This is really a disturbing, violent take on the benign St. Francis image."

"The sign by the door says 'fragrant meat' and 'mutton of the world.' That's what some European shops call dog meat. What do you think of the shop door?"

"Are those animal feet? They've been cut off and placed beside the shop door."

"Hoofs. Feet. Cows, pigs, geese. In old European style. In France they call a slaughter house *l'abbatoir*. The surrealists really fixated on this practice and made images of it in their club magazine. They used to put them beside the door for the poor beggars to make soup out of. Nowadays they're ground up into meat food product and used to make canned food products and sausage."

"I'll never eat vienna sausages again."

"The surrealists were fascinated with the play of light and shadows on the amputated cow hooves, especially. They looked like religious school girls in uniform lined up against the butcher shop wall. They thought the visual double-entendre looked like prostitutes working the street."

Jason looked at Medea like he had never really seen her before. "Yeah, I can see that now. They do sort of look like street walkers."

Medea said, "I'm visually quoting images from the Surrealist magazine, *Documents*. And I'm verbally quoting Giorgio di Chirico: 'To become truly immortal, a work of art must escape all human limits: logic and common sense will only interfere. But once these barriers are broken, it will enter the realms of childhood visions and dreams.'"

Miss Fulton confronted Medea after art class. She handed her the iconography project report which had been severely marked down, and included comments like "disturbing" and "degenerate," and assigned a very low grade.

Medea smiled at her and handed her back the grade report as she scrolled through files on her cell phone. "Some people during the period between the world wars said the same things about the Surrealists' works in *Documents,* photos, and writings, as well as paintings. It was so disturbing to them that they joined the Nazis in burning a lot of it. The works were deliberately disturbing to shock the petite bourgeoisie out of their complacency. I'm glad to see it still has that power, based on your reaction."

Miss Fulton said, "You're not Georgio di Chirico or Andre Masson. You're not…"

Medea pressed 'play' on her cell phone and an obviously pornographic stream of grunts ('Oh my God,' 'Oh, Baby') and passionate moans filled the classroom. Medea increased the volume and turned the screen to Miss Fulton so she could see herself and coach in the throes of consummated lust.

"Turn that off! Turn that off!"

"You guys were pretty hot and heavy, getting your money's worth out of that mail-order lingerie, I think." Medea turned the volume way up. "I don't really care what you do with your bored, tawdry lives, but you interrupted my smoke break, up in the rigging, and you made me late for class. It was just good luck that the contractor and the principal happened along when they did."

A student knocked at the art classroom door and started to enter. "Get out!" screamed Miss Fulton. "I mean, we're in conference here. Make an appointment online." *Oh My God. O, Baby. How pornographic.*

Miss Fulton turned scarlet with shame as Medea fiddled with her cell phone. "You Tube. Upload. Facebook. Status. Do I push 'send' which would send proof of your shame to 600 of my friends? Or do you give me the A that my project deserves?" She pushed the grade report in front of Miss Fulton.

"Let's turn that off. It sounds so wanton. So perverse. And in the school auditorium, no less. Ewww, I feel nauseous," said Medea. She silenced the cell phone.

Miss Fulton wrote A in a wobbly script on the project report.

"One more thing, Miss Fulton. I understand that you and coach are leaving under a cloud at the end of the semester. I'm sick of your Christer bullshit. Do not mention your degenerate religion in class for the remainder of the semester." She waved the cell phone at the teacher. "Or I push 'send.'"

Medea got a thrill of satisfaction when she successfully completed drivers education class and got her learner's permit. Morris agreed to be her licensed driver.

"Let's drive to the truck stop," he said and they borrowed Eshu's Ford F-150.

Alice greeted them with a menu. "Today's blue plate special is beef tips with two sides."

Morris said, "I'll have the chicken fried steak with fries and a salad. Coke to drink." He then excused himself to the bathroom.

"I want a cheeseburger, fries and a chocolate shake."

Alice left to turn in the order to the cook and returned with drinks, "So you're out here with another boyfriend. Lucky girl."

"Morris? Oh, no, he's…teaching me to drive. I've known him forever. We practically grew up together. I told him that if I could drive us out here without running over anyone we could eat anything on the menu. My treat. He begins his first year at University of Georgia this fall."

"How's Jason doing? Weren't you seeing him for awhile?"

"Not really 'seeing.' Jason's going for an Associate's Degree at the community college. Business major."

Medea was startled to look over her shoulder and see Morris directly behind her. He frowned as he sat down across from Medea.

"What?" said Medea.

"Miss Medea, white lady, say, 'Oh no. He's, er uh, teaching me to drive. I've known him forever. We practically grew up together.' Nothin' about my being your half-black, half-brother. Medea's version of 'Driving Miss Daisy Crazy.'"

"Morris, you're reading something into this that isn't there."

"Don't take me for a fool, Medea, and I won't take you for one. After all, I grew up here in Georgia, just like you. What I don't get is why wouldn't you want to claim a piece of this intelligent, handsome, hard-working, landed nigga. Oooohhh, that's it. Ain't it? The nigga thang."

"Morris, you…"

"Shut up. Just shut up and eat your food. It's a surprise to find it in my own family. That's all."

Earlier in the summer, Medea had received a letter from the principal refusing a charter for the Young Women's Health Issues Club. The Supervisor, the Board, and the Mayor replied by brief letters that they supported the Principal's decision. They were all on official stationery, and Medea had kept them. Her self-styled school uniform was usually black jeans with a black pullover. No makeup. No jewelry. Today a small brooch, a bright yellow flower with a black and yellow bee hid a tiny microphone attached to the left side of her chest. She knocked on the principal's door and walked right in.

"Medea, you need an appointment."

"This will only take about five minutes."

"Well, I don't have five minutes, I have another student…"

"I'll leave as soon as they get here. You refused the Young Women's Health Issues Club a charter. Why?"

"We explained in our letter that it seemed inappropriate—most girls talk to their mothers about this sort of thing." He beamed a grin like a good Baptist deacon who knew his answer was the correct, biblical one.

"Not in many cases. Mine for instance. I grew up with a bachelor farmer for a dad, and a half brother as the only other member of my household. No other female or mother figure to ask."

"You should have gone to someone in your church then."

"And asked what? I had no idea what a menstrual period was until I started bleeding on the bus."

The principal looked uncomfortable.

Medea said, "That's exactly the type of peer-driven information we want to provide for other girls who've not come from traditional homes. By the way, did you know that half of American homes are now single parent, with that parent working? Or from any home, really, where the topic wasn't discussed. We want to cooperate with the school nurse and the science teachers to provide accurate information to fill in the gaps surrounding women's health."

"Well, it's not going to happen. There's a bit of witchy content that many may object to. Next thing you know they'll want information and access to birth control and abortion. Condoms, for God's sake. Why, they'll be inviting Planned Parenthood up here to speak."

"Witchy? You object on religious grounds because you fear the club would practice witchcraft?"

"Yes. Exactly those concerns were expressed to me by a member of the PTA."

"So you voted down a school club for girls, for which there is clearly a need, based on one person's religious objections, one person's vote?"

"It wasn't voted on. It was tabled."

The other student, who was late for his appointment, arrived and Medea left. She locked herself in a stall of the women's bathroom and pulled up her shirt. She removed the recording device connected to the flower and bee microphone and pressed rewind, then play. The entire conversation was clearly audible on her ear plug.

Somebody came into the bathroom and pushed on the stall door.

"This one's occupied."

Medea dialed a conference call to the Cheatham Bugle and the regional editor of the Atlanta Beacon, which also owned a TV station.

She played the tape when she had an interested columnist from each paper on the line.

"I want to meet with columnists from both newspapers."

"Well, the Bugle would have to confer with the principal's office and we probably couldn't…"

"The Beacon will meet with you. Say when."

"Today or tomorrow?" said Medea.

"We want an exclusive on this story. This affects students all over the state, and will likely go to the Supreme Court. Bugle, since you've refused coverage, you can hang up now."

"But we want to be in on this story too."

"Too late. You've refused. Hang up now. Do it now."

There was a click.

"Ms. Medea?"

"Yes, I'm here. My name is Medea Cobb. Medea Royal is my stage name."

"I want to get the ACLU in on this. I think they will want to represent you. Probably for free. How soon can we meet?"

"Tomorrow? Tonight? Tonight. At the Three Roads Truck Stop. It's at the Cheatham exit. I'm the redhead dressed in black. I'll be in a booth to the right of the front door."

Two vehicles arrived at the same time, the media van from the Atlanta TV station, and an SUV with a motto printed on the side: "Because Freedom Can't Protect Itself." Both the reporter and the lawyer from the ACLU looked capable of verbally laying to waste anyone unfortunate enough to be in their crosshairs.

Alice put them in a private dining room and served beverages.

"Press this button if you need anything," she told them.

The camera tech lit it up and began recording.

Medea played the taped conversation.

"We need to be clear that we've gone through all the proper channels, the Principal, the Board, the Superintendent, even the Mayor," said the lawyer.

"Before that conversation you heard, we sent registered letters. Very brief responses came back stating that they stood behind the principal's decision in running his school as he saw fit," said Medea.

The TV reporter said, "How long ago were your letters sent?"

"Six weeks ago. Right after they all had refused the charter."

"It seems pretty innocuous, a club for women's health information," said the TV guy.

Medea said, "It was tabled—not even brought to a vote. We felt it would be helpful to fill in the gaps, especially for high school girls who don't come from traditional nuclear families and have no reliable source for information. For instance, I come from a family with a step dad and a half-brother, all men. No other women in the house. My first menstrual period began on the school bus and I had no idea what was happening. I don't want other girls to have to face that alone."

"After you petitioned for a charter, when did you receive the principal's refusal?' asked the ACLU lawyer.

"Six weeks. That's when I confronted the principal and taped our conversation. It seems there was a Christian fundamentalist member of the PTA who was afraid we would be practicing witchcraft and attempting abortions—her interpretation of traditional and herbal medicine."

"Witchcraft?" said the lawyer.

"Someone mentioned an ancient Greek goddess and it upset her Christian belief system."

"So they refused based on one person's religious convictions?'

Medea played the part of the recording about mothers, someone in the church, and witchcraft.

"It's flagrantly against the Establishment Clause. They won't have a legal leg to stand on."

The TV reporter said, "We will edit this tonight and have it on the morning news." He said to his crew, "That's a wrap. Send it to the station."

A few weeks later, after the All-State Vocal Competition in Atlanta, Medea looked back on the event. A disconnected, dreamlike sensation surrounded the whole weekend. It seemed like a fugue state through which she had sleepwalked. From the economical suite Miss Alma had booked well in advance, to the five minutes and ten seconds singing an aria from La Boheme in front of the judges and a packed auditorium, to the dog dream at one-thirty in the afternoon, there was a surreal quality of both pleasure and putrefaction.

Medea had stood in the center room of the suite, which Miss Alma called the studio, and tried to practice.

"Relax your throat. Open your nasal passages. Remember your head voice and your chest voice, and begin," said Miss Alma.

Medea sang, but badly.

"Stop," said Miss Alma. "Look at your base. Your legs and feet are wrong. You are uptight from the bottom up to your jaw. Standing like that you can't use your abdominal muscles to support your voice. It's visible."

"It's that yapper in the next suite—a little black poodle."

Medea tried again to concentrate by widening her stance, flexing and twisting her legs and torso. She imagined a rod from her head to the ground and all the singing parts aligned, but the yapper did not let up.

Miss Alma closed the bedroom door nearest the dog.

"Elongate your vocal cords, drop your chin for the high notes. Don't look up, and open your throat. Circle your hands and arms. Now shorten your vocal cords. Think of your chest voice and your head voice—and we begin."

Medea briefly let herself go into the musical Italian vowels. She sang well for a few minutes.

"Bramosia…occhi traspira…l'effluvio del desio tutta m'aggira."

"Very well. We're done practicing. Let's knock off until the competition."

Leaving the motel for lunch and shopping, Medea touched Miss Alma's arm to guide her to the other side of the stairs. She pointed to a fresh dog turd, still wet on the steps.

"Dog shit."

"Some people are trash," said Miss Alma as she stepped over the mess.

Medea looked at the window of the suite next to her bedroom. The tiny black poodle with tight curls and an artful coif scratched at the glass and barked at them as they passed.

Medea and Miss Alma ate a light lunch and shopped in a couple of stores before returning to their suite. Miss Alma wanted to take a nap before they went to the competition, but Medea needed to walk off some stress.

"I'll let you have it to yourself," she said and gathered her key and wallet. She slipped a small coil of nylon twine and a pocket knife into her jeans. From the tiny refrigerator she took a leftover sandwich and went outside.

The yapper scratched on the glass and its owner opened the door to let it run loose. Medea pinched a little of the sandwich and dropped it, then another and another as she walked towards the rear of the property. The Hansel and Gretel canine trail led to a little-used area behind the motel. There was a picnic table shaded by an umbrella. Only bathroom windows with frosted glass peered onto this plot. Cigarette butts littered the ground. It was the sort of neglected area she and Morris had used as playgrounds during her childhood, so she located it almost by instinct.

The Mexican housekeeper turned off her cellphone and stubbed out her cigarette as Medea approached. She pushed her cart past Medea and headed toward the other wing of the motel.

"Buenos dias, senorita."

"Buenos dias," said Medea.

Medea's skills in knot tying had improved since her early kills. No more granny knots—the thirteen loop hangman's knot she tied into the nylon cord could rival that of any executioner in the state of Georgia. The yapper stood in front of her, looking up at the sandwich. Medea bent down and scratched it's ear, then lifted it up into her lap. She had tossed the loose end of the cord over an aluminum bar of the umbrella and secured it with half hitches. She slipped the business end, the noose, around the little dog's neck and tightened it. Then she let the dog swing.

The dog twisted and squealed as the noose tightened to close its airway. Medea stood transfixed by the pathetic sounds and the dog's attempts at biting the knot. She unfolded her pocket knife and stabbed one of the dog's eyes, then the other one, and sliced its mouth at both corners. The dog went into a frenzy of panic and pain.

Medea's actions were mostly beyond her voluntary control. The autonomic nervous system had become accustomed to playing out the breathing, heart rate, flow of adrenaline, pupillary response, and ceded only the basic knotting and cutting skills to the icy fingers. Medea could no longer even recall her mother, ten years gone. Not her eyes or mouth, or any of her other features even came to mind. Medea's psychic mechanisms, working to displace the pain and loss associated with abandonment and grief, no longer connected on a conscious level. Her eyes rolled back into her head and she stood erect and trembling like a saint in ecstasy before a divine apparition as the spastic jerking of the small corpse stopped and the sounds of agony ceased.

Medea came to, standing in front of the bathroom mirror. An arterial spatter of blood dotted her face and another made a diagonal across her t-shirt. She washed her face and disposed of the t-shirt. Then slipped into another and quickly returned to the scene of her ritual killing. The body of the dog, the remains of the sandwich, and the nylon noose were gone. She could not remember removing them or walking back to the suite she shared with Miss Alma. She touched her front pocket. The knife was there.

Each of the contestants at All-State Vocal had been asked to prepare a solo which they could present if they won. When the competition began, the spotlight touched her, and Puccini's overture to Musetta's Waltz sounded, Medea felt herself come alive.

Five minutes and ten seconds later the audience erupted into applause and, beginning with other students on the front row, her competitors, they stood and shouted, "Brava! Medea! Brava!" It was like a junky's first shot of heroin—it tingled throughout her body then hit her heart and lungs, a flood of warmth. Every synapse of every nerve cell flooded with dopamine and screamed 'pleasure.'

When the judges called her name and put a blue ribbon across her chest and a bouquet of flowers in her hands, she knew she had arrived at where she had been called in life. She found Miss Alma just beyond the lights and blew her a kiss.

"This is for my instructor, mentor, and friend—Miss Alma Williams. Like many, I struggle with the Father God but encounter the divine in the Eternal Feminine."

Sancta Maria, mater dei
ora pro nobis peccatoribus...

She sang Shubert's "Ave Maria" and as the audience stood and applauded, she felt she had levitated to paradise and touched the face of a benevolent deity.

Next morning at the motel she wheeled hers and Miss Alma's luggage to the waiting shuttle. As she passed the housekeeper's cart with its piles of fresh towels and sheets the Mexican woman spoke to her over the noise of the trash truck onloading its cargo behind the motel.

""El perrito ruidoso, fabrico de mierda, se encuentra en la basura." She gestured toward the noise of the trash truck out back.

Medea did not understand all of what she said, but she got enough that she reached into her pocket for a folded twenty dollar bill. She smiled at the maid and said, "Gracias, amiga," as she shook her hand and slipped the twenty into her palm.

During the summer of that year, Medea turned sixteen, and enough interest had been generated that twenty-three high school girls attended a formational meeting of the Goddess Club at a community center. It would grow to 94 at the beginning of the school year. The ACLU held the principal's and the school board's feet to the fire. The school already had the Mousai Club, named after the Muses, so any reference to goddesses or any religious beliefs would be decided entirely by the girls themselves. The extreme Christians, the art teacher and the science teacher who had left in disgrace, created openings for two new faculty and a fresh start.

Medea brought down the gavel. "The first meeting of the Goddess Club at Cheatham High School is called to order."

They proceeded for three hours. At the midway break Medea had a glass of punch with Miss Alma.

"Thanks for acting as our temporary faculty sponsor. I know we will have two new faculty in the fall, at least, who don't have a student club to sponsor."

"I met Mrs. Solomon, the new art teacher, at a conference. Buttonhole her first. She seems like an open-minded and competent woman."

Reverend Whiteacre offered Medea a seat in his church office. Not one to carry a purse, she set her backpack on a small table. She sat with a view of both the street and a large safe with an open door. Medea inspected what she could see of the open safe. What most interested her was a stack of several bank deposit books which fell over on a shelf with a noise—plop, plop, plop: Banco Paraguay S.A.; Bank of East China, Hong Kong, Ltd.; Agribank Singapore, Ltd,; and Banco Carribeno Cayman, Ltd. The reverend returned with coffee and quickly pushed the vault door nearly closed.

"Alma said you would come by this week. I find that Monday applicants are the best."

"I could get a ride today. My stepdad comes into town to the Feed and Seed store on Monday."

"You don't drive?"

"I have a learner's permit." She took her new I.D. out of her bag along with her Social Security card. "Alma said you had two singing positions I might fill."

"Yes. Two? Well, it's just singing with the choir. You could think of it as getting paid to attend worship." He looked at her two legal documents and said, "You can put those away—we're less formal here." He chuckled. "You might even say God would be pleased and you would certainly enhance our spiritual community here at Faith Tabernacle, if you were looking for a spiritual home?"

"I think it sounds like two singing gigs rolled into one. Soloist is paid locally at $100 per service, and lead soprano, which is a separate job, is paid the same. That's a total of $200 per service."

"Medea, that's pretty mercenary. Do you think our Lord would—?"

"Your lord, not mine. I don't presume to think for him. Basically I'm not religious, but I have a hell of a voice and I love to sing. You, on the other hand, desperately need a good soprano for your revival this summer. Would you like to hear?"

She stood and prepared her voice. Daddy Carter had lent her his collection of gospel music this week and pointed out which hymns were most beloved by protestants.

"Here's my deep voice," she said and she sang from her chest:

A mighty fortress is our God, a bulwark never failing.
Our helper he amid the flood of mortal ills prevailing.
But still our ancient foe, doth seek to work us woe.
His strength and power are great, and armed with cruel hate.
On Earth is not his equal."

"Here's my passagio range. It actually goes much higher than this:"

"Ave Maria! Heaven's bride.
The bells ring out in solemn praise,
For you, the anguish and the pride.
The living glory of our nights,
of our nights and days…
Oh save us, mother full of grace,
in life and in our dying hour,
Ave Maria!"

"And here's my head voice. It's where I can really kick some ass:"

"Then sings my soul, my Saviour God to Thee,
How great Thou art. How great Thou art!'

Reverend Whiteacre wiped away a tear from his eye.

"We're protestant, so we'll have none that Mary stuff. I'll hire you for a three-month trial period at the rate of $200 per service. In the fall we will negotiate a longer contract."

"Sounds good. Just one thing." *I hope I don't blow it.*

"Yes?"

"I don't have a way to get here. We live way out in the country. There's only an old pickup truck. And I just have a learner's permit."

"So, you're trying to get your license?"

"Yes."

"That's good. A lot of young people nowadays don't even want a driver's license."

"They don't live as far out in the country as I do."

The reverend paused and paced with his hands behind his back.

A horn sounded outside on the street.

The reverend looked out the window at the old F-150.

"That must be the truck?"

Medea felt a churning in her gut. *I was supposed to be outside by now. Now the Rev will see Daddy Carter.*

Medea looked over his shoulder.

"I gotta go. That's Daddy's helper. He's finished at the Feed and Seed."

In a moment of clumsiness, she dropped her backpack.

"Let me see what we can do about the driver's license. I have a friend in Conyers at the driver's license bureau who might can get you a hardship license based on your need to drive to work."

"I'll think about it." *Don't let him come inside.*

Medea knocked over her coffee cup and continued to collect her stuff into her bag.

"If we can do that, we can also talk about maybe you driving some parishioners to and from services for a little extra money?" The Rev tore off a paper towel and cleaned up the coffee spill.

"I gotta go. Thanks."

She threw her backpack on to her shoulder as she rushed for the door.

Later that week Medea got a call from Reverend Whiteacre.

"Hey, Medea. I talked to my contact in Conyers and he said you definitely qualify for a hardship license. They're all about getting young people into the system."

"That's great. What do I do?"

"Alma has agreed to take you to the Drivers License Office for your drivers test, and if you agree to help out with driving parishioners and running errands around here, I'll get the funds for the fees. It's a paid position at $12 per hour. The van just sits in the parking lot most of the time and I think your driving it around town will be good advertising. We're getting a new logo and banner on the side for the revival. What do you say to all that?"

"I say yes. It will be good to have a summer job that involves singing. And it will definitely be good to have some wheels to get around."

Medea went to orientation at the Faith Tabernacle Church. Miss Alma's favorite word around any discussion of the Rev for the past week was *bamboozle*.

A live plant potted in a ceramic bullfrog coincidentally arrived in the church office with Medea. It was from a well-meaning member of the church and contained the usual assortment of soon-to-die plants: sansevieria, philodendron, variegated pothos, and a tiny dragon plant, all in one pot.

Rev signed for the floral delivery and handed it to Medea. "Take care of this will you?"

"What is it?"

"A live plant."

"I'm no good with those."

"No good with what?"

"Those. Live anything. I have a black thumb." She crossed her arms across her chest.

"Just put water on it once a week if it feels dry. The fluorescent lights are good for it."

He put it on her desk which was a table in the church library, then brought a phone which he plugged into a jack in the wall. It rang immediately.

The Rev looked at Medea.

Medea looked at the Rev.

One of the sansevieria spears drooped at a 90 degree angle like a snake poised to strike.

"A little help with answering the phone?" Rev said and walked back into his office.

Medea picked up the phone. "Hello." She sounded more surly

than inspiring and immediately thought it was inappropriate. "Yes, the Tabernacle. Hold on. He's right here."

She placed the receiver back on the cradle and looked at the Rev. "It's for you."

"You just hung it up."

Medea shrugged and wet the potted plant under the drinking fountain. It dribbled a stream of water from the drainage hole beneath its frog's butt.

"I'm hired to sing, not answer phones."

"Medea, we expect here, as in any work environment, that you be a team player."

"What team would that be? I've never played sports."

The reverend sighed and shut the door to his office. The phone rang again. Medea heard the Rev open his safe, and heard the phone ringing in his office, as well as here in the library. She unplugged her extension.

Agency was a word she had heard on a talk show: *The capacity of an individual to act independently and to make their own free choices.*

The potted plant drained a rivulet of water towards the edge of the table. It dripped onto the carpet. Medea picked up the ceramic bullfrog and dropped it into the trash.

Then she went to explore the building.

When the Rev came looking for her he was red in the face and chewing angry words. He heard singing in the sanctuary and walked toward it. He found Medea with a hymnal open, sitting at the piano, and singing:

> *"All hail the power of Jesus' name*
> *Let angels prostrate fall.*
> *Bring forth the royal diadem*
> *And crown Him Lord of all…*
> *Bring forth the royal diadem*
> *And Crown Him Lord of all."*

She noticed the Rev sitting silently in a pew and stopped singing. "Are you Zionist?"

"No. There is some apocryphal and end times language in old hymns, but we don't have an opinion on Zionism. They've been fighting in the Middle East for a long time."

"When does the choir meet for practice?"

"Thursday evenings. Sometimes on Saturday. Alma Williams will fill you in."

Medea pulled the new van into the handicapped space at the tabernacle and helped the wheelchair parishioners get loose from their safety harnesses. The community center was frequently used as a meeting place: Hospital dietary teaching, Alcoholics Anonymous, Al Anon, the garden club, life skills class. Rev charged rent for these events. As she headed toward her office in the library her cell phone chimed.

"Hello, Medea Royal?"

"Yes."

"I'm Lina Bryant from the Women's Health Club. You probably don't know me, you're so popular and all…"

"I never thought of myself as popular, Lina. You name seems familiar, but I can't recall your face? We've met?"

"Not really. I usually sit at the back and leave as soon as the meeting closes."

"Oh yeah, I remember you now. You're small. Very pretty and quiet. I've wanted to meet you, but like you say, you're out the door as soon as we adjourn."

"Carolina is my whole name, but my family sort of shortened it to Lina."

"Yes. I've seen it written out long on the membership roll. How can I help you, Lina?"

Silence for a long moment on Lina's end. "I have a problem. I hope maybe you can help me with it. But I would like to talk with you in person."

"Where do you live?"

"Crowtown."

"OK, then you live near the Three Roads truckstop? Maybe that would be a good place to meet? Would later this afternoon do?"

Medea looked over the dining room at the truck stop but didn't see Lina. She wasn't sure exactly what the girl looked like except that she was small and pretty. Then she noticed her waving from the back near the restrooms, and walked over.

"Yes, I remember you now. It's good to finally meet you." Medea smiled and shook the girl's hand.

"People tend to overlook me and I never know what to say in a crowd so I usually just leave."

Alice brought Medea a soda. "Hot day. You hungry? We got a chicken salad over greens cold plate."

"That sounds good, Alice. Have you eaten, Lina?"

"I've had a little upset stomach. I'll stick to just a coke. Thanks."

"So, what can I help you with—this big secret?"

"I heard the lecture on herbal medicine but I couldn't remember all the names of the herbs—tansy, penny royal, blue cohosh. I wouldn't know how to get them or how to take them. Infusion? Oil? Or how much. Would the health food store have them?"

"Good you didn't try any of that. It's dicey. These are traditional abortion drugs. You're pregnant?"

"Yes." A tear hit the top of her blouse.

"And you don't want to have a baby?"

"God no! My stepfather…" She lost her composure. After a few seconds she looked around the dining room to see if people were staring and seeing none, wiped her eyes on a napkin.

"Would it be like 20 drops of a tincture of blue cohosh root, 20 drops of an infusion of penny royal, 15 drops of tansy oil? And how would I know how strong the solution should be?"

"You wouldn't. And it would be taking your life in your hands."

"I don't know what to do? You seem so much smarter about these things. Can you help me?"

"Don't do anything stupid. There are safer ways to abort now. Five pills you take over three days. I have a friend who can get the drugs."

Lina grabbed Medea's hands and kissed them. "Thank you. Thank you."

"Call me Friday and ask if the marigolds have sprouted? Say that."

"Have the marigolds sprouted?" repeated Lina.

"If I tell you yes, meet me here on Friday afternoon. Meanwhile get a safe place to stay for about a week. You will cramp and your period will be unusually heavy. There's a woman, a deputy at the Sheriff's Office, named Philly. Go see her and tell her what's happened. She's a concerned, compassionate woman who will help get your stepfather off your back."

As the sun set, a peculiar light hit the old sign which read "Three Roads Truck Stop." Medea punched numbers into her cell phone. She had never thought about how old the business might be, but it occurred to her in that light that it was much older than she thought. The pentimento letters beneath the more recent paint showed through. *Trivium,* it said. Trivium is a place where three roads meet. Traditionally, suicides were buried there, witches met to boil roots and pour their tea, and musicians, vagabonds and such, made deals with the Devil. To some, that set of circumstances might strike fear into their heart and send them crossing themselves and reaching for prayer beads and holy water. Both Medea and Lina, women in search of women's help in a circumstance that only women can know, left with a feeling of empowerment and benevolence—a feeling that their life had been returned to their control.

"Pharmacy," said the pleasant voice on the cell.

The second week on the job, doing errands for the Rev, Medea was more than earning her $12/hour. Singing in the choir on Sunday was no sweat. She didn't care for the music really, but like a piano owned by a collective group she made sounds according to the keys punched. Two hundred dollars per service would never get her rich, but it was a start. She forced herself not to laugh at the delusional members who parted with their pension money or other hard-earned cash, never suspecting most of it went into offshore accounts belonging to Reverend Whiteacre. His most recent new toy was a Scout boat: 210 Dorado, F150 Yamaha with depth finder, livewell, rod locker, GPS, radar, and a tempered wind screen.

"Both Peter and Andrew were fishermen, and they walked with the Lord," he said to one of the deacons.

"The Lord walked on water. I guess they needed a boat to keep up," said the deacon, and laughed.

Medea watched and made mental notes of Whiteacre's slickness. People seemed to share in the pleasure derived from the recreational water craft, even though they weren't likely to be invited aboard and probably would not taste any bass or catfish he might catch. His Italian suits, Medea noticed, brought a twinkle of pride to the eyes of his less prosperous parishioners, even though they might only afford off-the-rack for themselves. *Pleasure by proxy.* His tricked out SUV with chrome wheels and Bose sound turned heads in time to see his bumper sticker, *Jesus Rocks!* She knew she would never have qualms about milking this big fat tabernacle tit.

Word processing—code for 'Can she type?' Medea, at her table in the church library, had had a gut full of it when she heard the office door open and whoever had been meeting with the Rev spoke to her right side. She listened but didn't look up.

"I need some information on the depletion of Cyprus' forests as a probable cause of the Bronze Age Collapse in about 3,200 B.C. Could you help with any books on that, pretty lady?"

"The fuck you just said?" asked Medea, and she wheeled around in her cheap office chair.

Jason stood there grinning.

"Jason! Oh my god. I've missed you." She hugged him. "How have you been? How's school?"

"Wow, quite a summer job you've got here."

"It's ok. Let's go out back so we can talk. You can tell me all about life at the Community College, and I'll tell you all about life studying for the GED."

The back entrance of the building had steps going down to a patch of weeds, and asphalt laid beyond that to make an overflow parking lot if crowds of worshippers ever became that large.

"Sit down here and tell me all about it," she said patting the top step beside her and lighting a cigarette.

"Not much to tell really. I'm going to CCC—business major. I arranged for some I.B. credit this summer while I work as a real estate associate with one of my dad's friends. I'm studying for my realtor's license. Hope to have that by the time I graduate with my Associate Degree. What are you up to?"

"Well, you know I went to Atlanta with Miss Alma, to Allstate Vocal Competition? I won first place!"

"Good for you. I'm so proud for you."

"Yeah, I sang their socks off. We've nearly got the Women's Health Issues Club at school. The principal has dug in his heels, but the courts are on our side. I guess you heard about that—it was on TV."

"Sounded like you kicked some Baptist butt."

"Always happy to see the patriarchy go down in flames. So now things are on track to get my GED in August."

"You dropped out of school?"

"School's a waste of time. It's bullshit. I can pick things up in half-an-hour on an internet website that the other fuck-offs in public school drag out for a week. Miss Alma's giving me voice lessons. I got my driver's license—hardship case. I have to drive to work."

"That reminds me. I want to show you something. Come on."

They walked around the building and stopped by a new pickup truck. "This is it," said Jason.

Medea read the logo on the door, *Golden Fleece Realty ~ Jason Carpenter.* "This is yours? Holy shit, you got an Onkyo sound system. Marry me, dude. I want to bear your children."

"You want to go for a ride? Out to the truck stop?"

"I need a break. Rev can answer his own phone."

At the truck stop Alice took their order and gave it to the cook. She brought back their drinks as Jason excused himself to the restroom.

"So you're seeing Jason again."

"Not really. He just dropped by the Tabernacle and pulled me away from my job. Rev will probably fire me before my first week is up. What do you think of Jason?"

"He seems like a go-getter. A couple of council members were in here the other day, talking about him. Said they wish more young people were like him. He looks for opportunities, like always looking in the want ads at land for sale."

"Must be nice to be well thought of by people in power. It's kind of a father-son thing, I believe. Like that new pickup. Do you think he could have got that thing without his old man's signature?"

"Word of caution if you're dating him—he's in here every other week with a new girl. Just saying."

"You think he's a player?"

"Don't put words in my mouth."

"Maybe I'll play him." She noticed Jason coming back to their table. "And I'll have a side salad as well, Alice. Vinaigrette. You want a salad, Jason?"

Jason sat. "Salad sounds good. Blue cheese."

Just then, Morris and his date entered and took a table on the far side of the restaurant.

"Excuse me for a second," said Medea and went over to their table.

"Hey, Morris. How's things in Athens?"

"It's school. They keeping me busy. This is Shirelle."

"I'm Medea, Morris's half-sister."

In spite of herself, Shirelle looked a little puzzled. "Pleased to meet you." She shook Medea's hand.

"Half-sister. The white half." There was a bitter note in Morris's voice.

"Daddy Carter's harvesting peanuts and hay. He'll be happy you're back to give him a hand."

"I miss the farm during the week. I'm not a city boy at all."

"Well, our food's on the way. I'd best get back before it gets cold. Pleased to meet you, Shirelle."

She headed back to the table where Jason had tucked into his salad. Morris waved to Jason and Jason held up his hand. *Back at ya.*

"Who's that? Isn't he the guy who helped you pass your driver's test?"

"Morris Carter. He's going to University of Georgia this year. That's his girl, Shirelle. Isn't she pretty?"

Medea watched as Jason evaluated Shirelle. *Like meat on a rack.*

"So, anyway, I'm dropping out of school," Medea said.

"Really? I mean, you're serious?"

"Not really dropping out—moving up my exit date."

"But you'll miss so much in social interactions. What about your club?"

"The girls will do fine. Their case is watertight. The bullshit is overwhelming. First the thing with Miss Fulton and the Coach. Then the court case. Students can't do anything creative without getting slapped down. We're just warehoused until we graduate and go on to college, or to work or trade school, or worse—to jail."

"I don't think that's wise leaving school, Medea. What do your parents think?"

"They don't have an opinion in this. It's my decision."

On Thursday Medea's phone rang. "Have the marigolds sprouted?" Lina asked.

They met at the same table. Medea handed her two plastic envelopes, one had one pill, and the other had four pills. Lina seemed more talkative and in control of herself.

"They didn't even leave me a full name. Lina—that's half a name. Carolina's my whole name. My mama's a drunk. She said I asked for it, always flirting with her man. I never flirted with that piece-of-shit. One look at him and you can see how far she's let herself go. Can't believe she calls that a catch."

"Do you have a safe place to stay for the next few days? Remember, you will have cramps and your period will run a bit longer, and be heavier than usual."

"My aunt's place. She's my mama's sister. You know, I went to the pastor at our church and told him what was happening. He said the Lord works in mysterious ways. And went on about original sin and how it came into the world through a woman named Eve. His God's a male. Too many of those in my family—four brothers and an all-too-present stepfather, and a long gone daddy. I guess he saw Mama crawling into that bottle of booze and pulling the cork in after herself before any of the rest of us. No help there. Too many penises in my family and it looks like God's got one, too."

"Here's an instruction sheet. You take one pill, mifiprex, on the day you want to start the process of terminating the pregnancy. Take a full week off and rest at your aunt's place. Then 48 hours after you took the first pill, you put two of the misoprostol tablets from the four-pill bag in each cheek. Total of four pills, two in each cheek, between the teeth and the cheek. You let it sit there and melt for half an hour, then you swallow the remainder with some water. Times vary on how fast the contents of the uterus begin to be expelled. It can happen as fast as two hours after you put the pills in your cheeks."

"Thanks for talking straight. The websites go off on 'baby,' 'murder,' 'a new individual,' 'product of conception,' and the one I really came to hate, 'your unborn child.' *Unborn child is an oxymoron.* This fertilized ovum, this blastocyst, this zygote, not even a fetus yet—this product of a rape is the parasitic thing in my uterus I want out."

"No argument here. These pills will end the problem."

"I called Philly down at the Sheriff's Department. She sounded like she actually cared. I'm staying at my aunt's till this is over. He gave me clap. I already got shots for that at the health department. I got a screen to catch whatever tissue comes out. I want them to do a DNA test. Then I'm letting the Sheriff sort it out, and I'm not looking back."

I'm letting the Sheriff sort it out, and I'm not looking back. Medea liked decisive thought. She had it on her mind when she saw Miss Alma again for voice lessons. Out the window she looked at the space above the garage as she sang vocal scales.

"Miss Alma, do you use that upstairs space, over your garage?'

"I don't even use the garage. I hate driving into that tight space and trying to get out of a sedan."

"I need an apartment, and a studio space, to practice."

"We'll look at it after your singing today. Continue with your scales. We'll practice rapid changes up and down the scales. Those will be important as you take on more difficult roles—maybe one day you'll get to the real fireworks like, Queen of the Night."

After practice they climbed the stairs to the one bedroom garage apartment.

"I had a wild niece whom I had for a summer. Her parents couldn't control her and I got tired of her night time ways, so I put in a kitchen and bath. When I gave her the keys I told her the next stop was juvie, motherhood, or college. She did better without an adult standing over her all the time. The utilities are on one account. We can work out something on rent."

Medea walked around the large space and looked out the windows. There was a screened gazebo in the backyard. "I like the open feel of the place. I don't think I would bother anybody with the singing and piano."

"No. You wouldn't. I like hearing your voice."

Medea had more work at the tabernacle than two people could get done—food bank, letters, phones ringing, people in-and-out to see the Rev—when a well-dressed, pleasant woman entered the library.

"I'm looking for Medea Cobb, could you tell me where I might find her?"

"I'm Medea. How can I help you?"

"My name is Sarah Hauptman. I'm from the Atlanta Lyric Opera."

"Ohhh, another music lover. Pleased to meet you." Medea shook her hand.

"We have a problem with our production of La Boheme. Musetta has laryngitis and her understudy had a traffic accident."

"That's a problem."

"A friend of the opera heard you sing at All State and she was enchanted."

"Musetta's Waltz is something I've loved since I was a child. La Boheme can be overwhelmed by pathos, but Musetta kicks it up." She sang for Mrs. Hauptman:

> *Cuando me'n vo soletta per la via*
> *La gente sosta e mira*
> *E la belleza mia tutta ricera en me*
> *Da capo a pie...*
> *Alli occulte belta*
> *Cosi l'effluvio del desio tutta m'aggira*
> *Felice mi fa!*

Sarah clapped and smiled. "Your Musetta sounds quite vain, and flirty. Is that how you see her?"

"Well, it's the first half of the 19th century. They're Bohemians in the Latin Quarter of Paris, so all are poor. Women rose on the status of their looks, and Musetta is quite attractive. She has a history with Marcello, whom she still loves, but she's dating Alcindoro. He's like a sugar daddy—she treats him really bad. She accepts gifts, vain coquette that she is, but she also generously parts with things, to help her friends, like when Mimi needs medicine. Pathos rules this libretto. It could be overwhelmingly sad were it not for Musetta stirring things up and adding some sparks."

"You come highly recommended after the All State Competition. Will traveling to Atlanta interfere with your school?"

"No. I have two jobs, both singing, and I support myself."

"If you take this offer we will need you as soon as possible for dress rehearsal. The offer is $2,000 per performance for three nights—Friday, Saturday, and Tuesday, and a matinee on Sunday. We cover transportation and lodging, including meals."

"Yes. Yes, definitely. My stage name is Medea Royal. Medea Cobb sounds so country, don't you think?"

"I like Medea Royal. It sounds like a professional entertainer's name. You certainly understand the character of Musetta."

"She grabs life and shakes it. She sees Mimi dying, and thinks romantic love with Marcello is passionate but probably hopeless. Alcindoro is the rich, secure alternative. She doesn't have the options that women today have."

"Not you at all?"

"No. I'm much more level-headed. I have a mirror over the sink in the bathroom and one inside my clothes closet. Boys are mostly just trouble. I am most alive when I'm singing in front of an audience."

"We're putting you up in the Georgian Terrace Hotel. It's right across the street from the Fox Theater, the venue for our La Boheme. This venture is part of our Outbound Opera series. We've put things out in the community at various sites to make them more accessible to everyone. It's our opinion that opera shouldn't be just for snobs in the corporate world but should make the whole city a vibrant and exciting place."

"What an innovative idea."

"Here's your credit card for meals. It's only $500, but it's only four days and you'll find reasonable places to eat both inside the Georgian Terrace and nearby. Downtown Atlanta has a dynamic restaurant scene."

Morris and Medea had come to terms with the demands of their summer jobs. Daddy Carter had finally let them alone about getting up with the chickens. They were not country kids at heart. Medea watched Morris over the rim of her coffee cup, slathering a biscuit with butter and jam, cutting bacon and eggs into bites. She could imagine him Daddy Carter's age: He would have high blood pressure, a cholesterol problem, and pre-diabetes. He would own a farm and have several children.

"What?" asked Morris.

"Oh, just thinking about the trip to Atlanta."

"We have five days' pretty weather. The hay is at 20% moisture—good for baling. If we can get this harvest in the barn and another—"

"I'll be in Atlanta, singing with the Lyric Opera, through Tuesday. I'll be back on Wednesday."

"I need some help with getting these bales in the barn. I need it today."

"Can you get temporary help? Maybe a kid on summer break who needs a little cash?"

"This is a family farm, Medea. We all got to work to make this thing go."

"Morris, can you even look at yourself in the mirror anymore without seeing Daddy Carter's genes staring back at you?'

"Yes. He shaves early. I get the bathroom later on."

"Oh god. You believe it now too."

"What?"

"Nothing. Never mind."

"Believe what?"

"I believe I can get the loft cleaned before I have to catch the plane. I'll be back next week."

Medea tied a bandana around her nose and mouth to keep out the dust and climbed into the hay loft. She carried a large trash can and a rake. This barn was never a comfortable work space for her—too many warnings: From her long gone mother that it was not a safe place to play, not to go there without Daddy Carter; his warnings that people can get hurt in barns; and the abysmal statistics that people die in farm accidents at a rate exceeding most other work places including construction sites. *How could so much junk collect in a space made for storing rectangular blocks of bundled grass?* She set to work cleaning.

An hour later the boards on the loft floor were clean and awaiting bales of hay, winter food for their livestock. Medea bent over to scoop up the last of the loose straw, mouse droppings and bird feathers. Her butt bumped a wooden rail that ran the width of the loft, high above a storage area for bladed equipment. The board swung downward in an arc toward the blades of a cultivator, spikes on a harrow, blades of a disc, a plow and other sharps. She stood above the well-kept equipment and imagined the violence it did to the earth and it's capacity to cut, tear apart and bring change to natural order. Like tiny spotlights the rays of the sun penetrated cracks and angled light onto sharp edges in the space below.

She pulled the loose board back into place and looked for a hammer and a nail to fasten it. The nail hole in the upright post looked like it had been loose for awhile and the board had been banged back into place. several times. She let it go and it swung again in its downward arc. She pulled it up and pounded it into place with her hand. Finding no hammer and nail, she decided to just leave it as she'd found it. It was getting on toward time for the airport shuttle.

Back in her upstairs bedroom that, for now, served as her studio, she checked the contents of her luggage and locked it. She played chords on her electric piano from sheet music for La Boheme and studied the role of Musetta until the sound of tires on gravel drew her attention to the airport shuttle.

At the regional airport she took her seat by the window and looked down to the tarmac and luggage carts. She heard a familiar voice on the aisle.

"Would you mind trading for an aisle seat so I can sit next to that pretty woman?"

As Jason settled into the seat next to Medea he winked at her. "Ma'am, I believe you're stalking me. You keep turning up in all my places."

"What a surprise, Jason. You're headed to Atlanta too?"

"Yes. Seminar on land development—How To Build The McMansion. It's a final requirement for the I.B. course." He looked at the cover of her program. "The Lyric Opera Production of La Boheme?"

"I'm singing Musetta." Medea thought he looked too unimpressed for such a big development in her life.

She asked, "You know Musetta? La Boheme?"

He shrugged. "I know real estate, football and deer hunting. Nothing about opera."

Medea eyed the emergency door. *Could I really slide down those inflatable things? Could I find and grab my luggage? How long is this flight?*

"Tell me about this course," she said.

"Oh my god. This presenter has made millions and millions taking rural land within 60 miles of a regional airport and building luxury homes on it. His gimmick is to leave some of the details unfinished so prospective clients can decide on things like primo appliances in the kitchen, cabinetry, bathroom, paint colors, flooring and all that. So he finishes with their input and they get a really swag home, custom built to their individual tastes."

The captain announced, "Good morning, Sky Connect passengers. Clear skies and sunshine in Atlanta. We're clear for immediate take off. Flying time will only be about forty-five minutes. Flight attendants please make your final cabin checks and we'll be airborne shortly."

Jason leaned into Medea's arm and shoulder and smelled the scent from her hair. She turned to look at him. He was too close in her personal space, even for a plane, and he didn't move away. "You have the greenest eyes I've ever seen. They look like emeralds."

"And yours are hazel, I think. Move over, you're crowding me. Do you use sunscreen on your face?" She pushed his shoulder. "I should take you shopping while we're in Atlanta. If you're gonna be big in real estate development we need you looking sharp. I think we can find what we need at a place called Buckhead." She gave him her cell number.

In the airport when they parted ways she said, "Don't wish me luck, it's bad luck to theater people."

He kissed her on the cheek. "Catch lots of bouquets." He turned to go.

"Jason, call me tomorrow."

"Where are you staying?" He turned around to walk backwards.

"Georgian Terrace."

"Happy coincidence. Me too."

Medea stood on a low platform as the wardrobe mistress took in the waist and underarms of the early 19th century French costume.

"It's a treat not to have to make fat girls look skinny."

"My brother says I'd forget to eat."

"This is gonna look great on you. Most of the other characters are poor artists, you know, Latin Quarter, Paris. Alcindoro's money is well spent on lavish gifts for Musetta."

"I like the way this fabric moves. Musetta likes this dress." She stepped off the platform and waltzed across the room.

"Take long strides with your legs to show the color and fabric, and when you turn, take the dress in your fingers and give it some air. You'll have pretty, ribboned petticoats underneath. Your red hair and skin coloring are just right for this costume."

"Oh, yes. I see. It sort of floats. Very light."

"Musetta is a bright spot in a very grim universe. Most people say they love La Boheme, but it's pathetic and too tragic. Creating this dress for the Cafe Momus scene is the only thing that has kept me from drinking lye these last few weeks." She gestured for Medea to waltz and turn. "Yes. It is beautiful. Your figure does it justice."

The director walked Medea through all four acts of the opera and listened to her sing her arias.

"We'll walk you through Act II. It's the Latin Quarter of Paris, in the street, outside the Cafe Momus. The buildings are painted on rising diagonal streets on the screen behind to give depth to the very shallow stage here at the Fox. Street merchants with their carts, including a flower vendor and haberdasher, display their wares. The soldiers climb steep stairs backstage and enter high and on a diagonal which gives the illusion of twice as much depth to the street scene. They appear to march down a street. We've built two runways over the orchestra. You do your solo, and the Act 3 *Addio dolce svegliare alla matina* is out here too, but it's the gates of the city and it's snowing."

"Which marks on the floor do I follow?'

"The yellow. Alcindoro will lead you through the crowds. You're here mostly, at the front of the stage, at the tables of the Cafe Momus. Wardrobe says dance in long steps, and when you turn around take the folds of the dress in your hands."

The Friday performance did better than expected. "When we got hit by a double whammy, laryngitis and a car accident, we didn't think this could be saved. But, thanks to our new Musetta—" said the baritone singing Alcindoro. The cast and crew gathered after the performance at a bar, Proof and Provisions, on the lower level of the Georgian Terrace, to toast Medea's stepping into the understudy-to-the-understudy role of Musetta. Realizing her talent lay way beyond understudy, they all laughed with great pleasure at the birth of, what many of them thought was, a new operatic star.

Saturday morning, Jason called Medea's room. "Hey, Musetta. I wanted to have coffee with you at Buffalo Bayou Coffee. It's downstairs. You're gonna love the write up in the Beacon. Half an hour?"

"This better be good, Jason," said Medea as the two met in the hotel lobby. He gave her a copy of the paper, opened to the arts and entertainment section. In the fourth paragraph they had written of her courage in flying to Atlanta and performing with only a walkthrough for a rehearsal. The critic said, "Her courage is only matched by her beauty in a world where dresses usually have to be let out and lazy sopranos trying to sing Musetta's role can't even laugh their way up a simple scale in the Act 3 quartet. In Puccini's La Boheme, pathos can overwhelm you unless you're blessed with a diva who can brighten a desperately poor Latin Quarter with her dynamic presence and voice. Many in the cast say they witnessed the birth of an operatic supernova at the Fox last night. We look forward to her moving beyond the soubrette roles into her natural milieu, lyric coloratura."

"Coffee?" said Medea.

When Jason brought it back to their table, Medea put down the paper, and read no further. "I've heard you should ignore critics' reviews, whether good or bad."

"Sale at Buckhead," said Jason.

"World class. I want you to get a couple of suits, some shirts, shoes, and some skin products, before you absolutely ruin your skin—Shiseido's good. They've got it at Neiman Marcus and Bloomingdale's. If you're going to sell real estate, you must have a good suit."

They finished breakfast and walked to the North Avenue MARTA station. Medea handed the agent her credit card. "Four day pass, please." Jason did the same.

"I thought you were just here for the weekend seminar?"

"You're here til Tuesday. I think I'll stay longer. I'd like to hear you sing onstage."

They took seats with great views on the train. Rectangular, chrome-colored cars painted with a signature orange, yellow and blue stripe, sped them in 15 minutes up the middle of GA 400 to the Buckhead Station. They emerged via a pedestrian tunnel into Lenox Square.

"It's enough to make you believe in God," said Medea.

They shopped and, while waiting for alterations on the suits, booked themselves for a couple's facial and manicure/pedicure at Aloe Jamaican Spa. Two nail technicians put them in reclining chairs facing each other to their left side. They soaked their hands in bowls of warm water that smelled like flowers.

Medea said, "I remember when I was little, maybe three-years-old, my mama and a man in a soldier's uniform posing for a picture under a Coca Cola sign somewhere here in Atlanta. I think he was my father, but I can't be sure."

"You're not sure if he was your dad?"

"No, I have false memories and true memories. It's difficult sometimes to sort them out. You know, you've heard things said so often—this or that happened—until it takes on a life of its own."

Don't you know who your dad was? What he looked like?"

"No. He was killed in Afganistan shortly after that day we were together here in Atlanta. I remember he had his arm around my mother's neck and I thought he looked like he was choking her. I was holding her other hand when someone snapped a picture on mother's digital camera."

"Didn't you see the picture?"

"Only on the display screen. I didn't have a picture myself. Mama was killed in a car accident about two years later and I went into foster care."

"That's terrible."

"I don't remember much about it really. If you're not engaged with the places and people, things just slip. I moved around a lot. Home-to-home, I mean."

The nail technicians finished with their manicure and both, Medea and Jason, took a bathroom break. When they came back their pedicures began with a similar foot bath.

"Tell me about your family. Now that you know what little there is to share about mine."

"Oh well, don't go to sleep on me. You've seen the old re-runs of the Beaver Cleaver family?"

"Very few. I preferred the Friday Night Frights."

"We were pretty nuclear. I have two older brothers. We lived in a ranch style home. I guess you'd call it a suburb, or an exurb of Cheatham. Four bedrooms, three baths. Mom and Dad had the master bedroom. We boys each had our own bedroom. Dad put in an extra bathroom with shower off the carport. He was a builder. Architect actually, but he had no illusions of making the cover of any magazines or winning any awards. He just said he wanted to build interesting houses that people could live in. He said it was a useful way to make a living. I guess that's where I got the idea to go into developing real estate. My dad put himself through college working construction."

"What about your Mom?"

Jason gave a Cub Scout salute, three fingers with palm facing out.

"She's a Cub Scout Mom. Her boys are everything to her. She wants grandbabies so bad she has offered $25,000 to the first one of us who puts a grandbaby in her arms."

"That's creepy. She sounds like a slaver offering $25,000 for a child."

" 'Make me a grandma and I'll make you rich,' she said. So far, neither of my two older brothers has popped. And of course I haven't either. I guess the offer's still good."

There was something relaxing and conducive to talking in the scent of the flower water, almost narcotic. The nail technicians completed their pedicures by massaging their clients's ankles and feet, most welcome after a day of shopping.

"Mom was a den mother all through our Cub Scout years. Baking brownies and making rice krispy treats."

"How sweet of her."

"She loved it. Bobcat, Tiger, Wolf, Bear, Webelos and Arrow of Light. All three of us went all the way through. Mom's an Episcopalian, and a Republican, but she's not overboard with any of it. They go to mass like twice a year—Easter and Christmas. She doesn't believe in holy days of obligation. Three times I guess, if you count taking the dog to mass on St. Francis's Feast Day in October."

Medea felt a shiver and the tech put a warm blanket over her legs. *I'll never pass muster with the Beaver bunch. She'll see right through me.*

They picked up their packages at Neiman's, made their way back through the geometries of concrete and chrome, and caught MARTA back to the hotel. They had more bags than Bedouin camels when they entered the lobby of the Georgian Terrace. Bell boys greeted them with carts and helped them to their rooms.

After the Saturday night performance, the Opera Guild sponsored a meet and greet during which Medea signed a contract to sing the soprano lead in *Romeo et Juliette* with Opera Chicago. By eleven o'clock she could feel her energy fading, so she slipped away from the crowd and called it an early night.

Sunday morning Jason called at nine a.m.

"This better be good," said Medea.

"Coffee's ready downstairs, and MARTA's rolling."

They met again at Buffalo Bayou. Jason handed her a coffee.

"You're almost house trained. I may keep you."

"I talked too much yesterday about my boring nuclear family. You mentioned a Coca Cola sign that you couldn't be sure was a real memory?"

"True memory or false memory. When I was three. My Dad and Mom, I think."

"The concierge told me something. Come with me. You're in for a pleasant discovery."

They caught MARTA and rode two stops to Peachtree Center, a deep tunnel with rock walls and huge escalators. They emerged into canyons of buildings and walked a few city blocks to the intersection of Pryor Street and Peachtree Street. He found the Olympia Building behind them as they crossed the street.

"Medea, I'm gonna cover your eyes and I want you to turn around. Just shut your eyes and trust me."

He put his hands over her eyes. She could smell a woodsy fragrance with undertones of leather. When he removed his hands and said, "Open," she went back in time. There before her was a Coca Cola sign several stories high. It sat on top of a two story building where a new Walgreen's Pharmacy had just opened.

"It was early summer and it was raining," she said and pointed to a spot down the street toward which she ran. "Here," she said, "Here's where we stood to let the man take our picture. People were crowded in to see them light up the Coca Cola sign. You'd think God had come back after years of vacationing somewhere and resumed his seat at the center of the universe."

She pointed another block down the street. "The park is over there," she said.

As she and Jason walked quickly toward Woodruff Park, Medea related her memories of that long-ago day. "People were playing chess on a giant chess board. You could walk around on it. People were doing yoga, and there was a soccer game. My favorite thing, well, two actually—was a curved fountain with water running down its walls, and a giant statue of a bird. Mama called it "Phoenix Rising From The Ashes," or something like that. There was a woman in a hoop skirts dress holding the Phoenix up as it took flight."

As Medea and Jason encountered these things for real, she became more emotional and started to cry. She heard the water tumbling in the fountain. "It's a true memory," she said. *It's a lie—he was a john.*

Jason handed her his handkerchief and she dried her eyes. Then she turned to him and hugged him. As they relaxed their embrace he kissed her. She tasted salt from her tears and coffee and his breakfast from Buffalo Bayou, cream cheese and citrus.

"Oh God, look at the time. I have a matinee. I have to be in wardrobe."

They ran for the underground train.

Enroute, Medea pulled out her cell phone and ordered Jason a ticket for the matinee. "You'll find this at least as interesting as deer hunting and football. You get to sit in the center, on the front row of the first balcony. I think you'll like the Fox. It's built to look exotic, like a Moroccan palace."

After the matinee performance, Jason met her in the lobby.

"Out of all the makeup and costume and wig nobody recognizes me as Musetta. I'm just another thrill seeker in downtown Atlanta. Thanks for this morning, by the way. That was sweet and thoughtful."

"You like soul food, right?"

"Am I from Georgia?"

"Mary Mac's is a classic. It's just four blocks from here on Ponce de Leon at Myrtle Street. I called for a table. You have to eat."

The building was one-story, gray, with flowers in window boxes blooming on the street. It was unremarkable except for the smells of soul food—vegetables in pots, bread baking, and things frying. Attached to the side of the building there was an L-shaped sign: Mary Mac's Tea Room. The windows were large with many small panes and an awning that shaded them from the afternoon sun. Inside, wide-bladed venetian blinds were drawn against the light and the prying eyes of the street. Photographs, many old and black-and-white, some sepia tone, lined the earth-colored walls, images of the famous and not-so-famous patrons, matted in soft white and framed in black. The tables and furniture were black and the table tops were covered with white cloths.

"Iced tea for me," said Medea to the black waiter in a crisp white shirt and starched red apron.

"Same here. Could we get two salads to start?"

"This stuff looks like the food at the truck stop."

"More desserts. Ummm… peach cobbler a la mode."

The waiter brought salads and tea. He placed a salad dressing server on the table and a basket of yeast rolls and corn bread muffins.

"This place is a keeper," said Medea.

They grazed their way through southern fried chicken, fried okra, mac and cheese, turnip greens and pot liquor until they had to stop.

"I wish I had two stomachs," said Jason.

"Want to split a peach cobbler a la mode?"

"Hurt me," said Jason, and he ordered coffee as well.

"Have you had time to attend any of your sessions at the real estate conference?"

"Yes. I got one in on Friday evening, regarding covenants. Then one yesterday after our shopping. That one was good, it was about custom kitchens. Today was better. I spent part of it with you."

"Awwww. Wherever you're hoping to go with flattery, that's sure to help."

"One more tonight on 'Infinity Pools, Plexiglass, and the Weight of Water.' Then I will have attended enough to get the lab credit for the I.B. course."

The waiter brought the ticket and placed it by Jason.

Medea reached across the table and took it.

"My treat today," said Jason.

"No. Let me. I have a credit card from the Opera Guild for dining expenses."

So Medea picked up the tab for the food. *Getting the check, and lighting tobacco products are art forms. Social power ensues.*

She felt free, not having obligations the following day, and slept soundly.

Ever faithful to his schedule, Jason called at nine a.m. They bought chicken biscuits and coffee on the way to MARTA.

Medea suggested, "Let's walk some? Or we'll get fat."

They caught a train to Peachtree Center from which they hiked several blocks west across Centennial Park. They stopped in front of a long, glass building with a bronze dome over the entrance that looked like a football helmet.

"You said you liked football," she said to Jason.

"Hell yeah. I'm a Georgia boy. This is the College Football Hall of Fame."

He hugged and kissed her.

They had to validate admission and choose a team on entry to personalize their experience. Jason chose Georgia Tech.

"I'm a CCC student, but just for shits and grins, I'll take Georgia Tech. 'Rambling Wreck from Georgia Tech.'"

"I'm a dropout, but I'll take University of Georgia. 'Bulldogs!'"

Their choices turned on lights among the teams represented on the two story Helmet Wall. Perpindicular to that was a giant mural of nearly equal dimensions. Their Georgia players' helmets lighted up as they approached.

Jason said, "My dad would like this one. Joe Hamilton, quarterback who went on to play with the Tampa Bay Bucaneers. He had gimpy knees and eventually went to play for a team in Germany. He played before I was born."

Medea said, "Same here. Jake Scott inducted 2011. I wasn't even born when he played college ball, and then for the New Orleans Saints. Jim Donnan was a coach for the University of Georgia until the year I was born. He was inducted in 2009. This seems like a tourist attraction for old men."

There was on open area with astroturf and play stations in the center of a large recreation area. It resembled a football field and covered an area about half as big. One end had a goal post where you could kick a field goal. Medea ran the gauntlet of skills challenges just ahead of Jason, and she came out with a better score. Her pass was a little less wobbly than his.

"Medea wins," she said and bounced up and down like a cheerleader. "Let's go kick a field goal."

Her first ball bounced off the goal post, but the second scored.

Both of Jason's went wide.

They walked outside. "The Georgia Aquarium's around here somewhere. It's a silver building that looks like the bow of a ship. I think it's about three blocks north."

"How do you know all of these things?" Jason said.

"Internet. Cell phone. Concierge."

They held hands as they walked toward the aquarium.

Medea said, "I have to sort out true memories from false memories."

"What's a false memory?"

"Sort of like a lie, but it's the way something ought to be, or ought to be remembered. Not necessarily the way it was though. Maybe it started out as a lie, or a half truth, and then it got told and repeated until it took on a life of its own. Maybe the people to whom it happened left, or died, but the story kept going. Eventually it didn't resemble reality at all."

"That's kind of strange. My parents, especially my dad, kept us grounded in reality. When we would get too far out into fantasy, he would tell us we could have anything no matter how high up it was as long as we could jump or climb and get it. He said we were like little frogs sitting on our butts wishing for the moon. He'd pinch our bellies and say, 'Ribbit.' Then, 'Leap, froggie, high as you're tough enough.' And we'd jump up and land on the carpet in the den."

The Georgia Aquarium was indeed designed to look like the bow of a silver ship. They decided to see two of the features, the Ocean Voyager, and the Behind the Seas Tour. The experience, walking around and through the largest tank, which was large enough for a whale shark and all things smaller. It was lit in dim blue light. The middle of the tank had an acrylic tunnel from side-to-side.

"It feels like we're scuba diving."

"You ever been scuba diving?" said Jason.

"No. But this must be what it feels like."

As the giant shadow of the whale shark passed over them, "It's as big as a boat," said Medea. *They must feed them well to keep that one from eating everything in the tank.* Her mind wandered back to days much earlier in her childhood with Morris, spent exploring ditches and streams.

The second part of their exploration, Behind the Seas, was a machinery and all tour of the working parts of the aquarium.

"We used to have a dolphin show, but it got shut down," said the scuba tech as she took off her flippers and headed for the locker room.

The sun was sinking behind them as they made their way across Centennial Park and back to Peachtree Station. They caught the Red Line train. Two stops and they were back at the North Avenue Station.

In the hotel lobby Jason's phone chirped. He had the speaker on as they sat on the lobby club chairs. It felt like a different era to Medea. She looked down at their sneakers and imagined correspondent shoes. It was Jason's mother. Medea picked up a newspaper and tried to ignore the conversation.

"Finally, I get you on the phone. I've got nothing but 'not available' messages."

"Medea and I have been on MARTA a lot. With the buildings and all, WiFi is spotty."

"Who's Medea?"

"Girl from Cheatham High. She's an opera singer. We sat beside each other on the plane."

"What kind of name is that?"

"What?"

"Medea."

"Greek I think."

"Sounds like a Tyler Perry movie. She's not black is she?"

"Mom... stop it. Of course not."

"Well, what is she?"

"It's complicated."

"That's what people say on Facebook when they're shacking up, or gay, or divorced, or a serial killer."

"Mom, why did you call?"

"Can't I call my youngest son? You were supposed to be back yesterday."

"Well, I stayed over another night. There was a good presentation on infinity pools. I got everything completed for the I.B. credit."

"A man, a minister? Has been calling you on the land line. Reverend Whiteacre. I don't know, he's some kind of evangelical."

"What did he say?"

"I'm not sure. That your money had come through? What does that mean?"

"It's for the realty company. He's buying a house. It's not important. I'll call him later."

"What are you doing?"

"Nothing. Sitting in the lobby reading a newspaper."

Medea looked over the newspaper. He leaned over and kissed her.

"When are you coming home? I was worried. You were supposed to be back yesterday."

"Tomorrow morning. I changed my flight. Stop freaking, Mom. Everything's OK."

"Who's this girl? This Medea?"

Medea watched Jason. *She says that like I'm a particularly revolting specimen in a lab jar.*

"She's an opera star. Her voice is fantastic. She got me a ticket to a matinee on Sunday at the Fox Theater."

He leaned over and kissed her again.

"The Fox Theater. Isn't that downtown? Oh my god, I thought you were safe out in the suburbs—Cobb County or somewhere. Theater people are very loose—you need to watch yourself."

"Mom. I'm right downtown in the middle of everything. I'm in imminent danger and you can read all about it in tomorrow's paper. Look, I gotta go. Something's come up. The police are here now."

He clicked off the cell. He leaned toward Medea but she backed away.

"Your mother sounds like a pill."

"We're her life. When she isn't trying to run the state of Georgia through the Cheatham County Republican Party she has her nose so far up our asses she thinks the world smells like baby shit."

"What's that about Reverend Whiteacre?"

"I don't want to jinx it. Just keep your fingers crossed. I'll see him tomorrow when I get back home."

Back at the Carter farm on Wednesday an operatic French aria drifted from her bedroom studio down to the barn where Morris parked the tractor and trailer with a last load of hay. Morris could see darkening clouds coming from the south. A flash of lightning set him to counting to thirteen before he heard the rumble of thunder. As he opened the barn door there came another flash and time to count only to seven before the thunder sounded.

Je veux vivre
Dans le reve qui me enivre

Ce jour encor!
Douce flamme,
Je te garde dans mon ame
Comme un tresor!

With her head full of intoxicating dreams of love kept in her soul like treasure, she practiced and commited the aria to memory. To give herself room to move and breathe in the heat, Medea had stripped to her athletic bra and leggings when an angry Morris burst into the room.

"This is still a working farm! Could I get a little help down at the barn before this hay gets soaked?"

Medea pulled on a work shirt. "You knock before you come in here."

"You just up here singing away, and there's a storm coming up from the Gulf. We're about to lose a whole day's work."

Medea poked his chest with an angry finger. "You knock before you come into my room." She pushed him onto the landing and slammed the door in his face. She watched him stomp back to the barn as she put on boots and work clothes. Then she descended the stairs.

Morris wouldn't let it go. "You think you all high and mighty cause Jason's playing up under your dress."

"You need to mind your own business. I don't have a future in this so-called 'family farm.' That's a cock-up of your future and Daddy Carter's past, no matter how big a fiction that is. It has never done anything for women but fuck us up."

She climbed the ladder into the hayloft as Morris pressed his argument. "I wonder if young Jason'd be so excited about his trophy woman if he knew what low roots you come from. Wonder what he'd do if I walked up to him some night at the truck stop in front of gossiping Alice and all of his white buddies and said, 'Hi, brother-in-law. I'm Morris, Medea's half-black brother. We was both born on the wrong side of the sheets to the town whore. Then dropped off like two stray kittens when the slut skipped town for the casinoes on the Gulf Coast."

Medea grew silent and trembled with rage as she looked down on Morris from the darkness of the hayloft. He looked up at her but the shadows hid her face. If he could have seen it, he would likely have run.

"Send up those bales. When I'm finished here I still have shit to do."

She pulled on work gloves and tied a bandana over her nose and mouth against the dust. Morris turned on the winch and sent the bales up. They both were drenched with sweat when the last bale ascended and Medea wedged it with her foot between the boards of the floor and a supporting post. The winch went into a high pitched whine and Morris shut it off.

"This last bale's stuck," she said. "We could get it loose but I need some help up here."

Morris climbed the ladder to the very narrow space left between the wall of stacked hay and the gimpy wooden rail above the sharps storage area. Medea placed him squatting with his back to the rail and dislodged the stuck bale of hay.

"Here catch." she said and swung the fifty pound bale of hay hard into his chest.

Morris felt his butt bump the rail, felt the rail fall away. He looked back to see sharp spikes rising to meet him. He fell onto a harrow.

Medea peered over the edge with more curiosity than horror at the multiple spikes poking out of his chest. His eyes seemed to try to focus on her as a bubble of blood formed on his lips and burst. "Medea?" he said, and his eyes rolled upward.

Medea's world felt frozen in time. *That heart has always beat near mine since I was born—now it is still. Or is it?* She climbed down the ladder from the loft, opened the gate to the sharps storage area, and reached for his neck. No pulse. Her own emotional numbness surprised her. If she expected something like a tidal wave of grief to wash over her, it did not. *What now?* She dialed 911 on her cell phone. Thunder and lightning cracked outside.

"There's been an accident at the Carter farm. Morris Carter has been killed." She listened to the voice of the Sheriff's Department on the phone.

"Yes. I've checked for a pulse. There's none. He fell from the hayloft onto some bladed equipment. We were stacking hay. Ma'am, I can't get to him to do CPR, he's impaled on a harrow."

Daddy Carter's return from the field just ahead of the storm coincided with the arrival of the Sheriff's Department deputies with their sirens and flashing lights. He tried to pull Morris off the harrow, but the deputies stopped him. His screams of grief were the closest Medea would come to the real thing.

"Sir, please. You can't move a dead body." The deputies caught his arms and moved him away from the sharps storage area.

A social worker, a woman, gently pulled him outside the barn. "Eshu, come with me. Come away from this with me. There's nothing you can do here. Let the deputies do their work."

Upon seeing the loose rail hanging against the wall and the single bale of hay beside Morris's body, Eshu visibly crumbled. "I should have fixed that," he said. "This is all my fault." Lightning turned the interior of the barn an eerie blue and thunder cracked before anybody could count to one.

Investigating the circumstances and assigning blame, if there was any, fell on Detective Erinye. In Medea's mind he would always be associated with her mother's leaving. Ten years on and his conversation with Medea appeared to be something he felt he could just pick up where he left off.

"So, Medea, was there any hostility between yourself and your, er… brother? Half-brother? Now, you have different names, but you're living here under the same roof, is that right?" The approaching storm blew dust around them and set Erinye to wiping his eyes and blowing his nose. "Damn peanuts," he said.

They took shelter on the porch.

"Which of those questions do you want me to answer?"

"Hostility. Was there what we legally call 'animus' between you and Morris?"

"No."

"No?"

"No. There was none."

"You both lived here with Eshu Carter?"

"Yes. Morris lived part time in Athens at the University. He jumped right out of high school into studying agribusiness. He mostly stayed on campus during the week and came home on weekends."

"Had you two recently had any spats, like between…what do you call that? Siblings? Yeah, sibling rivalry?"

"No. This farm is a big place. We both had our bedrooms. If

anything, we had been growing more distant. His life was moving towards the university, and he had a new girlfriend, Shirelle? Yes, Shirelle. I just met her last week at the Three Roads Truck Stop. And I have a new job, singing. I just got back from a gig at the Lyric Opera in Atlanta. Next I'm off to Chicago to sing Juliette in *Romeo et Juliette*."

"What were you two doing in the barn today?"

"Storing hay. There was a storm coming and Morris needed help getting the last of the hay into the barn."

"So you both had a stake in the successful running of the farm?"

"Morris more so than me. He was blood kin to Mr. Carter and stood to inherit the farm. I was no relation, so really I've had one foot out the door here since my suitcase hit the gravel in the driveway. I'm not related except through our mother, who left like ten years ago—but you know that."

Lightning was followed immediately by a clap of thunder, and the rain came pouring down.

Detective Erinye's investigation found the obvious: The horizontal rail had been loose and banged back into place several times. He also found Medea's fingerprints all over the barn, along with Daddy Carter's and Morris's. "Follow the money" was a favorite old saw of his, but there was no money trail—Medea was never included in the will, just Morris. There was also no life insurance policy on Morris. It appeared, if he thought Medea would somehow become closer to inheriting the Carter farm by Morris's death, that the opposite was true. Medea was closer than ever to parting ways. Indeed, the criminal evidence seemed to reinforce actuarial evidence: that farm labor in the last ten years ranks among the top ten causes of work-related deaths.

"Why'd your mother leave?"

"When you find her, you ask her for me."

"Where is she?"

"I believe you asked me this shit ten years ago. The answer then, and the answer now is the same, 'I don't know,' because she left without even saying goodbye."

Detective Erinye turned red, then blue and grabbed his throat. He fumbled with an epi-pen, and dropped it. Medea saw his eyes swell shut and heard his airway close. She grabbed the epi-pen and stabbed him in the stomach with it.

"Help! I need some help up here," she said.

One of the deputies came running with a first aid kit.

In New York, the police-appointed psychiatrist appeared to Medea to be floundering. Perhaps it was because so many psych problems stem from and feed on low self-esteem. While Medea had that for sure, she also had all the grandiosity that came with being a diva. She vacillated between both extremes. As the shrink was starting to see, it could be difficult to figure her out. "Could she, indeed, arrange the murder of her husband's mistress? And what kind of woman could arrange for the disappearance of her own children?" the shrink wrote in her notes.

"This was your second encounter with Detective Erinye?"

"Yes, he questioned Morris and me, as well as Daddy Carter, right after Mama disappeared. It was about the john she cut up and put in the hospital in Emory. I guess he didn't die. At least Erinye left us alone for awhile. I think it embarassed him, to have to ask us questions again immediately after the accident. Well, I say 'us' but there was no us anymore. Maybe that was what got Erinye so fixated on my dysfunctional family of origin and the blended family arrangement that came later— it upset his idea of patriarchy, there being no father at the head of the family. Did you know that in the ancient Middle East the worst crime was patricide?"

Medea's killing of Morris was an impromptu performance. No thinking ahead. No rehearsal. So she'd had no opportunity to think about how she might feel afterwards, how his death might affect her life. She decided her best strategy would be to keep a low profile. After all, her kinship to him had been the one great secret of her life. She bought a dress for the funeral. Dresses in black and gray being only and always for funerals, she looked for something else. A guide to funerals online said that purple was also a color for mourning so she chose one with a color tag that said *aubergine*. The store lights and the lights in her bedroom made the color look pretty on her, but she overheard a girl from the Baptist Church say when she stepped forward to sing eight lines of *Tristes Aprets* from Castor and Pollux, "She looks like a bruised eggplant that's been dropped in the grocery store and put back on the shelf."

Medea was sure that the locals in Cheatham knew little of the myth of Castor and Pollux, so she began with a brief explanation. "In the ancient Greek legend twin brothers were born to Leda, a mortal woman seduced by the lustful god, Zeus. The immortal twin, at the funeral of Castor, his dead brother, bargains in terms of light and darkness with their father, this philandering deity. Pollux renounces light and life to take his brother's place in the underworld for half of each year."

Tristes apprets, pales flambeaux,
Jour plus affreux que les tenebres,
Astres lugubres des tombeaux,
Non, je ne verrai plus que vos clartes funebres.
Toi, qui vois mon coeur eperdu,
Pere du Jour! O Soleil! O mon Pere!
Je ne veux plus d'un bien que Castor a perdu,
Et je renonce a la lumiere.

Medea had sat with the choir so she could sing her solo. The woman to her left, as soon as the minister had closed the service, turned to her and said, "That's an odd choice of music for a mostly protestant funeral."

"Bargaining with God is a bitch."

"This is a church. Profanity isn't necessary."

"This is a funeral home. It's a commercial business. You asked me a question in a value-laden statement. Our ego copes with the present reality of death by looking to the past and the future and imagining what could be changed. Bargaining, rolling dice with God, is a losing game. You're up against a loaded pair, a stacked deck, a fixed roulette wheel. Whatever terms you offer in this light-and-darkness bargain, God will have his pound of flesh. Both Castor and Pollux could again experience life and the underworld, but never again could they do it together."

Medea went through the receiving line like everybody else to shake

Daddy Carter's hand. He was too grief stricken to notice who had sat where, or that she had not sat in the section reserved for family members.

The day after the funeral Medea parked the church van on the gravel driveway and carried boxes upstairs to pack her stuff. She heard Daddy Carter's footsteps on the stairs slowly climbing, heavy like some wounded animal dragging its damaged parts. He stopped at her door.

"What am I gonna tell Tiffany when she comes back and ya'll both gone?"

He's pathetic. It was as close to sympathy as she could get. She opened one drawer of her chest and removed underwear and socks. She dropped them into one of the boxes and taped it shut and then labelled it.

"You still believe, in spite of everything rational, that Tiffany is gonna drive into the driveway one fine day and walk up those steps and say, "Eshu, I'm home"?"

"She gave me the responsibility to raise you and Morris until she got settled with her friends in Seattle."

Medea opened another box and wrote "pants" on the side. Then she opened a drawer of her dresser and dropped a stack of black jeans into the open box and taped it shut. She stacked it on top of the first box.

"She told you, 'Seattle' but she told me and Morris, 'both the coasts.' That would be Atlantic and Gulf coasts, not Pacific. Mama was a liar— if anybody knew her, and nobody really did, they would know that real quick."

"You all the time stirring things up with your brother. Between your mother and me. At school. In the news with your witch club. From your mouth to the ears of God."

"Old man, God's deaf, dumb, and blind."

She opened the third drawer and took out folded sweaters and pullovers. As she did that, the dresser tilted a bit and the long-ago framed picture of her mother fell and cracked. Now faded into unrecognizability, the image of her mother as Detective Erinye's *Wanted: Attempted Murder* subject of a one-time manhunt, lay in shards on the floor. She looked down at it and back at Daddy Carter crying at the door. She bent down and took the faded poster from the broken frame, brushed it off and handed it to him. It was the faded outline of a human head, no recognizable features.

"Something to remember Tiffany by. You know I wasn't the gatekeeper to Tiffany's motel room, but Morris and I were put out to sleep in the car plenty of times, so I have a good idea of the populist nature of mama's trade. Show her the money and she'd assume the position. Don't think you were the only black man she had sex with."

"You still doing it. Trying to drive a wedge between me and Morris."

"If you want to keep on believing a lie you go ahead, but know this: your chances of being Morris's father are about one in several hundred. The way your name got on the birth certificate is it's memorable. Mama had just pushed out a seven-and-a-half-pound baby, she was tired, and that nurse wasn't going away until all the paperwork was done. So she said 'Eshu Francis Carter' just to get the bitch out of her face."

She put the last of her stuff into the last box and taped it. She closed the top on her portable electric piano. She had a new garment bag that held everything from the closet. Her shoes were kept in a hanging bag on the door. As she took that down she touched the measurements on the door from when she was five-years-old.

"She never intended to come back, a fact she covered with lies to hide her intentions from all of us. You, me, Morris—everybody. She was a prostitute and a liar. She never intended to be found."

In several trips, Medea carried the boxes and the electric piano downstairs and put them into the van. Daddy Carter stood on the porch crying with the faded picture in his hand. She walked over to him and gently sat him on the porch step.

"When I was really little Mama once told me a bedtime story about a cow bird. It's a lazy bird that doesn't like to sit on a nest. They're not much on parenting either. They don't like to forage and feed their young. So when it feels it's time to lay eggs it looks around at other nesting birds and when they leave the nest it hops on there and quickly slips one in. Then it pecks a crack in one of the other eggs or rolls it onto the ground. Their fortunate young are larger and heartier than the smaller birds in the parasitized nest so they get the most food and fledge sooner. It's funny to see the unwitting parents, smaller than the fledgling by this time, poking food into it's large beak as it hops away and spreads its wings into low bushes."

Eshu Carter stood up and tore the faded paper image into shreds and let them drop onto the steps. Then he went inside and closed the door.

Medea drove to Miss Alma's place, parked the van in the driveway and carried her things into her newly rented apartment. She looked at the bare, freshly painted space and without enthusiasm said, "Home."

Two weeks later, with the Faith Tabernacle Church Revival half way through its week long run, Medea had been working hard. She dropped off the last passengers from senior fellowship just after one o'clock in the afternoon and realized she had not eaten all day. She stopped by the truckstop.

"You just missed Jason," said Alice.

"Oh my. And I had so hoped to see him."

"He must like redheads. You fit his template of desire, I think."

"Alice, you've been reading too many trashy novels. You need to get a real boyfriend."

"Glad you two aren't seeing each other anymore. He was in here last week a couple of times with a new girlfriend. She looked like you, but as country as a piece of shelled corn and plum dumb."

"You told me he was a player."

"No, you said that. All I did was make an observation of facts."

"He just left?"

"Yeah. He was going out to Singing Water Creek to talk to a man about some land."

"I hope he has good luck. He's working hard to become a developer."

"How's the revival?" said Alice.

"Rev's banking some real money. Alice, I'm too tired to read the menu. Order for me." She folded her arms and rested her head on them.

"Long day?"

"Busy at the Tabernacle. I didn't eat breakfast."

"Blue Plate special is chicken fried steak with gravy and two sides. We could get you a salad too."

"Sounds good. Iced tea to drink."

Alice turned the order in to the cook and brought Medea's salad and tea. Medea dived into it like a starving hog and only came up for air when Alice brought the rest of her food.

"Rumor's been going around in the Farm-To-Table Co-op that after his son got killed in that accident, the old man's just let things go."

"Who is this?"

"Carter I think's his name. His son is the one who tutored you when you were learning to drive."

"Oh yeah. I sang with the choir at his funeral. Very sad."

"Some farm-to-table restaurants up Augusta and Athens way are short of produce without his 300 acres of vegetables and stuff. People say he's so deep in grief he's just letting stuff rot in the field."

"That's land on both sides of Singing Water Creek, right?"

"You know Jason. He reads the newspaper everyday, checking the want ads in Land for Sale, so I told him about it. Seems kind of bad timing, but Jason thought he might go talk to the old man, put a bug in his ear in case he wants to sell. Jason says he got access to a big line of credit through some offshore bank—local lender nobody knows is a multi-millionaire. I heard literally millions of dollars are involved. If it don't work out with Jason, somebody'll develop it. That land is prime right now with people wanting country estates. And this has been Jason's dream for years."

"I hope it works out. Could I get some more tea?"

Alice refilled Medea's glass.

"You ought to come out to the revival. It runs through Sunday. I'm singing a solo. Miss Alma says the choir sounds better than it has in a long time. Rev's raking in the dough every night."

"You know you're my favorite church lady, right? But me and the Lord reached an agreement a long time ago. He'd stay out of the truck stop and I'd stay out of the church. If I showed up at worship it would make too many people nervous."

"How come, Alice?"

"'Cause I know who they were with on Saturday night after the Speakeasy closed."

Later that day, Jason called.

"You want to go on a ride out to the fire tower?"

"I gotta practice for Chicago."

"You sound sore. Did I do something wrong?"

"No. I'm just busy and I have to practice. This libretto is a lot to learn in a short time."

"So, you don't want to see me?"

"Jason, let's just chill for awhile. I like you, but you need to grow your morals to catch up with your hormones."

"What does that mean?'

"I'll let you think about it. We'll talk after Chicago."

She clicked off her cell and walked to the gazebo in the backyard. Miss Alma had surrounded the wooden structure with flowers and broken columns in a half circle. *What a pretty and peaceful place—it feels timeless, like it belongs to a different era.*

With the revival done and many new members added to the Faith Tabernacle Church, the Rev reluctantly let Medea have time off to travel to Chicago. She practiced the role of Juliette with the director in a small studio in the opera house.

"Open your eyes wide to lift your voice. Juliette is terrified. She is in her bedroom, but staring at the tomb, confronting her most horrible fears about drinking poison. What if she awakens before Romeo comes? Will she be pursued by the barely cold corpse, the ghost of Tybalt there in the dim light of the family tomb? Thousands of years of bones are buried there—that's a lot of family history. And we begin," the director said.

Medea sang:

> *Dieu, quel frisson court dans mes vienes!*
> *Si ce breuvage etait sans pouvoir, etc.*

"You have a light quality to your passagio and head voice."

"I use a steamer, and I don't do dairy before singing. Miss Alma, my voice coach, taught me the basics back in the ninth grade."

"Also, you are good with conveying emotions. Did you take drama classes?"

"No. I'm a natural liar. I feel like I've been acting all of my life."

The director leaned his head to one side and appeared to have a question, but Medea stopped him.

"Personal issues. Small southern town."

"OK. Let's continue."

Medea sang:

> *Amour, ranime mon courage,*
> *Et de mon coeur chasse l'effroi, etc.*
> *O Romeo, je bois a toi!*

"So she finds courage and drinks to her lover, Romeo. You have a deeper, more dramatic strength in your passagio and chest voice for the heft of the 'poison aria.' Couple that with the lighter requirements of 'Juliette's Waltz' and it's quite a package. It's a really desireable set of abilities in a lyric coloratura. "

"Thank you. Singing is what I do best."

"Knock off. Get some rest. I think our opera fans are in for quite a treat tonight."

Medea took a boat tour of the bridges and buildings of downtown along the Chicago River. Doing touristy things helped her to relax before the performance. The tour began and ended near her hotel. Then she took a brisk walk along the waterfront of Grant Park. Having grown up on a farm, she liked to walk out of doors. As she took the elevator to her hotel room, she compared the experience to Atlanta. *This would have been more fun with Jason.*

She returned to Cheatham with contracts signed, and new business connections. She would go in the near future to Sarasota, Los Angeles, San Francisco, Seattle, Nashville and Tanglewood. Her repertoire now included three roles if you added her current project, The Merry Widow. People really liked her voice, and, from a moderately full house on the first night, the rest of the performances were sold out. The critics gave her good reviews.

Deer season had begun in Georgia, so Medea had to curb her walks down country roads and through the fields and woods. Distant gunfire, shotguns and rifles, began with sunrise, and made her hesitant to even sit outside in the gazebo. Staying indoors so much gave Medea cabin fever, so when Jason called late in the day she was actually glad to hear his voice.

"Want to go for a ride? We could really blast this Onkyo."

"Sure."

"Why don't I pick you up about five? We could watch the sunset."

"Sounds like fun."

"Just one thing, I don't know where you live."

"Oh, I live in a church van. I have a sleeping bag and a camp stove. There's a mini-bar refrigerator and a little TV."

"No, really," Jason said.

"OK, seriously. The Rev has a sex dungeon in the basement of the church and when he's not using it I can crash on a mattress down there."

"You're not going to be serious are you?"

"Not at all," said Medea. "OK here's the truth. I'm really an international opera diva who travels the world from great opera house to great opera house and I live out of an endless series of hotels—sort of like Sartre's *No Exit.*"

"What's that?"

"You don't know Jean Paul Sartre?"

"No."

"You don't read much, do you?"

"Land for Sale in the want ads."

"Since I legally became an emancipated minor I've lived at Route 2, Box 18. Alma Williams is the property owner, she's my voice coach. It's about three miles north of town. I have the garage apartment."

"That's close to where Mr. Carter's farm is."

"He's a couple of miles further on. We're a little closer to town. Call me if you get lost."

Jason found the place. "Want to go out to the firetower? I know you nixed that before you left, but I was thinking…"

"Don't overthink things, Jason. Sounds great."

Medea put Franz Lehar's "The Merry Widow" into the sound system and the haunting legend of Vilja filled the cab. Medea sang for Jason:

> *There once was a Vilja, a maid of the wood,*
> *A hunter espied her alone as she stood,*
> *The spell of her beauty upon him was laid;*
> *He looked and he longed for the magical maid.*
> *For a sudden tremor ran throughout the smitten man,*
> *And he sighed as a hapless lover can:*

> *Vilja, O Vilja! O witch of the wood! Would I not die for you, dear, if I could?*
> *Vilja, O Vilja, my love and my bride! Softly and sadly he sighed.*

"I used to try to stand outside the practice studios, in the hall at school, and listen to you sing. The hall cop always busted me and sent me to study hall. So having you sing for me alone is a dream-come-true."

"We're not done yet," said Medea.

> *The wood maiden smiled, but no answer she gave,*
> *Just beckoned him into the shade of the cave;*
> *The lad had not known of such rapturous bliss,*
> *No maiden of mortals so sweetly could kiss!*
> *As before her feet he lay, she vanished into the wood away,*
> *And he called vainly till his dying day,*

> *Vilja, O Vilja! Oh witch of the wood! Would I not die for you, dear, if*
> *I could?*
> *Vilja, O Vilja! My love and my bride! Softly and sadly he sighed.*

"That's so beautiful, and so sad," Jason said.

"It's from 'The Merry Widow,' an operetta I'll be singing in two weeks in Nashville."

Jason had some firewood in the back of the pickup, and he had brought binoculars. When they got to the abandoned structure deep in the national forest, he dug a firepit and laid the wood in it. They climbed the firetower, which was closed down due to government cuts. The lock had been broken on the hatch door in the floor, so they climbed in. As they looked around they could see Cheatham in the distance, the sunset so red it looked as if it could burn the whole county. Singing Water Creek lay in the distance below them and Medea could see Daddy Carter's farm on both sides of it. Through binoculars she followed the creek to the ruins of the water-powered cotton gin. From that point, the land rose sharply, and she could see from this perspective the length of the old dam. *What a beautiful spot for a house.*

Jason had swiped a bottle of bourbon from his dad's bar and they sipped from the bottle as they sat on a table and watched the sunset.

"Something big has happened," he said.

"Oh?"

"I got financing to buy as much land as I can find."

"People around here think God stopped making land on the third day. They generally pass it along in a will when they die. Usually to the oldest boy, but more recently it's split up between all of the kids," Medea said.

"I want to build my house on Singing Water Creek. That's why this acreage is so special. It's sweet. There's an old man named Carter, Eshu Carter, whose only son died recently in a farm accident."

"I sang at his funeral. He went to our school. You've seen him, in fact—he's the one who came into the truckstop with his girlfriend, Shirelle?"

"Right. I remember. Well, since the boy died the old man has let the farm go to hell. He's so deep in mourning he doesn't even bathe and shave anymore."

"That's sad. Doesn't he have anyone? Any other relatives?"

"Apparently not. Maybe he's a widower or something. I've talked to him about selling. He has about three hundred acres on both sides of Singing Water Creek. That's named after Cherokee Indians. He's willing to sell it."

He pointed as Medea looked toward the creek which resembled a rivulet of liquid fire cutting the earth in half, or perhaps, she thought, it looked like blood. Jason offered her a drink of bourbon from the bottle. Her head was floating.

"The development's gonna be called 'Singing Water.'"

"I like that."

Jason took her hands and kissed her. His mouth tasted sweet like bourbon, with an underlying mint taste of toothpaste.

"I'm in love with you," he said.

"You poor man," she said and kissed him back. "Don't love me—you'll regret it."

Back on the ground, Jason lit the fire and spread out his quilt. The moon, slightly past full, rose above the horizon. Bourbon warmed their fingers as they unbuttoned and unzipped their clothes.

They lay naked on the patchwork quilt in front of the fire. Medea looked up into his eyes. *He's handy with unsnapping a bra.* He turned her onto her side and pressed his erection between her legs from behind. His weight against her back pushed her nose into the quilt and she took a deep breath. *I guess this is it.*

"What's that smell?" she said.

"What smell?"

She pulled away from him and smelled the quilt again.

"That smell like somebody's booty. Don't you wash this thing in between screwing people?"

"I took it camping last week. Maybe it's from then."

"If you can't operate a washer, maybe you can give your trophy quilt to your Cub Scout mama and she can do it for you."

"Medea, what are you talking about?"

"Some men carve notches on their bedpost for every woman they screw, but this takes a prize—a butt mark for every piece of ass."

She stood and threw up as she did. Then she pulled on her clothes.

"Get dressed and take me home," she said.

On the night of the new moon Medea sat in the screened gazebo smoking a cigarette and thinking deep, angry thoughts. The empty circle of the moon rose over the half circle of column fragments. She arranged three candles into a triangle and lit them along with some incense. She stood and raised her arms toward the dark moon. Then she tapped her chest over her heart three times. She tapped her lips with her fingers three times. Then she tapped her forehead three times and extended her arms again, palms up toward the moon.

"Hear me, O Hecate, Goddess of the moon. You're my goddess, you're my girl. I need your wisdom."

Medea heard a canine whine and panting just outside the screen. A large female, alpha wolf put her nose to the screen. Medea pressed her hand against the screen for the wolf to smell. The wolf sniffed and sat on its haunches in front of the door. Six other she-wolves circled the gazebo and sat looking out in all directions. Footsteps approached in the dark and all the wolves stood and wagged their tails. A woman in a dark cowl stood at the door.

"I am Hecate, goddess of the moon, crossroads, women's issues, hearth and home."

Medea opened the screen door and Hecate pulled up a chair across from her with the three lit candles between them on the floor. The flickering light made it difficult to see her face and the dark cowl appeared as shadows in motion. Her image appeared in constant change.

"Do you have a cigarette?" she asked.

Medea gave her one and she lit it off one of the candles.

"How's Lina?" she asked.

Medea found her tongue, but felt she was wandering in a fugue.

"She's OK. The unwanted pregnancy is ended. She's living with her maternal aunt, and her stepfather is in jail charged with rape of a minor."

She lit a cigarette as well.

"I need your guidance," Medea said.

"You do pretty well on your own."

"I don't know what to do about Jason."

"He cannot be faithful to one woman. He is like the male wolf who services all of these girls." She gestured around the circle of wolves. One growled, one yawned, one barked and one whined. "What is it that you desire?" asked Hecate.

"I want acceptance, I'm tired of living outside the circle. I want people to drive by my house and say, 'That's Medea Royal's house. She's a famous opera singer.' And I want my name on the deed to three hundred acres of the Singing Water development."

"You think I'm a genie living in a lamp? Just rub it and I pop out with three wishes?" She took a deep drag off the cigarette. "God this is good," Hecate said.

As she stubbed out the cigarette the wolves stood, circled the gazebo and formed two columns toward the woods. "I'll look into it. You need to be more careful what you leave behind. There's not always a Mexican housekeeper to clean up your messes."

Medea awoke uncertain of how much time had passed. She was chilled in the fall night air. All three votive candles had burnt out. She climbed the stairs to her apartment and pulled the covers over herself. She immediately fell asleep.

"What a strange dream," she said aloud when she awoke. It was nearly ten a.m. and the sounds of hunters filled the woods and fields all around. She made coffee in the kitchen and walked down to the gazebo. No candles. No ashtray. Two cane bottom chairs sat neatly placed on each side of a rattan table.

She sat down at the table and drank her coffee. The sunlight lit up a dull, pearl-colored spot on the floor. Medea knelt to check it out. She scraped it with her fingernail and held it up to the light—paraffin.

Two days later, Miss Alma loaded stuff into her car. Another school day. She saw Medea having coffee in the gazebo and came over.

Miss Alma said, "How's the apartment? Is everything in working order?"

"All the appliances seem to be working fine. I'm not much of a cook so I really haven't tried all the burners and the oven yet. They're delivering and hooking up the washer-dryer today."

"Good. Let me know if something needs my attention. The man who cuts the grass said he believes he saw wolf tracks out here. He thought wolves were extinct in Georgia, they may have been dogs. Whatever, he says don't leave any food scraps or garbage where they could feed on it. We are really close to the national forest."

"No food scraps. Got it. This looks good with the landscaping—kind of like those Mediterranean postcards."

"I noticed you had been burning votive candles? Please be careful. The gazebo would go up like a lit match. I'd hate for you to get hurt."

"Thanks for the heads up."

"Well, I'm off to play school marm. See you this evening."

"Have a good day."

Medea made good progress on memorizing the libretto and score for The Merry Widow. The delivery truck brought the washer-dryer and the guys had just hooked it up in the garage, when Jason called.

"Want to get some good, home-cooked food?"

"Sure. Truck stop?"

"My mom's cooking. She wants to meet you."

Medea's stomach knotted up. *She'll know everything. She's a ferret savant.*

"What'll I wear?"

"Jeans and a pullover. Your usual will be fine. We're very informal."

"Oh God. Who will be there?"

"Just you and me, and mom and dad. You'll like them, they're nice. Mom said if you had me for a three day weekend in Atlanta, she wants to meet you."

Singing for three thousand people was a pleasure and a thrill for Medea, but the thought of supper with Jason's parents made the lower part of her back sweat and sent her tearing through her closet.

"I don't have a thing to wear," she said to herself in the mirror and sat down on the floor.

At the door, Mrs. Carpenter extended her hand. She was casually dressed, coiffed, made up. Her social skills were country club, old Republican Party, Episcopalian. "I've heard so much about you, Medea."

Don't tremble. Don't throw up. "Jason tells me you were a Cub Scout Mom for him and his brothers."

"The boys all enjoyed scouts. I was never happier than when I was doing something with them. Something to drink? Tea? Coke?"

"Tea's good."

The Carpenter home was comfortable in a lived-in sort of way, twenty-eight years she would learn, and well-maintained.

In the kitchen, Medea and Mrs. Carpenter prepared supper for the table.

"What kind of name is Medea anyway?" said Mrs. Carpenter.

"Suburban Atlanta," said Medea. "Irish traveller?"

"It sounds Greek."

"I think I'm Irish." Medea looked at the freckles on her hands and held them up for Mrs. Carpenter to see. She pulled a lock of hair over her eyes and inspected its thick, curly texture and deep red color. "Pretty sure I'm Irish."

"Don't you know?"

"No." *Don't you KNOW?* "My father died when I was a baby. He was killed in Afganistan."

"Didn't your mother tell you?"

"Mama died when I was five. That's when I went into foster care."

"Surely your mother must have told you something?"

"Mrs. Cleaver, ummm, I mean Carpenter, not everyone has your secure, suburban, middle class privileges. My upbringing was a tragic mess. If my mama told me anything, or gave me any heirlooms, I don't remember it and I don't have them. I remember very little of my childhood and I'd prefer to forget even that."

Over supper, Mr. Carpenter made an announcement.

"I've been hired as a partner in a Naples development. Naples, Florida I mean."

"This is the first I've heard about it," said Mrs. Carpenter. "Shouldn't we have talked about this before our company arrived?"

"I just got word today."

"I didn't even know you were interviewing," said Mrs. Carpenter.

"I wanted to know it would pan out before I told you."

"Great, Dad. Congratulations. When does this start?"

"Soon. They've broken ground already."

"We've lived here twenty-eight years. I had hoped to see my grandchildren in this house."

"They can come to Naples. We'll drive to Disney World. It will be a period of adjustment, but it's only one state away."

Mrs. Carpenter folded her napkin beside her plate, "Excuse me," she said, and left the table.

"God, I was afraid this is how she would react."

Jason started to get up. "I should go see if she's all right."

Medea said, "I'll go."

"But you don't know her," said Jason.

"It may be a good time to get acquainted," said Medea.

Medea knocked on the bedroom door.

"Yes?"

"It's Medea. May I come in?"

"Sure."

Medea moved a box of Kleenex from the bedside table closer to Mrs. Carpenter and took a seat in the closest chair.

"Change can be hard," she said to Mrs. Carpenter.

"Tell me about it. Twenty-eight years here. Raised three sons in this house and now he wants to move." She took a Kleenex and wiped her eyes.

"Naples? That's Florida, not Italy, right?"

"Florida," said Mrs. Carpenter.

"I hear both have man-made canals."

"Yeah, and Florida has toxic algae, alligators, giant lizards, pythons, for God's sake, and sharks. If my grandchildren, if...ever? If my grandchildren come to visit I'm not letting them near that water, no matter how pretty."

"It must feel hard to give up twenty-eight years of living in the same place."

"My friends. The country club. This house. I wanted to grow old here. Hell, I'm forty-two, I'm halfway there."

"Change can be a bitch."

"It's a bitch."

"Or an opportunity. Your husband is pushing fifty and he has a skill set that's in demand. A lot of middle-aged guys are like dinosaurs five minutes after the asteroid hit. They put their heads down and keep on grazing, then wonder, if their reptilian brain can wrap around wonder, where the sunshine went."

"I can't look at positives right now, Medea. Sorry."

"No, your losses right now are too great. You have to grieve that."

"How did you get to be so wise at such a young age?"

"Good student. I took international baccalaureate psych before I dropped out."

"Good grades? How are you classified?"

"When I dropped out I had a 4.0 gpa. I got the GED soon as the next test became available. I need to get into some conservatory classes I think. My voice coach is my old high school chorus teacher. Sometimes I think we're reaching the end of what she knows about the operatic voice."

"I raised three kids all my adult life, and now they're heading out. Jason's the last one. So far no grandkids."

"They were 'headed out' the minute they were born. That's life. No sooner do they get to us than they're headed away from us. Creeping, then crawling, walking, bicycling. They're gone. Life is change. If you let go of fear and grab onto life in all of its change, it's good."

"You must have moved several times growing up?"

"You could say that. From the moment my suitcase hit the driveway I never knew whether to put my stuff in the chest of drawers, or back into the suitcase. Change was the constant with me."

Mrs. Carpenter fixed her make up and she and Medea went back to the den where Jason and Mr. Carpenter had looked up Naples online.

"I'm making coffee and we have dessert. Who wants some banana cream pie?" Mrs. Carpenter asked, and hugged her husband.

At Medea's apartment the next day, Jason raised the idea of cooking classes for Medea.

"But I don't want to learn to cook," said Medea after Jason handed her a brochure on cooking classes.

"Mom thinks it would be fun, and she wants to bond with you. She says we will have to feed our kids."

"Whoa! Who said anything about kids? Is this some kind of backhanded proposal? I don't want kids. And I certainly don't want to be married."

"Mama says they'll need vegetables."

"Vegetables are overrated. We'll take them to a salad bar. Besides did you ever know a kid who willingly ate vegetables?"

"I just want you two to get along."

"Well, tell Mrs. Beaver Cleaver to make an effort. She could start by minding her own business."

"We are her business. Her only business. She never worked. She was a housewife, a mom, a den mother."

"We'll get a microwave. Frozen dinners are so convenient. So balanced. It'll be cheaper than the classes, and I won't have to cook."

"I'll help with cooking and cleaning. I'm a very domesticated kind of guy."

"I don't want to be a housewife and mother—that's your mother. I'm a professional woman. I want to sing. Opera is my life, my only desire."

They hugged and kissed.

"Whatever you want, Medea. I love you so much. Sing if you want, travel, I'll take care of the kids. We'll get a nanny. We'll get a cook."

"Oh, Jason, you finally understand." She placed her hands on his cheeks and kissed his mouth.

Jason lunged into that like a ravenous wolf into red meat.

"Yes, Medea. I do understand." He kissed her ears and neck. He pulled her hair loose. "Oh my God! I love you. I love you. I love you."

"Yes, Jason. I love you too." She unbuttoned the top buttons of her blouse. Jason ripped off the rest and unfastened her bra. Clothes seemed like such a barrier to them both as they headed toward the bed, crashed naked onto it and consummated their lust in just under two minutes.

"Oh my god!" said Medea.

"Whew," said Jason.

"Water," said Medea as she walked naked to the kitchen. She brought back two bottles of ice cold water and tossed one onto Jason's belly.

"Ooooh!" he exclaimed.

She looked at his penis. "Ohhh, it got so small. Here, let me warm it." She straddled his pelvis. As she opened her bottle of water, took a long drink, and pulled back her red hair she gazed down on him. *We're lovers.*

He reached for her breasts. She thought of all the beautiful paintings she had ever seen of women's breasts, and leaned forward. She prayed for the grace of gravity and thought of ripe pears, nursing madonnas, courtesans with mirrors, *Les Demoiselles d' Avignon*, Playboy. *Hecate, help me out here. I don't know what I'm doing.* She bent forward and kissed Jason's mouth spilling cold water onto his chest.

He rolled her onto her back. "My turn to cool you down." Then he poured water from his plastic bottle onto her breasts and lapped it like a dog as he sat on her pelvis and held her wrists. This sexual play and exploration of each other's body went on for about two hours until they collapsed into exhaustion. He held her from behind and she held his arms and hands over her breasts and kissed them as they drifted into sleep.

When they awoke, Medea was lying in a wet spot of blood. "My God. My period is usually so regular." She woke Jason up and stripped the sheets from the bed, then took them downstairs to the garage to the washer. She was crying when he came looking for her.

"It's OK. Shhhh. It's Ok. This was your first time?"

"Yes. I'm so embarassed."

He hugged her and lifted up her chin so that she looked him in the eye. He wiped tears from her cheeks. "God, girl. I love you."

The next day, Jason drove her to the regional airport for her flight to Nashville. "I'll see you in a week," he said.

"Bye, lover boy." She kissed him. He stopped at the concourse gate and watched her retreating back. When she reached her boarding area, she turned and blew him another.

In Nashville all the dates to The Merry Widow sold out and the engagement was extended by one performance. Medea was $10,000 richer. The last day, a well-dressed man with a Dutch accent, introduced himself. Mr. LeJean Saphier, Entertainment, read his business card.

"Do you have representation, Miss Royal?"

"No. I really don't. It has just all landed in my lap this year. I won the Georgia All State Competition, and the calls started."

"Do you have professional goals set for yourself?"

"Well, everybody I know is in college now. I feel like I need to take my singing to the next level, whatever that may be, you know—tougher roles like Queen of the Night, Bellini, Donizetti, the bel canto stuff. My voice teacher is my high school choir teacher—I feel kind of disloyal saying this, but I think I've outgrown her abilities."

"Who manages your contracts?"

"I do. As much as they're managed."

"Miss Royal, based on what you've just told me I can offer you managerial services to include getting you more engagements, much better venues, better financial rewards, accomodations on the road of at least three-star hotels, restaurants, and a voice coach who travels with you to see that you are ready for your performances, and that you won't hurt your voice."

"Wow. That's a lot to promise."

"I want you to think about it. It's not a promise, it's a professional contract. I've watched you over three engagements now, and I think you're the caliber of entertainer we would like to represent."

Mr. Saphier gave her a brochure. "When you've had time to read our benefits brochure and think it over, contact me."

"I know it's bad manners to ask this on the first meeting, but how much is your commission?"

"Standard rate, twenty percent."

"You have a wonderful accent. Where are you from?"

"I was born in the Netherlands, Amsterdam. Dual citizen of the U.S. and, most recently, Canada. So, you see, I'm quite an international fellow. A citizen of the world, if you will."

Medea pulled her robe around her legs for warmth and sat on them. From the breakfast nook Jason had built in her kitchen she watched him cook.

"No eggs for me. Just coffee," she said.

"I'm cooking breakfast for us. I want this to be a special morning."

"Go ahead. Cook whatever you want. I'll just have coffee."

"I've made this huge omelette, with toast and fruit salad."

"Fruit salad sounds interesting. Where did you find fruit this time of year?"

"Supermarket. It's probably from Central America."

Jason plated food and set it on the table.

"What a pretty fruit salad. I may keep you."

Medea held out her coffee mug for a refill.

Jason put a tiny, gift wrapped box beside her coffee mug.

"I love you, you know?"

"Silly man, I've warned you."

She opened the gift, a very large diamond engagement ring.

Jason knelt beside her on the kitchen floor.

"Medea Royal, will you marry me? Will you become Mrs. Jason Carpenter and make a family with me?"

"Ohhh, Jason, what a lovely ring. You're sweet and so thoughtful."

She slipped the ring on her finger and held it up for him to see. Then she took his hands in hers and kissed them. She loved the smell of his hands—soap and breakfast.

"I've told you I don't want to be a wife and mother, but you're persistent. I should give this ring back to you rather than wear it and give you false hope."

"I'll take false hope. I'll take any kind of hope I can get. Will you just wear it and think about it? Think about marrying me?"

She kissed him and rubbed away crocodile tears.

"One morning I shall eat red meat and eggs for breakfast. You'll be the first to know, because you'll awaken with a hole in your chest where your heart once was."

After breakfast Medea played the musical prelude to *Habanera* and sang:

> *L'amour est un oiseau rebelle*
> *Que nul ne peut apprivoiser...etc*
> *L'amour est enfant de Boheme*
> *Il n'a jamais jamais connu de loi.*
> *Si tou ne m'aimes pas, je t'aime.*
> *Si je t'aimes, prende garde a toi*

Without giving Jason an answer to his proposal of marriage, she flew the following week to Sarasota to sing the leading soprano role in Carmen.

Medea continued her employment at the Tabernacle. Singing was lucrative, but it wasn't yet dependable. Opening letters and sorting out the Rev's correspondence made little sense to her. It seemed as much investment portfolios as the work of God. One letter caught her eye and all systems on her radar sat up and noticed—it was from a newly formed corporation called "Singing Water Country Estates" and it was signed by Jason Carpenter.

Hey, Rev!

I loved the fishing trip. Your Scout boat is awesome. Here's the new letterhead. We got the transfer of title notarized. Mr. Carter wants to leave Georgia, says the $10,000/acre (Nearly $3,000,000) we paid for the farm will get him set up in Chicago. He wants to open a farm-to-city market right near the lakefront in Chi-town. University of Illinois at Chicago is within walking distance, so that should be sweet for him.

Partner, Golden Fleece Realty is ready to break ground on this development as soon as you and I can talk to the Mayor. I'm wording a press release—no mention of you, of course. There was once a water-powered cotton gin on the place, and the old earthen dam is still a raised, long mound. What I propose is a new dam across Singing Water Creek that will form a lake. We can build this in time for the rainy season, and farmers downstream won't even notice.

All you and I need to decide now is how big the lots will be and how many. We're gonna be rich, dude! Can you say, "Lakefront Property?"

With the Rev out for coffee and the safe open in his office, Medea made a picture of the name on the offshore accounts, the number of each account, its balance and the name of the banks. It occurred to her there must be a reason for so much secrecy. If she could figure how to apply it, it might mean leverage in getting better pay for herself and Miss Alma, who had not had a raise in ten thankless years of directing a choir that, until recently, had sounded like caterwauling harpies. This deal was so good, the men could not lose, but it was time, as well, for the women to win one.

As the weather warmed, Medea and Miss Alma got together on a Saturday to work in the flower beds around the gazebo and beside the driveway.

"I'm an executive secretary for a very messy man," Medea told Alma.

"He's a bamboozler," said Miss Alma. "I've known him for ten years. He wore his off-the-rack suit and cheap brogans into town in an old Toyota. He had a preacher's certificate from a Bible college in Dallas."

"He gets statements from five offshore banks. I'm not supposed to open those."

"Offshore banks is about his hayseed sleazy style. He probably has a local bank for the Tabernacle account—whatever he doesn't skim off."

"I'm a grocery clerk in the food pantry, a social worker making referrals for poor people, and I sing on Sunday. That's all I'm hired to do is sing."

"And you do it beautifully. Our membership has tripled in a year."

"The offshore accounts are in the Cayman Islands, Hong Kong and a bunch of other places in Latin America, China, and the Caribbean."

They took a break and sat in the gazebo.

"I have juice or tea," said Miss Alma.

"Iced tea," said Medea. "If I thought it was dependable I'd quit the Rev and go full time with the opera singing." She took off her gloves and wiped sweat off her forehead.

"How's that going for you?"

"I get $8,000 to $10,000 per engagement. That's four or five performances."

"Wow. Congratulations."

"I hit the high notes. F6, up and down and up again with dexterity. Bel canto. Mr. Saphier has a voice coach on the gigs. I'm expanding my repertoire. But, I get a feeling it won't last. I can't explain it. Nothing good has ever lasted for me."

"I heard something good down at the Feed and Seed while I was getting garden stuff yesterday."

"Oh? Tell it—I need some good news," said Medea.

"You remember Eshu Carter, the farmer who sold the developer land for that new ritzy subdivision? His son got killed a couple of years ago in a farming accident?"

"I remember, yes. His son, Morris, was a couple of grades ahead of me at Cheatham High. I sang with the choir at his funeral."

"Well, Eshu's landed on his feet. He used the money he got from the sale of the farm and bought an empty building in downtown Chicago. He married a Latina woman and they've turned the place into what they call a Farm-to-City Market. Eshu buys directly from farmers in several states around there. They like him—he's one of them and gives them a better price per pound than corporate wholesalers. He tells the regular ones what kind of produce he needs months in advance, and they grow it and truck it in. UIC's near there, and a thriving Farm-to-Table bunch of restaurants that source their produce from Eshu every week—whatever's in season. Buskers play their music for tips. The Latina keeps him supplied with Central American refugees to package and sell the produce. And various craftsmen rent booths from him to sell their wares. It's an event on Saturday and Sunday mornings right downtown, near Lake Michigan."

"I didn't know Eshu, except through Morris. Glad things worked out."

At four o'clock in the morning of the day she was to fly to Santa Fe, Medea awoke nauseated. Coffee didn't stay down, tea didn't work, chicken bouillion landed in the toilet.

"I'm going to have to call and cancel," she said to Jason. "This has never happened to me—I've always been able to sing."

"Maybe flu? We'll call the doctor when they open."

She tried to sing, but her voice was dry and thin in the upper ranges. *I sound like an old woman.* Her tongue became sore at the base so her dexterity was off. She decided to go see Miss Alma.

"I think you may be pregnant," said Miss Alma.

"You've never been pregnant. How do you know?"

"Well I've taught for more than thirty years. I've seen pregnant women try to sing before. It's a disaster."

"Oh my god. What am I going to do?"

"What's wrong is hormones. You have progesterone making a placenta and preparing to nurture the fetus in utero. Your estrogen is out of balance," Miss Alma said. "The changes in your body are reflected in your voice as well. No part of us operates in isolation from its other parts. You will have a deeper voice, little ability to sing high notes, a sore tongue at the base, and you'll have no dexterity. Forget the word 'coloratura' for the next nine months—the fireworks aren't there."

She went to the urgent care clinic and did the pee test and had blood drawn. Sure enough, she was pregnant.

She returned to Miss Alma's sofa. Jason was building houses, and she did not want to be alone. "A few weeks after delivery, if you don't give the baby the breast," Alma said, "your hormones will return to normal. Your voice will have a broader range, and many women feel they have never sung better."

"Congratulations, even though you probably don't feel very good about it. Your insurance policy covers all things ob/gyn," said Mr. Saphier on the phone. "I'll cancel your dates and work up a press release. We will frame this as a welcome event, as good news. They will regard you as professional in your approach to your work, and they will welcome you back after your successful delivery."

Back at home in her apartment she put her head in Jason's lap and took his hand. "Let's get married," she said.

"When?"

"Soon as possible. We'll tell your mom and dad afterwards. I don't want a big ceremony. We need to be married so you can make medical decisions, and…" she started to cry, "I want this baby to be an heir, not a bastard."

The nausea persisted. Medea lost weight and had to be put in the hospital for intravenous therapy. They got the hospital chaplain to perform their nuptials, with the charge nurse and Miss Alma standing as witnesses.

"You're gaining weight," said the nurse as Medea stepped off the scales.

"That's good. I haven't had anything solid to eat for two weeks."

"That's not good. You're swelling, and your blood pressure is rising."

Jason, with Mrs. Carpenter along all the way from Naples to fret

Medea's nerves, took Medea to an ob/gyn doctor in Atlanta who specialized in at-risk pregnancies. Medea felt like she was on a flight from hell.

"Are you comfortable? Do you need to pee? I had to pee every fifteen minutes with mine," said Mrs. Carpenter. "I have the protein test strips here in my purse. You just let me know."

"I think I do need to go to the restroom," said Medea. Her mother-in-law was right behind her.

"Just take it easy, nice and slow. Everything will be fine," Mrs. Carpenter said. So there were two women in a tiny toilet, testing Medea's pee, which colored positive for protein.

"Oh my God. Oh My God. OH MY GOD! Help!" screamed Mrs. Carpenter, and pulled the emergency cord. She looked like a red-faced apoplectic when the flight attendant got the toilet door unlocked.

Sputtering Ps at the flight attendant, Mrs. Carpenter grabbed her by her uniform. "She's pre-eclamptic, pregnant, and pissing positive for protein. But they're married now."

Medea was crouched over the toilet protecting her mid-section from her hysterical traveling companion.

"Please calm yourself, ma'am," said the flight attendant. "Pregnant women with pre-eclampsia always test positive for protein in their urine." To Medea, she asked, "Are you all right? You're not bleeding?"

"I'm fine. That's the reason for this flight. We're going to the ob/gyn specialist in Atlanta. If you could just get her back to her seat. Look in her purse. She has a prescription for a sedative. If you could get her to take one all would be well."

Mrs. Carpenter snored through the remainder of the flight. The registration staff at the hotel had to bring her inside and up to her room in a wheelchair.

"Let's leave her a note telling her where she is. She can order room service if she wakes up hungry," said Jason.

"And that we'll be back from the doctor shortly. I'd hate for her to worry." said Medea.

Jason drove her to Emory University Hospital Midtown. They stopped at Valet Parking where an attendant with a wheelchair met them at the curb.

"Seems odd to be here in a wheelchair when just a few months back we were running all over downtown," said Medea.

In the lab collection area, "More needles," said Medea as the lab tech laid out collection tubes and sorted through lab slips.

"We can get all of these in one stick," said the tech. "Make a fist for me."

Through the labyrinth of the hospital, an ultrasound, and thorough physical, done by an advance practice registered nurse, preceeded the conference with the specialist.

"You're having twins, Mrs. Carpenter," said the specialist.

"Mrs. Carpenter's back at the hotel, please call me Medea."

"Medea, the ultrasound showed two placentas, each with an embryo. It's too early yet to know their gender." She pointed to two kidney beans in the pictures. "That's a tail, not a penis. It appears you are about five or six weeks pregnant."

"Twins?" asked Jason.

"Fraternal twins—each has its own placenta. That's the source of the problem, the placentas. Exact reason is unknown. Do you have a family history of pre-eclampsia?"

"My mother died when I was five. I know nothing, really, about my family tree."

"Pre-eclampsia can become life-threatening. Your pregnancy is already high risk, therefore you legally have access to pregnancy termination after a 24-hour waiting period. Have you considered this option?"

"No, we don't want that," said Jason.

"Medea, it's your choice. It's your health. What do you think?"

Medea was silent and thoughtful for a full minute. She looked at Jason, then the doctor. "If I get further along and we really get into trouble, is abortion still an option?"

"In Georgia, if the mother's life in in danger, yes."

"We will continue with the pregnancy and see how things go," Medea said.

"Ok. The presence of twins is itself a possible causative factor in pre-eclampsia. Whatever, the treatment is the same: medication for blood pressure, daily B.P. monitoring, bedrest mostly on the left side, daily weight and ankle measurement. We may want to monitor the fetal heart rate as the pregnancy progresses. Our goal is to get the pregnancy to thirty-seven weeks' gestation and then to evaluate the risks of continuing, if possible, or delivery by c-section. If you are currently at six weeks gestation, we have thirty-one more weeks of close monitoring."

"Am I going to have to come back here every couple of weeks, or something?"

"No, we have a community pre-natal clinic in Cheatham with a very good advance practice registered nurse. She specialized when she was here in high-risk pregnancy. You'll see her weekly. She will keep me up on your progress. You'll probably see me monthly.

Mrs. Cheatham was awake when they returned to the hotel. She came right to Medea's bedside. "Are you thinking of aborting this baby?"

"It's a high risk pregnancy, so it's an option."

"What did the doctor say?"

"That I'm five or six weeks pregnant. That we're having twins."

"Let me be clear. Abortion is not an option in this family. We don't murder babies. If I have to, I'll lock you in a cage for eight months. You're not killing my grandchildren."

"Mrs. Cheatham, if you had any idea what I did to the last person who threatened me…you're going back to Naples as soon as we get home and get you packed. This is my body, my life, my pregnancy. As of now you have no part in the discussion whatsoever. Now get the fuck out of my bedroom, I want to rest."

Back in Cheatham, Medea and Jason lay on her bed in the garage apartment. The mother-in-law was flying back to Florida.

"We need our house, our own house. I don't want to have to climb these stairs when I become a whale. Let's make plans for building one at Singing Water."

"Ok. How big?"

"Five bedrooms: you, me, the twins, and the au pair. Three bathrooms should be enough. No, four. Double garage. My studio at a far end of the house. Lots of light. We want an infinity pool?"

"Infinity pool, deck. A Spanish patio, enclosed and surrounded by the living space. Well, maybe open to the west, so the pool's plexiglass edge can align with the horizon and the sunset," said Jason.

"You'll need your man cave for watching football. And your kitchen, since you cook. What else?"

"I don't know. I'll get the architect right on it. Which lot?"

"A prominent one. Waterfront. I want people to drive by and say, 'That's Medea Royal's house. She's an opera star.'"

"Anything else, m'lady?"

"Transportation for one whale, and two twins. I'm quitting the Rev. Kiss me before I turn into an absolute hag."

They shared a quiet, affectionate moment.

Medea said, "I read somewhere, the paper maybe, that there had been a water-powered cotton gin at one time on the property—during Reconstruction?"

"Yes, that's how Mr. Carter's family kept the farm going after the Civil War."

"Are there gears and machinery still there?"

"Yes, they're really big, and they're pretty rusty, but they're still there."

"Save them. Don't trash them. And if any of the original wood can be repurposed, save that. I want to hire a sculptor to make something out of them. I read something in Architectural Digest about preserving heritage in a community."

"I think the gin's cypress. So's the old barn. I'm making Mr. Carter's old farm house into the sales office. It's where I've been staying since Mom and Dad sold out."

Jason bought Medea a Mercedes SUV to replace the church van. He had it outfitted with the best sound system available. He got a factory installed video with drop down screens for each kid seat.

"No use wasting drive time when the kids can watch educational TV," he said.

Medea, while she could still walk, took it to World Garage for its warranty check up. She sat in the tiled and vinyl customer waiting area, reading the libretto to Mozart's *Die Zauberflöte*, which she hoped to one day sing, when a wave of nausea sent her walking outside the building. She had her head down trying not to throw up when she rounded a corner to the back of the building and ran into a heavily tattooed mechanic with his shirt off. He was catching some rays.

"Heads up," he said.

She looked at his tattooed face, empty and filled stylized teardrops on his cheeks. He had an executioner with an ax on his right shoulder, and a heart pierced with a dagger over the left side of his chest. Another dagger was inked through his neck. The word "Assassin" was written across his upper back. He was smoking a cigarette.

"Oh my God," she said, "You've no idea how I've wanted one of these."

She took the lit cigarette from his fingers, drew it deeply in, and handed it back to him.

"Keep it," he said. "You seem to be in need." He lit another.

"You have an accent," said Medea.

"Berlin. I got here on a skilled technician's visa. The Americans couldn't pass the test. My certification keeps this place open."

Medea exhaled smoke and sighed.

"When are you due?" he asked.

"Not soon enough."

"Yours is the new SUV?"

"My mommy wagon."

"I've just finished servicing it. All the warranty checks and an oil change. My stamp of approval and your warranty's good. Wulf Botolf. Nice to meet you."

"How did you know it's mine?"

"Die Zauberflöte on the Bang & Olufsen, and you have the libretto here in your hand. I love Mozart."

"I love Mozart too. One day I hope to sing him again, but it's hard to push out babies and F6s at the same time. Nature has a way with hormones."

Medea finished her cigarette and stepped on it.

"One question," she asked.

"I wasn't there," he answered.

"No, seriously. What does 'Der holle roche kocht in meinem herzen' mean?"

"'Hell's wrath boils in my heart.' The Queen of the Night has lost her daughter to a kidnapper and wants him dead."

"Girl's gotta do what a girl's gotta do."

Medea felt better on her blood pressure and anti-nausea meds, so she decided to check in with the Rev at the Tabernacle. When she knocked on his office door she heard rock-n-roll turn off and meditative hymns turn on. *He doesn't even realize how transparent he is.*

"Hey, Medea. Jason said you two got hitched in Atlanta while you were at the hospital."

"There are no secrets in this town."

"Sorry to hear about the problem with the baby. Is everything ok now?"

"Nothing that complaining will help."

"Coffee? Tea?"

"If you have some hot tea?"

While the Rev went to the kitchen, Medea reached inside the safe and took out his bank books. She laid these out on his desk.

His jaw went slack when he saw them.

"I had a chat with a lawyer while I was in Atlanta. He has photocopies of all of this. Don't worry, I'm not blackmailing you. Well, not exactly. But if anything unfortunate should happen to me, the lawyer will contact the paper, the IRS, the local sheriff, and the Georgia Bureau of Investigation. Whether I'm dead or alive, they're gonna look at your $70,000 Scout boat. I don't think they're buying your line about Jesus walking on water and you just trying to keep up."

"Spill it, Medea. What do you want?"

"Nothing for me, really, but Miss Alma has labored in your Lord's vineyard for ten long years at low wages with no raises. I checked salaries online and, for churches with our recent membership increases, choir directors average $62,000 per year. That's from Christianity Today, your favorite magazine, right? No, wait, yours is Bass Fishing Monthly. I don't think Miss Alma gets that much. If you just gave her a raise and a thank you note, I'm sure she would be a devoted servant of the Lord for life, and nobody from the IRS would want to audit your finances."

"Now, Medea…"

"Shhhh. I don't need mansplaining. The IRS lets you get by as a 501C3, whose rules state you are not to personally benefit financially. They have rules regarding collections and expenditures. They can smell fraud faster than a fart in church if their suspicions are raised."

"Medea, I don't think…"

"You didn't think you'd get caught out by a little church secretary, choir lady? Well, color that past tense because your mule done sat down right in the middle of your vineyard. I'm not able to sing for awhile, or type, or answer the phone, or open mail—all of that causes me stress and messes with my blood pressure. So I done quit. Jason doesn't know, by the way. This is all my little scheme and it's to my benefit that it continue. None of this is for me, but Miss Alma is gonna get a big happy raise effective immediately. Understand, buddy? Any questions?"

"No."

"Call Miss Alma right now while I'm listening and tell her the Lord done inspired you to gratitude and generosity. This new $62,000 salary will make her day so much better."

"I'm a blimp," said Medea as Jason lifted her swollen ankles and put a pillow beneath them. "One behind my back, and under my head, so I can watch the soaps."

"The healthcare assistant will be here anytime to check your blood pressure and weigh you. Rest until then." As he brushed away hair from her eyes, she held his hands to her face and sniffed. *He smells like a carpenter: fresh cut lumber, cement, power tools.* He kissed her forehead and gave her the TV remote. He disappeared to his man cave overlooking the infinity pool.

The symptoms the specialist first described, floaters, colored flashes of light, headaches, blurred vision had been constant. Signs like swelling, rising blood pressure, weight gain and vomiting were obvious and anyone familiar with pre-eclampsia knew them well. They had tried with some success to keep her blood pressure beneath 140/90. Their goal of thirty-seven weeks gestation was four weeks out, and it seemed self-evident that they weren't going to make it.

The healthcare attendant measured her blood pressure and listened to Medea's list of symptoms. Her ankles were larger and nothing relieved the dizziness, which left her unable to tell which side she was lying on, or indeed, if she was even in the bed.

"Let's get you up at the bedside and see how much you've gained. Tell me if you get dizzy and we'll let you lie back down," said the attendant.

It was the last thing Medea heard as she stood up on the scales.

The medical record, and later the legal record, would show that Medea's legs started shaking while she uttered a sustained "aaaaaaaaahhh" sound. Then the attendant said she started to flip like a fish out of water. She landed back on the bed and the ambulance was called as the proper precautions for status epilepticus were taken. Medea's seizure would last twenty minutes. It ended only when the emergency medical technicians had started an intravenous line and administered magnesium. The record would state that she was incontinent of both urine and stool during the seizure.

As soon as the EMTs wheeled her into the emergency department, "The twins' heart rates are both way above two hundred fifty beats per minute, they don't fluctuate at all."

The doctor said, "The surgery crew and the ICU team are ready in surgery. Let's get these twins a c-section."

Medea's blood pressure rapidly approached their goal of 140/90 as soon as the placentas were removed from her uterus. The twins were boys, both low birth weight and requiring two weeks of round the clock care in the ICU.

Medea's recovery room was the next cubicle where she remained in a postictal state for a full twenty-four hours.

Medea had allowed her medical records released to the court-appointed psychiatrist. The evidence pointed to confused perceptions about her postpartum, postoperative, and postictal state of mind, and was backed up by all of the hospital staff.

"Medea remembered nothing at all for at least twenty-four hours, and afterwards she probably suffered from postpartum depression, if not outright psychosis," the shrink told the judge.

"If Medea seemed disinclined to bond with the twins, it matched their headlong efforts in utero to destroy her ability to sing. She had repeatedly told Jason she had no desire to get married, that is, to be a wife and a mother, but his determined sperm (two of them) had fatefully gotten through. Much drama played out as she was laid out by doctors orders and her own betrayed and parasitized body. The results? A pretty, talented soprano turned into a bloviating whale," the psychiatrist's report stated.

"Coincidentally, there was Dixie DeKalb, slim, red-headed, skin like freckled cream, derived of Irish stock. She had been hired by Jason to answer phones mostly, and pass along messages. She gave a good presentation on the real estate products offered by Singing Water, and at Jason's bidding, she happily assumed whatever position he told her to assume. Medea smelled her before she ever saw her. All time seemed nebulous during her recovery period, but that exact moment, Medea would remember: when Jason finally showed up at the hospital with the requisite bouquet of red roses. Her nose was primed for flowers representing love and passion, but the smell on his hands was of another woman's sex," the lawyer had written.

"I won't say you've embellished the truth, but your florid writing style is more in keeping with purple prose," said the judge hearing the case. "Hereafter, please use standard legal terms, and less from pulp fiction."

"Wash your hands before you touch those babies," Medea said to Jason, according to the nurses' notes.

The nursing staff heard that and entered a mistaken nursing diagnosis: "Readiness for enhanced child bearing process: a pattern of preparing for, maintaining, and strengthening care of newborns." This was part of her medical record which the shrink would enter into the legal record.

"Where were you?" she asked Jason when they were finally left alone.

"I went to the store for some popcorn. We were out. The healthcare attendant called the EMTs."

"Liar," said Medea. Her head was already a cauldron of toxic waste.

If the nursing staff had gathered correct information they would have arrived at quite different nursing diagnoses: insufficient attachment behavior, and unsafe environment for infants.

The babies, Mark and Paul, with their red, pinched little faces looked exactly like every other baby Medea had ever seen. She listened to the news on TV.

"A series of auto thefts has hit the Cheatham area. Patrons in supermarket parking lots…" She turned it off.

"Aren't you even going to hold them?"

"No. Did you find an au pair yet?"

"Three more interviews tomorrow. They all seem like such airheads— more interested in whether or not Cheatham has nightclubs, and 'How far is Atlanta?'"

"Maybe you've set your standards too high. If they can hold a bottle and feed them, and change a diaper, they're qualified."

"You have no natural affection for these children?"

"None. I told you I didn't want to get married or be a mother."

"Well, plans and reality have changed. You need to get used to the idea."

"No. Indeed, I intend to contact Mr. Saphier and resume singing as soon as possible. I'm getting a tubal ligation so we won't have any more of these little slip ups."

"You can't just walk away from your children."

"Watch me. I'll be moving into the extra bedroom. You can do whatever you want with whoever you want in yours."

He looked at her with horror and loathing. "You're not normal."

"Hire a nanny, and learn how to work those child seats. I'll be traveling."

Medea thought she heard a strange noise from the Mercedes so she took it to World Garage. She tried to describe the noise to Wulf.

"I'll give it a thorough inspection. If there's something wrong, the computer software will find it."

She hung around behind the building in the same break area, still littered with cigarette butts. Her voice was returning to normal, and she had a strict physical routine to get herself back in shape. She was practicing the "Queen of the Night Aria," scaling up and down, when she found herself having difficulty with a note.

"You're singing again." It was Wulf on a break. "And you've lost some weight."

"It's not a diet plan I would recommend."

"You still have dreams of singing Mozart one day?"

"Dream's coming true. My manager says it's time to get back into the opera game. I'm in New York in a month—Queen of the Night. I undermine the patriarchy and claim the Circle of the Sun."

"I admire ambitious women." He lit two cigarettes and handed her one.

"Thanks." She looked closely at his facial tattoos.

"What?" he asked.

"The tears tattooed on your face. Some are inked in. One is still empty. Doesn't that mean you've killed people in revenge? And that you have one more to do?"

"I have one left to kill, yes."

"Will you?"

"I hope so, when I go back to Germany. He's quite contented and lazy, living outside Munich now."

"Do you work for hire? You have 'assassin' across your back, as I recall. I mean for money, rather than for revenge?"

"Depends on the needs."

"You saw me when I was fat, pregnant with his kids?"

"Yes, you were having a tough time of it."

"He became disgusted with me and took up with his secretary. He was fucking her when I went into seizures and got carted off to the hospital in an ambulance. I wonder if you could arrange an accident for her. I would like to see him suffer."

"There are factors to consider."

"I would provide you with information and whatever money you need. Name your fee."

"Let's meet away from here. There's a biker bar called The Devil's Dam on the highway east of Cheatham, about ten miles out. What night can you meet me there? We will talk more then."

"I can meet most any night. Tell me when's good for you."

"How about Thursday? Around eight? Here's my cell number."

Medea found The Devil's Dam and parked the Mercedes SUV near the back on the side away from the road. The bar looked dicey for a woman alone so she called Wulf.

"I'm here. Can you come to the door?"

He walked outside holding two beers. "We can probably talk better on the patio."

There were two lovers, sloppy drunk and making out, oblivious to the world around them. Medea and Wulf took a table toward the back. Mulch and cigarette butts covered the ground, and empty beer bottles covered the tables. Wulf threw several in the trash and wiped the table with a handful of napkins. Strings of white skull-shaped bulbs strung from leafless tree to leafless tree, lit the night.

"Pull up your shirt and turn around." He felt around the edges of her bra and visually inspected her torso. "Pull your shirt down and drop trou." He felt in the elastic of her underwear and looked her pelvis over. "I needed to check that you weren't wearing a wire. Sorry for the inconvenience and embarassment. Here's to business." They clinked beer bottles and took a sip.

"So you want this woman…?"

"Dixie DeKalb."

"…dead? You must have loved your husband very much."

"I may have at one time. Now, this is about revenge. I want to hurt him as much as humanly possible."

"Hereafter, think of me as a death merchant. You are the consumer."

"I can deal with that."

"I prefer an arranged accident. Does she drive?"

"She drives a yellow coupe. You can see it parked at the sales office of Singing Water Realty. I'm not sure of the make and model."

"I'll find out. There's a device called Nottatakata, a bomb made like an airbag, but there are some differences. Both explode when an electrical current ignites some chemicals, sodium azide and potassium nitrate, inside the steering column. Normally the explosion, at about four hundred p.s.i.

happens in a split second, and deflates the airbag as fast as it blows it up. The Nottatakata has way more explosive, and its airbag has no vents, so it doesn't deflate. This device, which I can get from an acquaintance, doesn't require a collision but activates with ignition of the automobile. The beauty of it is the driver is leaning forward to crank the car, and the device is aimed a little higher than the chest—toward the throat. It's a module which fits quickly into the steering wheel. The cover is not soft plastic which explodes harmlessly, but very hard plastic designed to shatter into blade-like shrapnel. It will, at least, cut all the major blood vessels of the throat, if it doesn't decapitate the target all together. They're designed to use in espionage."

"How soon can you get it?"

"I will need a $10,000 deposit which will finance the acquisition of the device and act as good-faith money. Delivery of the device will take about a week by Fed Ex. It looks like delivery of another auto part. When we are ready you will bring me another $10,000 dollars and tell me her location. We will not see each other again. Which bank do you use?"

"Cheatham State."

"Withdraw $10,000 tomorrow afternoon. Put it in a backpack and call me when you leave the lobby of the main branch downtown. Understand?"

"Yes, I'll see you tomorrow afternoon."

"No. You won't see me. I'll tell you where to leave the money. In about a week when the device is delivered, I'll call you and say, 'Your auto part is here.' You will receive final instructions and you will tell me her location. Come on, I'll walk you to your vehicle."

Late night news filled the SUV with more noise than Medea's head could take, "...drivers should be aware and not leave their doors unlocked or their keys in the ignition. One victim at Southland Mall actually left her car running while she dashed into the quick stop grocery..." Medea turned it off. She was shaking after her conversation with Wulf.

Medea left the twins in the care of the nanny Jason had hired. As she drove past Daddy Carter's old farm house, enroute to the new bypass to the city, it scarcely resembled the farm she'd grown up on. Asphalt had been laid for parking, the house had a bright new coat of paint and new windows. The barn had been reduced to neat piles of lumber, and there was not a single farm implement in sight. Strings of plastic red, blue, and yellow triangular flags, an affront to the color green, flapped in the breeze. The frog pond had been drained. "Singing Water Estates. Sales Office Open" welcomed the curious, and potential buyers. Medea noticed Jason's pickup and Dixie's yellow coupe parked side-by-side on the newly striped asphalt.

She had no place to go, so drove toward the new bypass route into Cheatham. A busy, quick stop grocery had sprung up at the intersection with four sets of gas pumps and an apparently lively trade. Medea decided to explore a new route to the truck stop. It had been weeks since she had seen Alice.

"Hey, Church Lady. I heard you were a mother now."

"Hey, Alice. I got a craving for peach pie a-la-mode."

"You sure you're not pregnant again? You know what they say about cravings."

"If I'm pregnant again, I'm suing the doctor. No more of those little slip ups for me. And I'm not a church lady anymore—I quit the Rev."

Alice set the pie on the counter with a cup of coffee. "You look like you're recovering nicely, but you don't look content and happy."

"Jason's taken up with his secretary."

"The wife is always the last to know."

"How long has this been going on, Alice?"

"Since you got sick, about four months now."

"Spill it, I hear her name's Dixie DeKalb. What do you know?"

"I'm not one to tell you 'I told you so.' Actually, I'm really sorry, and I hope she gets what's coming to her. She's all the time with Jason now. Right hand girl, I guess. He's bought her a double wide and put it on a big, cleared lot right by the edge of the National Forest. I'd be scared to live that far out of town by myself."

"Who is she?"

"Little miss nobody from nowhere Georgia. Got some secretarial skills at the community college and set her cap for any man she could catch." Alice wiped the counter, leaving a smell of vinegar floating in the air. "Trouble with being the other woman is, what do you do about the next woman."

"Yes. Well, I'm working on that. Where is this trailer on a lot?"

"Indian Ridge Road. If you're going toward the firetower, a blacktop road cuts over towards Burkstown. Her place is about a mile down that road on the left."

Medea put twenty dollars on the counter. "Keep the change, Alice. My stomach's still a little tetchy."

She cranked the SUV and tuned the radio to local news. A bulletin warned motorists of a gang of 'travellers' operating around Cheatham, "… they operate in teams. One stands look out. Another boosts the car, and a third comes right in with a truck that they load the stolen car into." She turned off the radio and adjusted her rearview mirror to miss the child safety seats in the back.

On Friday, Wulf called. "Your part is in. Where is the car?"

"It will be at the sales office all afternoon. Jason has a meeting with his financier. That mean's they'll be fishing. Dixie will be at the office by herself."

"Leave the package on the bench in front of city hall at eleven o'clock." The phone clicked off.

The au pair had a fever and nausea, so Medea put the kids in the car seats in the back and plugged Teletubbies into the video. She drove to the bank and withdrew the money, then left it in a backpack on the bench as instructed. She drove around the block and caught a glimpse of Wulf, makeup covering his tattooes, getting back into a van with a magnetic sign on the sides "Auto Repair and Warranty To Go," He headed toward Singing Water.

Medea took the new bypass and stopped her car about a block from the sales office. She walked around a new house under construction until she could clearly see the coupe and the front door of the office. She wanted to hear too, so left the twins in the car with the engine, A/C, and gadgets running.

Wulf drove into the parking lot and walked to the door with a clip board in his hand, and knocked. His coveralls said 'Auto Repair and Warranty To Go' just like the logo on the truck.

"Dixie DeKalb?" he asked.

"Yes."

"I'm from your auto manufacturer. Here to fix your faulty air bag?"

"I didn't order that."

"No ma'am. The manufacturer ordered it. You heard about the recall? They pay to fix it. It takes like ten minutes to replace."

"Well, I haven't heard anything about that. I'm not just going to give you the keys to my car and let you steal it."

"Oh, no ma'am. I just need to get to the steering wheel so I can replace your faulty airbag. I don't need to crank your car. If this is a bad time, we could just let you make an appointment at the dealer's garage and take it in yourself. Or I could do it here in about ten minutes. If you'll just unlock your door is all I need."

Dixie clicked the auto control device. The car beeped and the lights flashed.

"It's unlocked," she said.

Medea walked back to her SUV and left. She drove around town until she felt the need for a cigarette. She pulled into the new quick stop grocery and felt a little uneasy—there was a man in a hoodie at the corner of the building, and another standing on the sidewalk, keeping watch. Further down the road she could see an unmarked truck parked on the shoulder with its emergency flashers lit.

She looked at the twins. Then looked at herself in the mirror. She turned up the air conditioner, pumped up the volume on the video and drove to the side of the building most hidden from the street. As she exited the SUV she left her door open and the engine running, and very loudly said, "Mommy will be right back. I just need to get some cigarettes."

She had no sooner entered the store than the first thief climbed into the driver's side door and drove off in the SUV. The lookout spoke into his cell phone, and the truck down the street raised its back gate and lowered a loading ramp. The Mercedes disappeared into the back of the truck.

Medea watched through the store window as the Mercedes disappeared. She went to the refrigerated display case to choose a microwaveable sandwich. She read the instructions then set the timer on the microwave. She selected a drink from the cold drinks case, then looked at items on the nearest shelf to the front window. The truck made a u-turn and headed toward the interstate. She added condiments to her sandwich. A lighter and cigarettes completed her shopping.

"Cash or card?" asked the clerk.

Medea handed her a Mastercard.

Outside the front door she peeled the cigarettes open and lit one. At the corner of the store she stopped with a puzzled look on her face. Then walked to the other corner of the store and looked panicked. She ran into the middle of the parking lot and looked back and forth at the corners of the store, dropped her groceries on the pavement, and started to scream.

"My babies! My twins! Someone stole my SUV!" She sank to her knees as a crowd gathered.

An ambulance came and took hysterical Medea to the hospital. In the emergency room it would appear her grief would result in self-harm.

"Oh my god—they've stolen my babies!" she continued to scream. "They stole my car and the twins were in the backseat."

She grabbed the nurse's scrub top and ripped it. Medea fell against the wall cutting her forehead. The smell and sight of blood triggers a release of adrenaline in all who witness it.

The nurse paged a social worker and the physician ordered an injection of diazepam.

"Let's wrap her in chemical restraints. Get me a suture kit too."

The sedative put Medea in a fog through which characters floated in and out like a Fellini movie. She came to in a hospital room and tried to focus on Jason as he talked into his cell phone.

"I was on the boat with the Rev. Tell me it's not so. Tell me they didn't kidnap my sons. No…No! I can buy another car. Those babies have to come back. Have they sent a ransom note, or called? Oh please God, I have to get my twins back!"

In her drug-induced stupor Medea tried unsuccessfully to form words. *Get some more children by your whore.*

"Get mmm more," she mumbled but her tongue was so large and dry the words would not form.

"She needs some ice chips," said the nursing assistant and she spooned ice into Medea's dry mouth. "Keep your head to the side so you don't choke, OK?" she said.

The five o'clock news headlines came on TV. Jason turned up the volume.

The news anchor began, "Two tragedies today in Cheatham. The latest in a string of auto thefts results in the disappearance of twin boys, and a faulty airbag explodes, killing a Cheatham woman as she leaves her workplace. More details when we come back." Video footage showed the sales office parking lot and Dixie's car, and the quick stop grocery with crime scene tape around the corner of the building.

Medea focused enough to see Jason jabbing at numbers on his cell phone, "Dixie, answer your phone. Dixie, please pick up the phone. Answer, God damn it!"

He slammed the phone to the floor as close up video of the inflated air bag covered with blood began the news coverage. He watched and sank to his knees, pulling his hair and raking his fingernails into the skin of his face. Fingers disappeared into the corners of his mouth. As his knees hit the floor his body developed an elastic quality. He pulled his face into a contorted mask of tragedy.

Medea smiled through the velvet cloud of sedatives. A warm rush of satisfaction hit her heart and spread throughout her chest, a feeling second only to taking a bow after a performance as she sees beyond the footlights, the audience rise to its feet and the applause and bouquets fill the stage.

The End

Claire

CLAIRE WALKED AWAY from the Academy of St. Agnes without so much as a backward glance. Second-guessing and petulance were not her style. One must, having started something, see it through. For Claire, St. Agnes was *through*. Twenty-one pages of dress code for the senior prom, and one page was for the boys. *Eve bit the apple first.*

Three weeks earlier she had set it all in motion. Lize and Sami had kept her company over herbal tea at Dharma Pot. They had been to the hospital to help their schoolmate, Meg, get discharged and settled in back at home. Meg had dropped a bomb on them—she would be leaving for Montreal to stay with her mama's sister.

"How long will you be gone?" asked Sami.

"Awhile," said Meg. "I need time to sort some things out."

Her wired-together jaw made talking a chore.

"A week? Months?" said Lize.

"I may enroll in French immersion classes. My aunt's family speak French. I'll take the GED online."

Meg put on her bland, inscrutable look and let her lips, a natural bow, turn slightly upward at the corners. It could have been a smile, or merely a banal contentment, but her eyes cut to Claire. *Get them out of here.*

"We should let you rest," said Claire as she put away the last of things from Meg's suitcase and turned down the bed covers. She straightened up, looking at the things on Meg's bulletin board. What caught her attention was a frond from Palm Sunday, folded origami style into a cross. *We learned to do that when we were eight, in catechism class.*

Lize suggested the Dharma Pot. The eggplant bruises on Meg's breasts and throat, and her wired jaw, leaped around Lize's mind like hell hounds after a witch. From their favorite corner booth the three watched intermittent lines of students' cars cruise up and down Stadium Drive. Plaid skirts, white blouses, and oxfords set them apart from their peers. None of them spoke until Sami tuned her laptop to the WiFi and thuds, crunches and angry shouts emanated from the Queens of Mean video game.

Claire looked at Lize.

Lize looked back and ground her teeth side-to-side.

Both looked at Sami.

"Could you turn that off?" asked Claire.

Sami pushed the power button on her laptop. "What?"

"Those bruises. And her jaw. She was attacked," said Lize.

"She sure didn't get those falling down the stairs like she said," said Sami.

"She said it was an 'unfortunate encounter' but she wouldn't say anyone's name," said Claire.

"More often than not it's somebody you know," said Lize.

"That creep jock, Matt Connor," said Sami. "She's been out with him a couple of times. I'll bet it was him."

Four boys entered. Their wet heads suggested the end of practice and a recent shower. Matt was among them.

"We'll have four kavas with ice mints," said Matt, who took it upon himself to order for all of the group.

"I want a caramel chaser," said one of the boys to the barrista.

"You don't have a hair on your balls, Harold," said Matt as he squared his shoulders to bully the kid.

"I don't like mint. I want caramel," whined the kid. He might play football but he wasn't an alpha male.

"I'll have a ginger kombucha, no kava for me," said a lineman.

"What's with you pussies—got an estrogen rush?" said Matt.

The lineman stepped close to Matt, then stepped closer, like young gorillas beating their chest and thumping the ground. Matt stepped back and seemed to grow a little smaller.

"Quarterback, you can tell me where to go in the huddle, but when I need your help ordering from a coffee house menu, I'll let you know." He leaned in close to Matt's face and made a sucking, kissey sound.

Matt frowned and swallowed.

"Three kavas. Two mints, one caramel. And I'll have a ginger kombucha, please." The lineman handed a debit card to the barrista. He turned his attention back to making Matt uncomfortable.

"I just heard from State. I'm in the lineman stable. Full ride," he said.

The other two jocks high-fived him.

"Your fast pass and fast ass got any offers yet, quarterback?"

Everybody looked at Matt. Red crept up his neck.

"No," he said.

"Naw? I didn't think so. Where you boys wanna sit?" asked the lineman.

They claimed a table near the three girls by placing their football jackets over the chair backs. As the girls looked at them, they glanced back and tried not to stare.

Claire studied Matt. She noticed scratch marks on his right cheek and the side of his neck.

Football? Then she thought of Claire's broken fingernails she had helped repair in the hospital. *Meg had blood under her nails.*

He looked up and caught her eye.

"How's it going, Claire?" he asked.

"Fine, Matt. You ready for the chemistry exam?'

"Yeah, I been hitting the books with the tutor. You?"

"I think I got it under control." Claire smiled at him over the rim of her tea cup.

Lize's mouth tightened as she watched Claire flirt with Matt.

Sami turned her tea cup around and around on its saucer.

"Maybe we could get together sometimes before the test and compare notes?" said Matt.

"Yeah, that would be great."

"Great."

The three girls got up to leave. As they passed the boys table, Matt's hand grazed Claire's knee.

She stopped and leaned her weight towards his hand.

"Call me," she said. "We'll set up a time to meet at the library."

"Cool," he said.

The girls walked towards the door and he squeezed his crotch.

Outside, as they unlocked the car, Lize said, "I don't believe you, hussy. Didn't we just decide that he was the one who attacked Meg?"

"Yes."

"Then, what the fuck are you thinking?"

"I'm setting a trap. That was bait."

Late Saturday afternoon, Claire sat on a pew at Holy Family. She had genuflected on the kneeler and twice tried to pray, but her mind wouldn't go there. She watched as the confessional light went on, a penitent entered, and in a few minutes the penitent came out. Claire dumped the contents of her purse onto the pew and raked through it until her fingers found a palm frond, origami-folded into the shape of a cross.

Palm Sunday, the kingship of Jesus until the ashes of Lent. From dust you come...

She turned this over and over with her fingers as she thought of the edges of the bruising on Meg's breasts and throat, how they spread beyond the eggplant borders to green like oxidized copper. She had seen the cut marks over Meg's shoulder blade when the nurse changed the bandage.

"M.C." she whispered. *Matt Connor.*

Father Theo sat down beside her. She looked at her watch as it neared time for mass.

"No confession today?" he asked.

"I can't get all the crap out of my head."

"Crap?"

"Stuff. You know. Meg. She went home today."

"How is Meg?"

"She's hurt. She may be moving to Montreal. I don't know if she'll come back."

"What happened?"

"I think a boy she was seeing raped her."

"You know this boy?"

"He's at school. A protestant."

"You should pray for him. Jesus tells us to pray for those who would spitefully use us."

Claire looked at Father Theo. "That would be a good thing to do, father. You pray for him. I'm laying other plans."

Father Theo looked at his watch.

An acolyte stopped at the end of the pew, "Ready?" he asked.

"Tell Meg I'll see her this week."

Toward the end of the mass Father Theo looked to where Claire had been sitting, but she was gone. She had neither made confession nor taken communion.

Claire asked her friend, Luis Torres, who worked at the slaughterhouse, for the backbones of three large hogs.

"Espinas cerdos? Porque, Claire?"

"Anatomy. I need to practice dissecting the spine, and identifying the parts of the central nervous system. Can you help me?"

"They use those in canned meat products and weenies."

"I need them as soon as possible. The test is right around the corner."

"Puedo por ti, Claire. By tomorrow, OK?"

"Gracias, Luis."

On her way home Claire stopped by the hardware store and pulled some axes off the shelf. She liked the design of the Hudson Bay axe. She lifted one and took a soft ball stance. As she put it to her shoulder and prepared to swing, the clerk quickly approached.

"Easy, Ma'am. You don't want to hurt anybody."

"No. We're going camping and nobody can find an axe." Clair grinned a hypocritical grin and let the axe drop. It didn't cut her leg when it bumped, but she said, "Ouch."

"We leave a safety sheath on the sharp edge. That's why you're not on your way to the E.R. right now."

Claire turned the axe over in her hands.

"Do you see what you did?" asked the clerk. "You weren't aware of your stance, the distance to what you're cutting, and the arc the axe would travel. All three are important things when handling an axe."

"Who knew?" said Claire.

"Here. Let me show you."

"Can't I just sign a release of responsibility and take it home?"

"You can do what you want. I just don't want you to get hurt, OK?"

The clerk sounded proficient with an axe: Control the swing, stance with knees bending as the arc comes down, closed-toed shoes, goggles or glasses over your eyes, covered legs, carry the blade pointing outward…

Is he flirting with me? I think he's flirting.

When she got the hogs' spines, Claire waited until everyone had left the house. She tied one to a tree in the backyard and imagined the arc of her axe as it circled towards the hunk of meat. It hit too broadside, spraying her face and clothes with pink, cool spatter and slipped from her hand. The meat swung back and forth in the breeze, like a school child at play on a swing.

"You're not getting the best of me," she said as she retrieved the axe and aimed again at the carcass.

Just then Lize and Sami opened the gate. Lize dropped her smoothie and screamed, and Sami stood frozen to her spot, mouth open.

"What are you doing?" asked Lize.

"You look like Carrie on prom night," said Sami, taking in Claire's blood-spattered face and clothes.

"I need a syringe with enough tranquilizer to knock out a football player," said Claire.

Sami's dad, a veterinarian, practiced out of their basement. His stock of medicines was locked in an old-fashioned clinical cabinet.

"My dad darts cows and horses. They're sedated quickly and stay out for about half an hour. He calls recovery, 'a soft landing,' because they wake up without anxiety or memory of what happened."

She ran her hand along a high shelf beside the cabinet until she found the door key. From the cabinet she took a dart-syringe and from a rack on the wall she took down the dart gun. Sami handed them to Claire and began to explain how to use them. Claire had never shot a gun.

"You know how to shoot this?" asked Claire.

"I'm a very good shot," said Sami. "Dad insists that me and the boys know how to handle guns."

Claire handed the dart and gun back to Sami.

"Then you're the shooter. I'm the chopper."

She put an arm around Lize's shoulders. "You're my muscle. You help with the lifting. We'll do this at the rave warehouse."

Outside they swore themselves to sisterhood silence with palm slaps.

"Not a word, ever," said Sami.

"Not a word," said the other two.

In the anatomy lab at school Lize stood lookout while Claire reviewed the central nervous system of the human on the anatomy dummy. She searched for the neurons ennervating the groin and lower extremities and where they exited the central nervous system. The diagrams all pointed to lumbar one as the area she wanted to target.

Then she searched for anatomical landmarks.

"Take off your blouse and stand here," she said to Lize.

"What if somebody comes in?"

Sami locked the door and covered the narrow window. From behind Lize, Claire placed her hands on both sides of Lize's navel and brought them straight back until she felt the bony prominences of the pelvis. The anatomical landmarks led her toward her target like the red and white circles of a bullseye. Following a straight line to the backbone, she located L3.

"Two vertebrae above there is L1. That's the sweet spot."

"Sweet spot? For what?" asked Lize as Claire pressed her fingers along the ridges of her back.

"If the spine is cut in half there, the victim becomes paraplegic. He'll never walk, never take a normal dump again, or control his pee..." said Claire.

"Or use his penis as a weapon," said Sami.

The girls arrived at the library earlier than the scheduled meeting time. Claire parked out back in a remote lot surrounded on two sides by overgrown bushes. Lize's car was a little bigger, so she parked between the library and their spot, blocking the line of sight of anyone who might be looking.

"Sami, take the gun and hide in there," said Claire pointing to some thick bushes about twenty feet away. "Do you think you can hit him from this distance?"

"Easy," said Sami.

"Lize, go with Sami. You two have to be absolutely quiet for this to work. OK?"

Matt was fifteen minutes late. He carried a go cup of cappucino and his chemistry textbook.

"Me and the tutor been working on this for weeks. I still don't get it. You just seem to understand it without any effort."

"I like chemistry. And math. The natural world can be your friend if you pay attention."

"Everybody knows girls can't do STEM."

"That's news to me," said Claire. She looked towards the bushes and nodded. *Thwack!* The dart hit Matt squarely in the side of his neck. His cappucino hit the pavement.

"Goddammit!" he jumped and looked around.

"What, Matt?" Claire watched him join his coffee on the pavement.

Lize's car signaled, and the trunk opened. The three girls put Matt inside and slammed the lid.

"The warehouse," said Claire.

The rave warehouse was the late night place to party. Isolated. Unlocked. Deserted industrial area. Nobody around during the day.

Claire checked the time. She didn't want Matt waking up. She was counting on the amnesiac effect of the anesthesia dart.

They cut off his clothes as they strung him up by his wrists to a supporting beam. Claire pulled a ski mask over her face and put on her safety glasses. She pulled coveralls over her clothes.

"Stand way back," she said to the other two and calculated the distance to L1. Claire imagined the arc of the axe and adjusted her stance. She buried the axe in his back and he flipped back and forth like a landed fish. The stench of feces filled the air and a stream of urine splattered on the concrete floor.

They let him down from the beam. His skin was ice cold.

"I don't want him losing his hands to gangrene before the ambulance gets here."

The girls gathered what equipment they had brought including latex gloves and the dart, and put everything in a lawn and leaf bag. As they drove away Claire called 911 on a disposable, pre-paid cell phone.

"Hello, 911? A boy has been attacked at the rave warehouse," she said into the phone. Then she stuffed it into the plastic leaf and lawn bag along with her ski mask and coveralls.

Lize's parents were away from the house so the three perps built a fire in their BBQ pit and disposed of all the evidence there.

"Remember, not a word to anyone," said Sami.

"Not even God," said Claire.

"Especially not that gossiping Father Theo," said Lize.

The halls of St. Agnes buzzed with two hot items: the quarterback at St. Michael's had been paralyzed in an axe attack, and the sisters of St. Agony had published their dress code for the prom. The girls were summoned to the chapel to review the document and acknowledge their compliance. Feedback from the girls was not a desired outcome.

Claire dressed in jeans and a muscle T-shirt with no bra for the occasion. She had put an indigo blue streak in her hair. Lize tried hard for the iconic Marilyn-over-the-subway-grate thing, and Sami shaved the sides of her head into a mohawk. She had a new piercing through her nose and wore dance leotards and a tuxedo top. When Eve bit the apple first, the Bible said the first couple's sin was that they became as gods, and knew good from evil. The patriarchy didn't have anything against eating fruit, but agency among teenage girls scared them shitless.

The threesome slouched near the front of the chapel, chewing gum, their feet propped on the pews in front of them.

The nuns and their teacher's aides handed out the Revised Prom Dress Code. Twenty-one pages, one for the boys.

Sister Iggy gave the three girls a surprised, stern look and pointed to their feet. "Down," she said, like commanding pet dogs.

Claire popped her gum. As she sat up she pulled her t-shirt tight to show her nipples free of the usual confines of a bra. She scratched her nose with her middle finger.

Lize sat up and crossed her arms beneath her breasts, then leaned forward to show Sister Iggy some cleavage.

Sami stood up and stretched so that her tuxedo shirt rose above her butt. The lovely globes and gluteal cleft left little to the imagination beneath the bright fabric of the dance leotards. She rubbed her new nose ring.

Sister Iggy said, "Detention. All three of you. Principal's office immediately after assembly."

Sister Vangie carried a yardstick. She had, at one time, hit girls with it, but parents had begun to frown upon that. Nonetheless, it was a comfortable prop for Sister Vangie.

"You're all A students who are usually well-behaved. What's going on?"

All three girls tossed their copies of the revised dress code onto her desk.

"Twenty pages for the girls," said Claire.

"Only one for the boys," said Sami.

"We're all withdrawing from school. We will study at home and take the GED at the next opportunity."

"You can't do that. What about our graduation statistics? You're all A students. We can't lose you."

"Sister, you've already lost us," said Sami. "You're a dinosaur who just put its head down to munch some more grass, five minutes after the asteroid hit."

"All three of us have already been accepted to our colleges of choice. None are Catholic," said Lize.

"So, Sister, we're done here. These are our notarized letters of intent to withdraw and complete the semester in home schooling."

They put the letters on her desk.

"You... you... you have to complete paperwork before you can go."

"No, Sister, you have a lot of paperwork to complete. And a lot of statistics to re-work," said Claire. "Good luck with that."

The three walked out of the office and slapped high fives.

"Dharma Pot?" said Lize.

"Dharma Pot," said Sami.

"Dharma Pot it is," said Claire.

The End

Author Bio: Brit Chism

BRIT CHISM LIVES on the west coast of Florida. Quite balmy. He is a writer of short stories about women. This fascination with half of humanity grew from his childhood during the McCarthy era at a truck stop on the highway. The most important people to him have always been women: two sisters, a mother who was a battered alcoholic, classmates and co-workers in nursing (from which he is now happily retired).

Mr. Chism earned baccalaureate degrees in registered nursing, and English/communications. He despises television. Life-long learning is a passion for him. He doesn't own a car, but rides public transit and a bicycle. Other fascinations are gardening and cooking.

Made in the USA
Columbia, SC
03 February 2018